MONA LISA
BECOMING A GHOST

A.L. MENGEL

Mona Lisa, Becoming a Ghost
A.L. MENGEL

A NOVEL BY A.L. MENGEL

THE ASTRAL FILES

Mona Lisa, Becoming a Ghost
A.L. MENGEL

A.L. MENGEL'S BOOKSHELF

Ashes
The Quest for Immortality
The Blood Decanter
War Angel
Ballet of The Crypt Dancer

The Wandering Star
The Europa Effect
The Arrival of Destiny
Battle of the Trinity

The Mortician

Curtains and Fan Blades
The Other Side of The Door
#Writestorm
#PaintTheWorld

Mona Lisa, Becoming a Ghost
A.L. MENGEL

VIDEO VAULT

VIDEO PRESENTATION PLAYLISTS

#TheEraOf: How Art Learns from Life

#Unmasked Video Diary Series

J.D. Estrada's #MarchofTheWriters (2021, 2022)

Take a Journey (2018 Book Tour)

#Haunted Video Blog

VIDEO PRESENTATIONS

A Thief in the Night

The Aura of the Soul

The Aura of Dreams

Finding Inspiration in a Post COVID world

How A.L. Mengel's 'War Angel' Was Connected to the Pulse Massacre

Videos are available for free viewing on A.L. Mengel's Facebook and YouTube channels. Follow A.L. Mengel on social media.

Mona Lisa, Becoming a Ghost
A.L. MENGEL

From the Author

To the Wanders and the Crypt Dancers,

I've said this before, I believe.

Throughout the years when I have published novels, I have always said how each book was challenging to create. I did not only present the creative writing and research obstacles which I needed to overcome working on the project, but I also presented marketing challenges which each project had, and some other projects which had unique marketing challenges (such as *Colonia's The Arrival of Destiny* and *Battle of the Trinity*).

Destiny had not prepared me for the challenges that I would be presented with during the creation and writing of *Mona Lisa, Becoming a Ghost*. Not unlike the character Pedro, I shared a similar misinterpretation of my own creative muse. This was the only project that I almost didn't finish; this was the only project where I had thought of retiring as an author.

In retrospect, I don't believe those frustrations that I felt with my creative career were founded; rather, it was the similar expression of characterization which had found its way off the page and into my everyday life. It's those times when I must take a step back and re-examine my purpose, my destiny, not only as an author, but also as an individual. With the creation of a character like Pedro, I empathized with the struggles of a start-up creative artist, whether they be a writer, or a painter, a performer, dancer or musician. For I have been there. I know

11

what passion goes into those projects, especially in the beginning.

It's in those early creative years when an artist has the most to dream about and the least to lose. They have yet to be discovered; they are searching for the fulfillment which they crave, following a dream which they must never lose sight of, and embarking on a journey of which the young artist or writer may not know, will be filled with challenges and obstacles which might seem insurmountable.

There will be times when the writer or artist may consider giving up their dream, shelving their creative inspiration and aspiration, and choosing a more "practical" and "sensible" direction. Creative careers are threatened frequently by the expected responsibilities of daily life. Long gone are the days when one can live truly "off the grid", in this age of technology and economic pressure. In these times, people generate financial liabilities from the moment of birth, with currency governing society, and determining whether an artist or writer can truly follow their passion – or succumb to economic expectations.

Is the idea of the poor and struggling artist from a bygone era?

Are the days when an artist, or a writer, or a musician, long cherished as translators of creative expression, with unique interpretations of the world and its people, over?

In *Mona Lisa, Becoming a Ghost*, the inspiration is the classic Da Vinci masterpiece. As many artists have been inspired by the creative works of the legendary artists – be they painters, composers or authors – that can be where the dream of the new creative can be born. Pedro experiences what many artists can and do; the call of the world *away* from the art is significant and has the potential to steer the artist in many different directions, in essence, disrupting focus and creating self-doubt and discouragement. In my days when I was a new writer, I had many phone conversations with my mother, mostly on days when I was feeling discouraged, and she always reminded me that discouragement is a tool of the devil.

Regardless of what one's beliefs are – or non-beliefs – that theory rings true. It's easy for anyone to feel discouraged, especially when new at something, whether it be a craft, a practical career or raising a family. There are many things which we try and feel that we are making progress in our craft. That despite the setbacks and obstacles, and the demand of time away from the craft, we feel we will, someday, get there.

Today as I write this, I am still reeling from the news of the loss of world-renowned author Anne Rice. While I never had the opportunity to meet her in person, she was the author, along with Stephen King, who inspired my dream of becoming an author. When I was much younger, I devoured Stephen King's books, and read several of Anne's as well.

I discovered *Interview with the Vampire* while still a student in high school, read the book and fell in love with her series. I also loved *The Witching Hour.* Those were probably my favorite books of hers.

But it was Anne Rice who inspired me to dream of becoming a novelist, and, years later, after I had written my first novel, I approached Anne online by sending her an email.

I was elated that she'd answered personally and gave me some wonderful advice...to just keep at it. It was during those days when Anne and I sent a few emails back and forth when I was trying to get an agent, and my first novel, *Ashes,* was still years from making its publication debut.

Mona Lisa, Becoming a Ghost is a story about a broken promise. As some of the characters in this story feel as if the world has not kept its word, has not provided a means to express their passions, it also holds an important caveat; that the journey continues. It moves onward, regardless. And it will take you to extraordinary destinies.

If you allow it.

A.L. Mengel

From the world of The Tales of Tartarus —

When the offices of The Astral's Paranormal Investigations Unit were destroyed, their files were stolen.

When they were recovered, the content was examined and analyzed in detail.

Here are the stories found inside…

THE

ASTRAL

FILES

MONA

LISA

ETERNAL *Moment*

The immortal mirror stares back at she who gazes upon it,
amoral morality shadows the quest,
but without remorse
it dances on the grave of the spectre
which casts long shadows on the living.
The paint lives, and the painting exhales slowly,
A fine, ancient dust emanating, covering the area with a fine
layer
...be careful not to take too deep a breath.

This is how the dead come upon the living,
if, indeed, the living of whom we seek,
are not already of the deceased – animated corpses,
wandering,
without soul or thought.
Thus the hope of night is mangled,
twisted within the lingering debris of light
which lays scattered,
and as I look about me,
rays meet my gaze from mirrored detritus, and
the eyes which glare back at me,
are mine own –

-    ROBERT CANO

BECOMING

A

GHOST

THE BONES OF THE CONVENT

THE GHOST WRITER

PORTRAIT OF A WOMAN

ARRIVAL OF THE PATIENT

THE WIDOW AND THE TAXIDERMIST

SKIN+BONES+BODY

RESURRECTION

SCENT OF THE GRAVE

Mona Lisa, Becoming a Ghost
A.L. MENGEL

FOR BEV

The one who taught me how to show my story

AND FOR ANNE RICE

1941-2021

A wonderful and thoughtful mentor

A SPECIAL THANK YOU TO JACK NOWICKI FOR
BELIEVING IN MY CRAFT AND MAKING AN INVESTMENT
INTO THIS PROJECT.

THE BONES OF
THE CONVENT

TRAVELING

HE MET WITH THE TAXIDERMIST in the weeks which preceded their trip to the abandoned convent in Florence. It was in the catacombs, beneath the halls of the crumbling building, where her final resting place was reported to be. The convent was an archaeological masterpiece of sorts, dilapidated columns of stone amidst sand and dirt.

Hidden treasures and untold stories would be the fruit of the explorer, he thought. He knew the mystery and speculation which surrounded Leonardo da Vinci's classic Mona Lisa painting; despite the sense of a desire to create which washed through him, as he remembered when he stood, watching her watching him, he remained focused on the purpose of the mission. Indeed, she was inspiring. She was powerful and held a stronghold over his creative life.

But he knew that he wasn't a painter.

Although he had aspired to be of the talent and magnitude of the classic artists which hung in the museums of Madrid and Paris and Rome, he had not believed that he'd had a muse.

"I am Pedro," he would say, back in the days when he used to go to the art classes which Valentina had suggested. As he would join the other aspiring artists at the painter's club in the basement of the church, the same nervousness washed through him which he believed was an affliction of novice artists venturing out into the light of day, to share their work in front of other equally struggling beginners.

He watched them watching him, as he hastily set his canvas in front of the easel. He could feel his heart pound in his chest; the eyes pierced his back, as he felt his cheeks grow warm.

He looked over at the instructor, who was a tiny man. His silver-hair was mussed and stringy, yet he still exuded an era of sophistication and confidence despite the colorful exterior. He was an artist, clearly, and his appearance showed it. Pedro noticed dried paint on his hands. The instructor stood in the corner; hands clasped around his chest.

"Now paint for us," the instructor said. "That is what we do here, Pedro. We paint for each other. We inspire each other. And we offer a critique of one another's work. How do you handle critique, Pedro?"

Pedro raised his head and looked up at the instructor. The instructor approached the canvas and took one of Pedro's brushes from the cannister. Pedro watched as he dipped it into a cup of black acrylic and slid the brush on the canvas.

Pedro's mouth dropped open. "What? My canvas?!"

He watched as the instructor dropped the brush on the table, never breaking eye contact with Pedro. "Look at that," the instructor said. "Look at your canvas."

Pedro turned for a moment and looked at the other artists, who sat at their stools, watching him, as if knowingly.

They had their canvases; they held their brushes. And now he was standing in front of them, preparing to paint for them.

He took a breath and looked at the canvas.

There was a swath of black paint assaulting the bright white canvas; it felt as if it were a criticism of his process before it even had begun. Pedro paused as he felt the instructor's hand gently cup his shoulder.

"Now," the instructor said. "What do you see?"

Pedro cleared his throat and shifted from foot to foot. He clasped his arms across his chest, took a breath, and sighed. He looked at the paint. It was a blotch, really.

"It is something that we all must look at," the instructor said, leaning close to Pedro's ear, and then turning to face the other artists. "Look at the details, Pedro."

Pedro leaned in closer and studied the splotch of paint. He examined the crevices where the bristles had been; how it added color to the page.

"Tell me what you see."

There were fine details that he hadn't noticed; tiny lines which revealed the placement of the bristles. "I see a splotch of black paint," Pedro said, after a few minutes. He turned to face the instructor.

The instructor took a step back and faced the other artists. "For an artist," he said. "It is always important to see the beauty in what *can* be beautiful. In what has the potential to be great. That is how art is born. Look at the canvas, Pedro."

The instructor took a few steps closer to the canvas and turned to face the class. Some of them were sitting on their stools, their elbows resting on their knees, leaning forward, peering around their own canvases.

The instructor folded his arms, addressing the class.

"And the rest of you, look at Pedro's canvas as well. When we take a first glance, yes, all we see is a splotch of paint. But therein lies the work of the artist. It is our destiny to create something out of that. See the beauty in the details of the ridges in the paint left on the canvas by the bristles on the brush; but also, the artist sees far beyond that. The artist is the one that allows that splotch to become something beautiful. The artist is the one who blossoms that butterfly. So, what can be beautiful? That is up to you, Pedro."

He looked at the splotch on the canvas and took a breath.

He slowly grabbed the brush, and dipped it in a few colors, and started mixing in his tray as the instructor approached. "Everything has the chance to be something," he said, leaning in close to Pedro. And then, as Pedro started adding color to the canvas, he glided his brush on the canvas, and dipped it in his brilliant mixture.

"Turn it into something," the instructor said. "It wants to be something more than what it is right now. Far more than what we perceive it to be. Help it become the butterfly that it wants to be."

As Pedro furiously painted, the instructor turned to the other artists. "Paint your canvases," he said. "And start with a blotch of paint, just as I did with Pedro here. Because everything really does have a chance to be something. A blotch of paint can turn into da Vinci's Mona Lisa, and a word can turn into a story. But only if the artist allows it to happen. For the creativity to flourish. And that is what we do as artists, no matter what the medium."

Pedro painted as the others painted, as the instructor walked through the room, his hands clasped behind his back, looking at the canvases, and studying them. He stood by each student for a moment, leaning in, providing instruction, as the student would turn and nod, and return their attention to their artwork. And then the instructor stopped at Pedro's canvas, as he focused on his work, and the art, and the bright colors that he was added to the canvas. The instructor folded his arms as Pedro took a step back. It was a bright, colorful butterfly, which had had created from the small splotch of black paint.

The instructor leaned close to Pedro.

"You, see?" he said. "Everything has the chance to be something. You have to allow it, Pedro."

In the days long after Pedro had become an artist, he was living with his beautiful Valentina in their shared flat in Madrid.

It was not far from the *Museo Nacional del Prado* and he remembered when she would stand over his artwork and encourage him as he painted, even if he didn't see his own talent which she clearly thought he had. It was also during the days after Pedro left Madrid, and Valentina, that he developed an infatuation in the immortal community, after studying their doctrines while in school.

Years had passed before he found it necessary to meet the taxidermist.

And it was one particular immortal, Antoine Nagevesh, who had become a leader in their society, who had taken Pedro under his wing. Antoine had the charisma and confidence which Pedro dreamed of. However, the one who had drawn him into the society was Darius, with an extraordinary promise of talent.

The immortals, who existed alongside the human population of the world, yet mostly undetected, exhibited members who were nothing short of extraordinary.

And Pedro desired that.

In the days in Madrid, Valentina could never give him that, yet she continuously believed in him and his work.

But when Pedro had to travel from his home in America to Lyon, France, where Antoine kept his chateau, his aspirations changed. He was to meet with Isaiah, the taxidermist from Tel Aviv, who Antoine said was the world's finest, to plan the resurrection and reconstruction of his long-lost muse. Pedro was to meet with both Antoine and Isaiah at the chateau.

And then they were to travel to Florence, Italy.

For that was where the convent was.

It was where the mysterious woman who was the subject of one of Pedro's most cherished and inspiring painters, Leonardo da Vinci, in his most mysterious and classical painting, Mona Lisa, lived and died. It was where she had lived as a nun, and Antoine insisted that her bones must be exhumed, to use in the largest and most significant resurrection in the immortal community.

"Skin, bones, and body," Antoine had told Pedro. "If you want her to return from the grave, then each of the components must be given equal consideration. At least according to *The Code of the Immortals.*"

Pedro knew all about the code.

And the book as well; he had procured a copy from his local library.

Casually, he forgot to return it; but he received a knock on the door seeking its return. "It was strange," Pedro had told Antoine. "I so desperately wanted to keep a copy of that book."

"It's the book that governs us," Antoine said. "It's powerful. And respected."

After he met the taxidermist in Lyon, and before Pedro and the others boarded the train to Florence, in search of the convent, he thought of the time when he first saw the woman in the painting.

She was the Mona Lisa, the enigmatic woman in the painting. She presented mystery and inspiration. Every time that he would venture from his flat in Madrid to Paris, as frequently he made pilgrimages to the *Louvre*, to study the work of Leonardo da Vinci.

He had remembered the art classes he had taken while still studying the legends, at the University, when the Professors had spoken about Lisa Giardini del Giocondo.

The mysterious woman had been married to a silk merchant in Florence. Pedro had always longed to travel to Italy, and now he was realizing that dream, yet for a different purpose.

When he was in Paris, he remembered standing at the museum, mesmerized by the painting, ignoring the throngs of tourists around him, gasping at its plain, simplistic beauty.

As he took a few steps to the left, her eyes seemed to follow. It was if she knew something which he did not; a mystery continued in the precious oils which comprised her likeness on the canvas.

Pedro's obsession was a desire to create, as a Spanish artist, from Madrid. He waited for the inspiration to thrust himself into a new life, away from his muse. A promise was made on a night when he wished he'd had the talent of the classic inspired artists who had long since passed away yet lived on within their paintings. But the promise came from an unexpected source of his infatuation.

Pedro knew the reason why he had to meet with the taxidermist, who was referred to him by the enigmatic Antoine Nagevesh, whose charisma was far beyond his own. It was rumored that Antoine was an immortal; that he was, in fact, centuries old, yet he resembled Pedro's age.

Youthful, vibrant, passionate and inspired with dreams of the future.

Pedro knew better than the assumptions of others; he had studied the immortals throughout his youth, possessing an infatuation with their kind and their code that few people had.

He knew who Antoine was in their hierarchy; and Pedro was confident that Antoine was, without a doubt, an immortal living within the human population.

But Antoine possessed a wisdom far beyond his youthful appearance, and Pedro became enamored with him in the years prior to their meeting. Was Antoine truly immortal? Was there an actual group called 'The Inspiriti', based in Rome, which was a group which governed the immortals? Did immortals walk among the people, seemingly undetectable?

Those were questions which Pedro had initially asked himself, and after the years he spent in his electives at the *Universidad Complutense* in Madrid while earning his degree in Theological Studies. But as Pedro became increasingly infatuated with the immortals, and the Inspiriti in Rome, he became aware of the many sources which proved that the immortals did exist in the human population, and in many instances, were seemingly undetectable.

Had immortals been living within the populace since the dawn of civilization?

Pedro recalled the days of his youth when he had first discovered the immortals, and the mysteries which surrounded them, and the books which mentioned them in the libraries of Madrid. He would stand in the tall, wooden stacks, holding the book which he had learned about, and it was clearly a copy, yet dusty, the pages yellowed and worn, no publication date on the interior. He held it in the dim light of the basement shelves. *The Code of the Immortals*. He carried it over to the nearest table, sat and turned the pages.

Pedro sat on the train, as it wound through forests and farmlands.

Antoine had insisted that they travel in a private, First-Class sleeper suite. Nothing but the finest of accommodations for Antoine, of course, but then he was accustomed to those types of surroundings. Pedro turned to face Antoine, who sat in a deep, leather seat, leaning back, with his eyes closed. Pedro knew he wasn't sleeping, Antoine rarely slept, and when he did, he slept the sleep of death, as he did in his chateau in Lyon.

Pedro stood, stepped over Antoine's extended legs, and parted the interior curtains, which covered the glass windows on the small wooden doors. He stepped back as the door slid open and Isaiah stood in the aisle.

Pedro noticed his long, white hair, still tied back behind his head. The man was many years his senior yet had a youthful vibrance about him.

The taxidermist Isaiah, from Tel Aviv.

Pedro hadn't thought that a taxidermist would originate from the Middle East.

Not long after the train had left the station in Lyon, as they settled into their sleeper car, after Pedro and Isaiah had exchanged pleasantries, Isaiah leaned in close to Pedro, as he leaned his arm on the armrest.

"One of the biggest, most grand taxidermy projects was in Israel," he said. "You can see my work there. All of the animals. Two of every kind. You ever hear of the story of the ark?"

Pedro "Ark?"

Isaiah nodded. "When God flooded the world. They saved two of every animal, do you remember from your studies?"

Pedro nodded. "Yes, I remember."

"Taxidermy is an art," he said. "It's no different than a painting or sculpture, really. Just the medium."

Pedro watched as Isaiah looked at him with a smile. "What is that?" Pedro asked.

"Well, the dead body, of course, Pedro. The body becomes my canvas."

Pedro glanced across the cabin and saw that Antoine had opened his eyes, yet his arms remained crossed over his chest and his legs were extended outwards on a small ottoman which the conductor had brought for them. "He is the most qualified taxidermist in the world," Antoine said, before closing his eyes again.

Pedro turned back to Isaiah who nodded.

They sat in the seats next to each other for hours as Isaiah explained the nuances of taxidermy, and the art, and the passion which he brought to the craft.

"And I can certainly bring back your beloved Valentina," he said, with confidence, to Pedro. And then Isaiah looked over at Antoine. "Of course, with your help, that's the only way it can happen."

"Of course," Antoine said, "And Jacob as well. A trip to Miami will be in order. The Waxley Mortuary is set up just for this sort of thing." Antoine adjusted his position and closed his eyes again.

Pedro leaned back in his seat and sighed as he turned to watch the forests pass through the window. He wondered about the mysteries the woods contained, as he recalled his studies of *The Code of the Immortals*, when he had learned about the mysteries of the forests. And the secret crypts which were placed around the world, for the immortals to serve their coffin sentences, in a system of justice which Pedro found fascinating.

But they weren't there to explore the mysteries of the hidden crypts; they were heading to Florence, to a centuries-old tomb, beneath an old, decrepit, crumbling convent. Beneath a church, near the altar, there was the reported entrance beneath the stones, to the catacombs which housed the tombs.

And her bones would be there. The bones of the woman who was rumored to inspire da Vinci's classic masterpiece.

But the three of them weren't heading there for the archaeological discoveries; Antoine had said that the city planners had granted permits to the Universities in a joint venture to excavate the catacombs beneath the building, and that is how Antoine and Pedro had identified the opportunity to move forward on the project.

Pedro had been told that the bones would be beneath the crumbling church; that the graves had been undisturbed for centuries. Yet now, after he met with the taxidermist who hailed from Jerusalem, with a unique and mysterious character, there had been a sense of trepidation for Pedro.

Should he be desecrating her grave?

Were the bones of the subject of the most mysterious painting of all time as powerful as they were rumored to be?

She was the Mona Lisa, he thought.

At least reported to be.

Could it be possible that the subject – and inspiration for – the most mysterious painting of all time be a common nun? If they didn't explore, though, he knew that his mission would be hopeless.

His longing for Valentina consumed him; she was the one who he had lost, the one who he had left, and the one who he had taken for granted.

And the bones would permit her return from the grave.

Or so he was told.

As Pedro cast his thoughts back to when the three of them were preparing for the mission, he fought with the thoughts swimming through his mind. He watched as Antoine and Isaiah, the taxidermist as he called himself, prepared their supplies next to the voluptuous Mercedes sedan outside of Antoine's chateau.

Pedro watched them roll the shiny, steel tools in a large, brown fabric bag, but couldn't motivate himself to assist. The drive from the chateau to the train station would be a long one, and he would have plenty of time to address his reservations in the car.

As he thought of the repercussions of the mission, he was reminded of the days when he had sat in his art studio in his small flat in Madrid, wishing for the muse to visit him. He longed for inspiration, yet as each sun would set, as the sky would liven and usher the end of the of the day, Pedro would hang his head in defeat, his long, black locks hanging over his shoulders. Another day lost, more failed inspiration.

Yet when he discovered the visitor in Madrid whom he was destined to meet, in the middle of the night, on an evening when he hadn't expected it, he had forgotten about the muse who had been gliding next to him.

It was she that continuously was watching his delicate strokes of the brush on canvas, dancing around him, her hands caressing the sides of his face, as he would concentrate on the minute details of his craftmanship.

Valentina.

She had always been there, she had purpose.

The one he had left, without a word, without a trace. She was the inspiration that he had lost without a warning.

But would she ever return?

Would the grave release her into his arms again, as the delicate clouds had promised to him?

The answers would lie within the convent, he hoped. There was an uncertainty which washed through him like a stone which upsets the delicate balance of a still pond.

Pedro knew that he needed Isaiah's help, if there was any hope for success at the convent, his services would be needed. But Isaiah was known by Antoine, who was the immortal who possessed the knowledge. Who said he worked directly with the immortal leadership in Rome, known as The Inspiriti.

Antoine had mentioned that they approved the mission, and the resurrection rituals, as Pedro's interest had provided the immortals another opportunity to repopulate after a devastating assault by a hooded figure carrying a crystal decanter full of blood, which brought death to the immortals.

It was agreed throughout the immortal community that Isaiah was a talented taxidermist, and now, that Pedro was seemingly forever alone, lost in the lazy summers in the endless Miami humidity, he knew that he needed Isaiah's talents for this mission. He was Spanish and blended well with the Hispanic culture in South Florida, but he knew that his love was across the ocean, lying in a cemetery in Spain.

It was time to recreate her.

Valentina, his long-lost love.

The woman he had so foolishly left for an infatuation, without a word. He had always been loving and faithful to her, never had an affair. At least not of the romantic kind. Pedro, though, had been fascinated with the immortals since he was a child. When he was offered the opportunity to join them, at a moment when he least expected it, during a time when he was at a creative end, Pedro knew that he had to follow his ambition.

His quest for knowledge, acceptance and destiny seemed to originate with the immortals. They had seemed to offer it.

And in this final project, he sought their assistance.

Mona Lisa had been buried for centuries, and the hopes of locating her bones, amidst the crumbling stone, dirt and rubble, would require the talents of a skilled archaeologist.

And Pedro knew of none. Perhaps one of the immortals in Paris or Rome might be of help. But Pedro knew, at the very least, that he needed Isaiah's help. He was, in fact, the finest taxidermist in Israel, and possibly the world.

And Pedro also needed Jacob Benjamin's help. Antoine had advised Pedro to visit the Waxley

Mortuary in Miami. Jacob was a mortician and had assured Pedro that when he returned to the Waxley Mortuary with both the bones, and several bodies, that he *might* be able to do a reconstruction along with the guidance and assistance of the most talented taxidermist in Israel and also in the world.

Both Isaiah and Antoine had claimed that yes, it was possible, if her bones could be located, and procured, that it *just might* be possible to use them for Pedro's massive project. His questions about why only Mona Lisa's bones would suffice had yet to be answered.

He didn't care.

He still wanted to proceed.

But it was Antoine who made the final promise.

"You will have to perform a ritual," he said. "If you want her back. And we can help you. You've proved your allegiance to us, which was inherent to the code. And you have also shown loyalty to the Inspiriti. That is paramount amidst our kind. And for that, you will be rewarded."

"I see…"

"And Pedro," Antoine continued. "Jacob can help you. He has been running the mortuary for quite some time now. But you have to make sure to only take the bones – and the bodies – to Waxley. And we will help you with that as well."

"And how will I get the bones there? And the bodies. The bodies will be even more challenging."

Antoine scoffed. "Do you have no confidence in me?"

Pedro sighed.

"I think it's more myself. I seem to have a curse against me, of some sort. It's everything since Madrid. The same dark cloud which seems to hang over my head."

"You don't talk like that as an immortal. You have more confidence. That is part of the code."

Pedro shook his head. "Then what is wrong with me? Why do I have these feelings?"

Antoine did not answer.

"Listen to me, Antoine. When I was in Madrid, I was worse off than I am now. But I have grown, I promise you. I have moved further in my life, I mean, I am a writer now! Isn't that something to be celebrated?"

Antoine nodded.

"Of course, it is, writers are cherished. If that is your destiny, then it is to be celebrated. But artists are cherished as well."

Pedro thought again of his time in Paris, and of the art classes in Madrid, and the days in his flat when Valentina would glide around his art studio, watching him paint, encouraging him to continue, and he did not listen. A feeling of regret tore through him as the night when he left, without a word or a whisper, flashed through his mind.

"But I feel like I lost my muse."

"You made your choice," Antoine said. "Choices come with consequences. But it does not mean that things cannot be fixed."

Pedro felt the pierce of his words, but Antoine was right. He made his choice, so many years ago, back in Madrid, before the days in America and then again in Paris, Pedro had made his choice.

He could still see the flashes of his art studio in his mind, in the small flat which overlooked the *Sierra de Guadarrama* mountains, and beneath was the cityscape and the bustling activity of cars and people scurrying on sidewalks and dining lazily in small tables at cafes.

He remembered the streetlamps, which ignited when the sun set and skies darkened; and he remembered Darius, when he waited and leaned on the iron base, watching his flat, waiting for Pedro to emerge.

My promise to you can never be kept.

"Darius made a promise," Pedro said.

And there was a moment in Pedro's mind which thrust him back to the night in Madrid, when the promise was made. When he was faced with a choice which took his life towards the destiny of his infatuation; an honesty which he faced, when the promise was broken.

But was Valentina his long-lost muse? He wished he could travel back in time, back to the days when she would dance, he always remembered when her skirt billowed out as she twirled through his art studio, as he would hover over his canvas. But when his memory fought for a semblance of who she was, the vision vanished, and he scarcely remembered her beauty.

The fire popped and cracked, and he was carried back to the present. Back in the front parlor of Antoine's chateau. Yes, he remembered now. Lost in his thoughts, he always knew he tended to become so wrapped in his musings that he forgot, for a moment, where he was.

Antoine was sitting across from him with Isaiah. And Giovanni was placing another log on the fire. It raged as he adjusted the logs with the poker.

"You are faced with another choice," Antoine said. "And this decision will stretch the limits of your moral judgement far more than you have ever experienced, I would imagine. But you must be certain...*certain*...before moving forward with this. You may experience the same fate I did when I resurrected Darius."

Pedro paused to consider Antoine's words.

He had heard about Darius, and how he died, which seemed so foreign for an immortal to *die*...but, as he slowly discovered...it was possible. That much he knew. But for Antoine, to have knowledge of a ritual to bring an immortal *back* from an eternal death sentence...then could that be extended to someone who didn't once possess the gift? Could the threat of death, somehow, be surmounted?

"Of course, we can die," Antoine said. "An immortal can die just as every other living creature. We are not walking with death, as many believe. We possess the gift, the immortality. The purpose and responsibility that comes with it."

"The responsibility?"

"Yes," Antoine said. "We immortals have many different abilities. Many are great World Leaders. Others are artists. Influencers in some way, in many respects, depending on their specialty. Some are great Theologians, and still others excel in their line of work, or their craft. But we have a responsibility to the gift. People look to us for guidance in many respects."

"But there are those of you that do not follow that guidance?"

Antoine nodded. "There are those, yes. And we have a system of justice. The Inspiriti brings order to our society. Most humans do not realize that we coexist with them peacefully, just a sacred few."

Pedro beamed. "And the talent you possess."

"Those are all part of the gift," Antoine said.

Giovanni headed to the others and offered more wine. As Pedro held up his glass, he looked directly at Antoine. "I definitely want the gift. I have been waiting for it far too long. I want to exist like you exist, know what you know. Experience what you do. I cannot express it enough."

He placed his glass on the table as Antoine and Isaiah exchanged a glance.

Antoine looked directly at Pedro with an intense stare.

"It bears a resemblance to the existence beyond the physical. We won't feel physical pain, of course. But the eternal isolation…" Antoine's voice trailed off for a moment.

Pedro thought Antoine may have been lost in thought, his eyes open, staring forward, yet no reaction when Pedro called his name. And then Antoine started to speak again. "…and darkness…can bring a searing and piercing…the eternal screams…"

Pedro looked up as Antoine raised his head. He lifted his hand, reaching out towards Pedro, his eyes wide, and a cold and desolation. "I can show you the gift, if that is what you wish to see."

"I want the gift. I've read so much, learned even more, and I want it more than even I could imagine."

Antoine paused.

"What you will see," he said "may lend you to reconsider. But you will use your own best judgment, I know you will."

Pedro felt a powerful force enter him as he squeezed his eyes shut and covered his ears.

The screaming...I cannot take the pierce of the screaming!

He felt the chill of a frigid wind against his face, and he knew that there was no escaping this vision.

Antoine had meant for him to be here; to see this.

He dared not open his eyes, yet the feeling that washed through him was that of trepidation, the glorification of evil, and the screams.

Too many cries of desperation.

He heard the soft dull roar of waves crashing on the shore, as he felt himself descending, deeper it seemed, perhaps into madness, with a certainty of desolation.

And then opened his eyes.

The sand was wet, cold against his cheek.

His eyes had struggled to focus, but he noted an emanating light, the sounds of a nearby shore, the methodic waves casting their deep melody towards his senses.

A beach.

"It's always a beach. Where you first descend. A putrid sea, that's all it really is. Guarded by a mist. But if you choose to proceed…the chaos…and the screams…will intensify."

He took a breath, coughing. It was Antoine's voice. His eyes slowly adjusted, and he held his breath for a moment.

Bright red blood.

Tiny crimson droplets on the sand; he couldn't have coughed up *blood,* could he?

"Don't let it consume you, Pedro."

He stared at the droplets as Antoine's voice tore through his mind. There was something about this place; he was right. There was nothing to be afraid of, was there? In this distant, dark place, in this seemingly forgotten realm?

There would be no pain here. No physical pain, at least.

That is what he had been told.

He lifted himself up on his elbows as his eyes continued to focus, and he saw.

There wasn't physical danger here.

But even with the calm façade of the delicate shores, as he watched the sea waves lazily approach the sands, his line of sight ended shortly after; a thick fog, a deep haze, concealed what was beyond.

Antoine spoke in his mind again. "Do not let it get inside your mind, Pedro."

And then he knew.

There were times during his studies of the immortals, and the resultant consequences of *the gift*; but here…things were different.

He stood, slowly; the aches in his joints a stark reminder of the physical world, but this was the spiritual, or so it seemed, and could there, in essence, be pain?

His thoughts remained and the questions as he finally straightened his posture, placing his hand on his back, feeling far beyond the years which he was.

Yet he watched the haze which levitated above the water and the smooth waves. He stood in the sand, taking slow steps forward until he felt the chill of the water on his bare feet.

There was a dark figure in the distance, out in the sea, in the white mist, someone approaching.

He held still.

As he scanned the area with his eyes, scarcely moving his head; he saw that it would be fruitless to make an attempt to hide. He looked out towards the sea once again, and the figure had approached closer. Could it be a ship?

No, it was too small.

It had to be *someone*.

But it was too large to be a person. Some of the immortals that Antoine and the others had schooled him about may have been larger in stature.

He watched and waited as the figure approached; it seemed to hover over a jetty of rocks which reached outwards into the sea, in a straight line, traversing the distance through the mist.

As the figure approached and gradually came into focus, he gasped.

It was a woman.

Dressed in black and white habit, she stepped down into the sand, taking slow steps toward where he stood, watching, and waiting. He scarcely considered his breathing, though his breaths were heaving his chest.

And then he saw her.

His mouth dropped open as she approached silently; the only sound being the lull of the waves. She emerged from the swirling, white mist, and he saw her. Yet she was somehow different; it wasn't the Valentina he had remembered from Madrid; she had an aura of mystery.

"Do not cross the stones," she said, as she stood in front of him.

Her habit was concealing and bulbous, flowing in the wind.

Pedro watched her face; there were scars running down her cheeks, and stitches. She was a nun at one point, but this was not the land of the sacred. She lowered her eyes and her head, and he watched her face; the skin was pale and bloodless, yet a tear streamed down her cheek. As if someone were inside, fighting for release, trapped in a hidden destiny.

"We are all different here," she said, as she slowly raised her head. Her eyes remained closed. "Do not cross the stones."

Pedro dared not speak.

"If you cross the stones, you will seek atonement for your sins."

He took a step back as she cried tears of blood, bright red streams down her pale and sullen cheeks. "If you cross the stones, you will be cast into the sea!"

Pedro awoke and gasped. Antoine sat next to him on the sofa, and he cradled Pedro in his arms, placing his head on his shoulder. The fire popped and crackled in the fireplace, as Giovanni stoked it and dropped another log in the chamber. Antoine stroked the side of Pedro's head as his rapid breathing slowly subsided.

"What did you see, Pedro?"

Pedro's eyes were wide, and he took a deep breath. "I...I am not sure. I *think* it might have been Valentina. But she seemed...so...it was as if she was...I can't even *explain*!"

"What is it, Pedro? What did you see there?"

Pedro shot up from the sofa and stood in front of the fireplace, staring at the flames.

He closed his eyes for a moment.

She was there, standing before him. He could hear the waves, he could see her, dressed in the black and white habit of a nun, appearing as if she were sewn together.

Reconstructed.

She took a few steps closer to him, placing her hands on his shoulders. He pulled back, wincing at the frigid chill. Her eyes were clouded, her stance rickety, yet she moved with a certain grace which only seemed to apply on the beach where he stood.

She leaned close to his ear.

Her breath stank of excrement.

"There is no physical danger here," she said. "There is only a slow and sure descent into madness…"

Pedro gasped, breathless.

His eyes shot open as Antoine and Isaiah got up and approached him. Giovanni rushed over with a small wet towel, placing it on his forehead. Antoine slapped him on his cheek lightly.

"Pedro! Pedro, don't leave us."

Pedro watched as Isaiah and Antoine appeared to be having a conversation, yet he heard nothing. He slammed himself back on the couch, reached up and grabbed them both by the arm. His eyes widened. "*She's in Hell!* Rotting like a demon!"

Antoine grabbed Pedro's shoulder. "Calm yourself. You wanted to see what the gift was. And now you have."

Antoine and Isaiah returned to the opposite sofa as Giovanni patted Pedro's forehead with the wet towel gently. Pedro's breathing slowly returned to normal. Pedro leaned back, closed his eyes, and listened to the crackle of the fire.

It was in the days and weeks before Pedro had flown across the Atlantic, from America, to Germany, to head to Antoine's chateau in Lyon, France, secretly by car, to meet Isaiah.

The waiting taxidermist was the one who would be recruited by the Inspiriti to bring Valentina back to life, Pedro had always recalled Antoine and his voice of authority.

Each time Pedro thought of Antoine's words, he felt a chill run through his spine.

Antoine was a leader in the immortal community, and he was always direct. His words reverberated through Pedro's mind as he boarded a widebody jet from Miami to Frankfurt in the weeks before their mission to Florence; Pedro had learned, over the years, from

The Code of the Immortals, that Frankfurt was the preferred landing airport when using commercial air transportation.

The waiting black Mercedes sedan met him at the terminal, as it always had. And always would, provided he remained loyal to the immortals, and to the Inspiriti.

He took a breath of the crisp, cool air in Germany.

The car was stunning, a large and voluptuous sedan.

Relentlessly overstated.

There would be many hours in that car for the trip south towards France, but Ramiel knew that Antoine insisted because the Inspiriti had insisted; there had always been dissension between the humans and the immortals, at least those humans who knew of them. And that had created the purpose of the secrecy. It seemed unnecessary, Pedro thought, but completely mandatory, for if the Inspiriti were to become aware of any diversion from their instructions, there would be swift repercussions.

That is what he had been told.

As he ran the regulations through his mind, he watched as the driver inched the car closer towards the sidewalk, as the chorus and chaos of traffic resounded nearby.

The luxurious sedan was as it had been requested for him, and the destination was Lyon, France; it was arranged by Antoine Nagevesh, leader of the immortals, the former coffee harvester from Sri Lanka, who would be waiting in the chateau. There were discussions of the taxidermist during the time Pedro and Antoine had spent together in Miami, when The Inspiriti had approved the resurrection, and Pedro had felt a sigh of relief that he would experience the encouragement of his muse once again.

"Valentina," he said, as Antoine had finished calling to reserve the plane to fly to Germany. "That was her name," Pedro added.

Antoine nodded. "Yes," he said. "And Rome has approved this, as you have been told that you receive the gift, and you desire the talent. Monsignor Harrison, who is in the highest position in The Inspiriti, had declared that we need to strengthen our population, especially after the threat which Darius succumbed to. For more immortals drank from the decanter. Lured in by that imposter. Luring us to our deaths."

Pedro stood behind Antoine as he sat in a small, upholstered chair, holding the phone in his lap, resting his chin in his palm on the arm of the chair. "You will be transformed, Pedro. You will receive your gift as it was promised to you. And you will uphold the code, and our doctrines, and be eternally loyal in return."

"Will you transform me?"

Antoine looked up at Pedro and shook his head. "You don't want to be a part of my lineage," he said. "It's cursed. Which is all for the better that Darius did not keep his promise, because he was my maker."

Pedro gasped. "He – "

"Yes," Antoine said. "He was. And this was not the first time that he has left me over the centuries. Dying, as he has. He's always been a bit of a rebellious immortal. They've punished him and banished him to the coffin several times."

"He sounds like an interesting character."

Antoine nodded and stood. "Yes, he was. Of course, now he's gone and done it. Doesn't help much when one dies mortal, you know. There's no returning from that kind of death. A sentence to the coffin becomes eternal, his body will rot and decompose, and there will be nothing left to resurrect."

"Unless we do something like what we are doing for Valentina."

Antoine glared at him. "We are doing that for *you*. There are no options like that for Darius."

Pedro placed his hand on Antoine's shoulder. "I understand. And I do appreciate what you are doing for me, Antoine."

Antoine nodded and headed down the corridor. "Be sure that you are ready within the hour. I've chartered you a plane and it leaves tonight."

"What about you? You're not coming?"

Antoine paused at a far doorway, turned and looked down the corridor at Pedro. "Don't worry about me. All of our gifts are different, Pedro. You will learn. But I have some additional business to take care of here before I join you. But by the time you arrive at the chateau, I will already be there."

He awakened in the back seat of the sleek black sedan, surprised that he could doze for so many hours after sleeping on a plane. He gazed out the window as the driver lowered the dividing glass. "Just passed Strasbourg, signor. Several hours remain. Do you need a stop off?"

Pedro nodded and waved an acknowledgement.

When the driver had pulled out of the Frankfurt airport, he had told Pedro that Antoine was already at the chateau waiting for him, and that the drive would take nearly six hours. There was wine and beer in the rear console, should he choose to partake, the driver had said. Pedro opened the center console, and selected a can of German beer, and popped the top. He relished the cool, crisp feel of the liquid, the warm and fuzzy feeling as the alcohol gripped his senses, and the delicate, floral aftertaste of the finish of the lager.

He didn't remember his eyelids becoming heavy once again, and as he opened his eyes, picking the grit out of the corner of one of his eyes, he watched as the car pulled up to a winding slender driveway, which was nestled in the center of a thick forest of trees. Pedro peered through the rear window as the driver eased the car closer towards the clearing in the trees. He could see the stone structure; it was clearly the chateau he had heard about. He knew that Antoine had lived there, reportedly for centuries, with his lover Darius, but now only Antoine remained.

Pedro stared at the chateau for several minutes as the car stopped. He watched as the driver lowered the smoked glass divider.

"*Estas aqui*, Maestro Dominguez," he said. He raised the divider, and Pedro watched as he opened his door, walked around the car and stood outside of his door. Certainly, an immortal, no doubt. One of a lower sect. Of a service lineage, most likely. He wondered what his bloodline might be. But Pedro did not understand Antoine's lineage. Antoine appeared to live as royalty, with extraordinary gifts, yet he had told Pedro that he had once been a coffee bean harvester from Sri Lanka. Certainly, that was a noble origin, but not that of opulence and royalty. It was of hard work, and dedication to the craft of coffee.

What had drawn Antoine to the lifestyle he currently possessed?

He watched as the driver reached out, slowly opened the door, and stood off to the side, clasping his hands at his waist, possibly sweltering in the black suit he must have been required to wear. It was late afternoon, and the sun was setting in the sky, but western Europe had been under a brutal heat wave. Pedro then returned his attention to the Chateau; it stood, nestled amidst the trees, seemingly formidable.

It could have been a castle, yet it was not. It resembled a mansion yet made entirely of stone.

It soared upwards towards the sky, and Pedro focused on the soaring wooden doors which centered the building, noticing their heavy and weathered look, and wondered if Antoine would be welcoming or not. He said he would, but they had parted in Miami with the irritation while Pedro had inquired about Darius. Antoine seemed to be inviting and helpful, for the most part. But Antoine was grieving himself.

Pedro also knew that Antoine insisted on him meeting Isaiah, who had flown in from Tel Aviv, and according to Antoine's messages, the taxidermist was already waiting inside, and eager to discuss the project.

As he approached the stone steps which rose up towards the massive wooden doors, he heard the car door slam and the engine roar to life.

The Mercedes pulled slowly along the winding, circular driveway, and Pedro turned back to see the sedan through a patch of trees, heading back towards the road.

Now he was alone, and he had no choice but to enter the chateau, as the sedan pulled away.

Pedro was thrust from his musing as he heard the heavy creak of a door from behind him. He looked up the steps and saw two men. Antoine nodded at him, and next to him, a much older looking man, with a long, white beard which nearly reached his waist. It was tied at the bottom.

Antoine gestured his arm outwards as Pedro slowly ascended the steps. He focused on Antoine. He was the eternally youthful immortal from Sri Lanka, the one who said someone would transform him. But not into his lineage. He could tell Antoine was gifted with near perfect bone structure, a slender body in his traditional black suit, and long, dark locks, which flowed downwards over his shoulders. Pedro hardly noticed his mouth dropping open, just slightly, as he extended his hand slowly, feeling the chill of Antoine's palm, as the immortal grabbed him close, wrapping his arms around Pedro in a wordless embrace.

"You made it, I see," Antoine said, releasing their embrace. "Of course, you must understand, I chartered you that plane as I had some business to take care of in Miami before leaving. But I also know that, as a mortal human, that you could not travel the way I am gifted to."

Pedro slowly nodded, drawn to Antoine's eyes. He cast a glance over at the other man, who appeared to be decades older, standing on the opposite side of the porch with his hands clasped at his waist. His hair was silver, long, and tied behind his head; he was slender, lanky.

Antoine extended his arm towards the older man. "This is the taxidermist, the one your fine mortician Mr. Benjamin told you about," he said.

Pedro slowly nodded. "Yes, Jacob Benjamin. At Waxley, of course. I remember him well."

The man livened as he and Pedro shook hands respectfully. "My name is Isaiah Mizrahi. Antoine called me several days ago and informed me about your predicament. I can certainly be of assistance. And I know Mr. Benjamin – Mr. Jacob – quite well, in fact. But I am here at your service. My talents are for your mission."

"He flew in from Tel Aviv just this morning," Antoine added.

Isaiah nodded and scoffed. "Yes." He then looked over at Antoine. "If you would have transformed me like you *promised* then I wouldn't have to fly in a plane and I wouldn't have this long grey beard!"

Pedro watched as Antoine grinned.

"You know we must all fly that way. Transforming you wouldn't change the code."

"But what about you?" Pedro asked, as Isaiah nodded.

Antoine pointed towards the doors and cast a glance back to Pedro, nodding his head.

Antoine glared at both of them. "Let's go inside. There are more important matters to discuss."

Isaiah shook his head and they all headed inside the grand foyer. Antoine led as Pedro followed. Isaiah called inside from the rear. "You need to keep your promises!"

Antoine sighed.

He looked over at Pedro, speaking in a hushed tone. "We have a bit of a history," he said.

Pedro slowly nodded. "I see."

Antoine spun around as Isaiah stepped inside and swung the heavy door closed.

"And he is the *finest* taxidermist in all of the Middle East. Possibly Europe too!"

Pedro watched as Isaiah approached Antoine and placed his arm around Antoine's waist. Isaiah leaned close towards Antoine's ear. "The world," he said.

Antoine looked over at Pedro. "You must need to freshen up from your travel?"

Pedro shook his head. "No, I'd rather get right to it."

Isaiah nodded. "I agree. I came here for the ultimate artistic project."

Antoine shot a glance back to Pedro. "And where are your things? You brought nothing?"

"I brought nothing. There was no reason to."

Antoine smiled and nodded. "Yes," he said. "Yes, I understand. You are one of us now. The code, of course. All that is mine is yours."

Pedro didn't care about Antoine's material possessions, although he did appreciate the acknowledgement.

Antoine showed them into the front parlor and introduced Giovanni, who stood next to a wet bar, on the perimeter of a grand rectangular room with soaring windows, heavy cranberry drapes, and a matching rug which nearly completely covered a stone floor. As the three sat in the matching sofas, Giovanni rushed over with bulbous glasses of red wine.

"This is how I receive guests," Antoine said. "You will be greeted in the front parlor, next to a crackling fire, with my finest glass of Beaujolais."

Pedro watched as Giovanni offered wine to each of them. Antoine was the gracious host and clearly, they respected him as the leader of the immortals. Pedro knew of the years when Antoine had been the leader of the Miami sector, but he didn't yet understand how Monsignor Harrison fit into the equation. Antoine had said that the monsignor had been in a high position in Rome, as a leader in The Inspiriti.

And, for that matter, Pedro didn't yet understand how The Inspiriti related to the immortal community, but from what he had deduced, The Inspiriti governed the immortal community. Those were tumultuous years; it was when the immortals had been assaulted by The Hooded Man. Pedro had learned of that in his studies, and even more when Antoine had been telling him the stories when they were together in Miami.

It was how Darius met his demise.

The immortals were gifted yet despised.

As they settled into the sofas with their glasses of wine, Giovanni tended to the fire and retreated. Pedro and Isaiah waited as Antoine took a sip of his Beaujolais.

He closed his eyes, and Pedro assumed he must have been holding it in his mouth. Antoine appeared to swallow, opened his eyes, and looked at the others.

"We are here for Pedro," he said.

Pedro had been examining the tiny clear bubbles that hugged the side of his wine glass and looked up. "Yes, thank you, Antoine."

Antoine stood.

"There is not much time if you want to arrive in Florence by mid-day tomorrow. The convent is abandoned. You will be able to enter and procure her bones. But we must leave shortly if we are going tonight."

Pedro and Isaiah looked at each other, making eye contact. Isaiah spoke first. "It's the convent of Sedosera. It's abandoned and decrepit. It's crumbling, and an archaeological excavation site, so we will have to go through the cover of darkness to reach her tomb. It's near the altar of the cathedral, underneath the floors, in the catacombs. But it is rumored her bones are there."

Pedro nodded.

"Then we shouldn't be sitting around and drinking wine. We should be leaving to catch the train, no?" He looked over at Antoine as he set his glass on the table.

Antoine took a slow slip of his wine, and then looked at Pedro. "Relax, dear mortal. We have plenty of time. And before we leave, anyway, we will be going to the crypt at *Les Enfantes*. Darius is entombed there. I thought you might want to pay your respects."

"You have told me why he couldn't keep his promise to me, so yes, provided we have the time, yes, that would be fine," Pedro said.

"Good then. And I will join you in Florence," Antoine said.

He nodded and continued. "You will need my assistance, anyway. And once Isaiah has finished reconstructing her, we will place her in the crypt here in Lyon where Darius is buried. I have experience with resurrection. But I must warn you. Because it will be you, and only you, that can perform the ritual. And you will be pursued."

Pedro's face shifted as he lowered his glass, placing it gently on the table. He looked up at Antoine. "Pursued?"

Antoine sighed.

"Yes," he said. "There is always a means to collect payment."

Pedro followed Antoine as he stood. Antoine took a breath and looked at Pedro directly. "If you do this, you must realize that the demons will come. There is a price. For the resurrection, you see."

Pedro placed his hands on his knees, and as he moved, he could tell his underarms had become moist. His heart was beating fast. "I was told that I could bring the remains to the Waxley Mortuary. Jacob told me. That they have a special cremation chamber there?" Pedro looked up at Antoine expectantly.

Antoine scoffed as he glanced over at Isaiah. "Right. They sure do."

Pedro shook his head. "Then what am I supposed to do?"

Antoine returned to the sofa next to Isaiah as Giovanni discreetly refreshed their Beaujolais.

"You are to make a decision," Antoine said. "And you must know every parameter so you can make an intelligent and informed choice. I am sitting here telling you that, if you proceed, there very well may be a cost for your incantation. I speak from experience."

The sun was long set, and the darkness had overtaken Antoine's chateau as Pedro quietly stepped down the corridor which lined the first level rooms which led towards the massive grand foyer. The train was scheduled to leave soon, and Antoine had not emerged from his quarters.

Pedro turned as he heard the approach of footsteps.

Giovanni approached and leaned close to Pedro. "Master Antoine will be ready, do not worry," he said.

"Isaiah and I are starting to gather the equipment. The car is waiting outside."

Pedro nodded and followed Giovanni to the foyer, where Isaiah was placing the bags near the front door.

Giovanni rushed over and picked up one of the bags.

"Let me, sir. You are a guest. I will bring these all to the car. Master Antoine will be emerging from his suite shortly, and you can catch your train to Florence."

Pedro and Isaiah jumped in to assist Giovanni, and the three of them loaded the sedan. The tools clanked as Pedro tossed one of the bags into the trunk.

Giovanni slammed the trunk as Antoine appeared at the front door, his hands on his hips. "Let's get going," he said. "It's an overnight train," he said, looking at Pedro. "If you need to sleep, I booked a sleeping car, so there will be plenty of time for you to sleep."

"I don't think I will be able to sleep."

Antoine shrugged his shoulders as he glided into the front passenger seat. "It's up to you. We are going to be full speed ahead once we arrive in Florence, so be sure to get your rest."

Giovanni closed up the chateau doors and headed towards the car as Pedro and Isaiah each took opposite ends of the back seat. Antoine turned to look at them as Giovanni pulled slowly away from the front walk of the chateau, but said nothing, before facing forward again.

Pedro exchanged a glance with Isaiah, and then Pedro leaned back in the seat, closed his eyes, and listened to the slight rumble of the road, which lulled him to sleep.

FLORENCE, ITALY

The train hissed as it slowed to a stop at *Stazione di Santa Maria Novella.*

Finally in Florence.

Pedro raised his eyes and looked across the car as Antoine was resting his head on his hand, gazing out the window. Isaiah fidgeted next to Antoine, on the opposite bench. The train stopped and the whistle sounded as the conductor made an announcement over the public address system in Italian, declaring their arrival at the station.

Pedro took a deep breath as Antoine cast his gaze across the car and made eye contact. It was now or never. Pedro knew that Antoine knew what he was thinking. The warmth of the wine back at the chateau in Lyon had long worn off; the stark reality of what they were about to embark upon was now staring them straight in the face like a morning hangover in the bathroom mirror.

Pedro knew of the risks.

The demons may come.

"No, they will," Antoine reminded him, as they all rose and headed towards the glass sliding door.

Isaiah brushed past to the corridor as Antoine leaned in close to Pedro. "The demons will come," he said. "They will come for your soul. But you've made your choice. And we will return in a waiting car, which will be provided to us from Rome."

Pedro took a breath and exhaled as he watched Antoine follow Isaiah towards the end of the car. Antoine was right. The mission he had chosen was not without risks. And the rules remained, that had been in place for centuries, if not millennia, in the immortal community.

Resurrection requires retribution.

One of the rules of the code.

Antoine had reminded him of the book repeatedly, after they had finished in the parlor, and finished their wine. Antoine had led the three of them down into the cellar beneath the estate. Nestled in a set of old dusty bookshelves, in the corner of the dark, stone walls, was a copy.

Antoine reached his hand towards the shelves, and Pedro noticed that the book seemed to reflect the light more than the others.

"It's *The Code of the Immortals*," Antoine said and slowly pulled the big, heavy book from the shelves, and hoisted it over to a small wooden table. The others watched as he flipped through old, dusty pages. He paused at a page as Isaiah leaned in more closely.

Pedro felt a chill run through his body.

"Resurrection requires retribution," Antoine said, laying the book open flat on the table. The others leaned in closer to examine the section on resurrection.

"And this is what I am going to do," Pedro said. He looked closer and saw the incantation specifics but felt a shudder as he saw the expected results of the ritual.

"Asmodai is the demon of lust," Antoine explained. "He is the demon that pursues me."

Isaiah raised his head. "A demon pursues you?"

Pedro looked at Antoine.

He saw that his eyes fell, and Pedro knew the answer. "For many years now," Antoine said.

Pedro's thoughts were thrust back into the present, as he watched Antoine retreat with Isaiah down the narrow corridor which bordered the First-Class roomettes.

They were past the point of no return.

He was surprised that Isaiah had agreed to continue with the exhumation after learning of the immortal code.

But the feelings of uncertainty remained.

They were like an unwelcome visitor, a feeling which Pedro knew would not dissipate, nor offer any resolution even if they were to fade away.

As he waited for a group of elderly travelers to ease themselves from the front cabin, he watched Antoine and Isaiah through the nearby window.

He parted the sheer, white curtain, and watched them wait for him on the platform. He could see they were discussing something, but despite his attempts to read their lips and posture, he couldn't determine any specifics.

Save one.

It was the demon which Antoine spoke of.

The demon of lust.

Asmodai.

As they gathered on the boarding platform at *Stazione di Santa Maria Novella,* Pedro paused and looked around.

Expansive windows, as if a glass ceiling, soared above the bustling atrium. Travelers dashed in many different directions as Pedro slowly lowered his head, taking notice of the small shops which lined the edge of the platform.

"It has ushered in the cosmopolitan era of the city," Antoine said. "Such an astounding contrast to what it once was."

"And in some ways, still is," Isaiah added.

Pedro gazed upwards towards the glass which filtered in the daylight. Outwards, towards the city, were the small stucco buildings, the low-rise windows and the bustling cobblestone streets painted a soft, pastel contrast to the modern, bustling train terminal. It was as if they were inside the destiny of a city, stepping outwards towards the past. But Pedro's thoughts remained with the destiny with which they would collide at the convent.

The crumbling stone church: an excavation site now, Antoine knew. He always knew. It was something about him that appeared all-knowing, as if Antoine had advanced to a level of which Pedro may only dream about.

Antoine and Isaiah both turned to face Pedro. "I think you are lost in a daydream," Antoine mused. "But we must hurry to the Cellai."

Pedro followed as he heard Antoine speak of the famous Hotel Cellai. He had learned of the luxurious boutique hotel, just steps from the Cathedral, as a favorite of traveling immortals. He had never been there, however, and Pedro hoped to discover why it was the first choice of accommodations in Florence.

Pedro watched as Antoine and Isaiah appeared to be in deep discussion, and he watched them, and followed, as they navigated the busy crowds.

Antoine turned around but kept moving forward. "Not much farther now," he said. "No need for a car. In perfect walking distance."

The sky livened with color as the sun began to set; it sank down towards the horizon as Antoine charged toward the famous Boutique hotel, a few mere blocks away from the station. Antoine led the trio, as Isaiah walked at a slightly slower pace, smoking and easing himself between the people who walked the opposite direction. Pedro followed them, watching them, wondering what mysteries the hotel might contain.

But Pedro was not bothered by the walk.

And as he watched Antoine and Isaiah come together, walk side-by-side and return to their conversation, he lost the curiosity to discover what they were discussing.

To him, it no longer mattered; and even if was about him and what they were planning to do, there was even less of a reason to care. He had made his decision; they were assisting with the plan.

He had no choice but to trust Antoine and his judgement; Antoine was now one of the highest-ranking immortals, commanding great respect in their governance, throughout the world and time.

While they waited to cross the thoroughfare, the rays of the setting sun warmed his face and he closed his eyes and saw Valentina gliding across the hardwood in their old flat back in Madrid, years ago.

He could see how the sunlight glistened in her hair as it flung outwards as she twirled, making it appear less brunette and more golden. So many days, when the sun would settle in the sky and usher in the evening, she would dance as he painted, huddled over a canvas, studying the tiny strokes of his brush.

Valentina would dance, sing, and lightly touch his cheek when she passed close to his small wooden stool.

Antoine and Isaiah stopped in front of a nestle of small, iron tables on the edge of the small, busy thoroughfare, against the tan masonry of a building. Pedro raised his head and saw the steel lettering above the arched doorway.

HOTEL CELLAI

He had heard about this tiny boutique.

And when the three immortals entered under the small, scalloped awning, they stepped into terracotta opulence. Potted palms nestled between high backs of small sofas and upholstered side chairs, and grand archways leading into cozy rooms off the main greeting area, a bar and library. Pedro saw the literary connection, and the theory that he had studied many years ago was now starting to reveal itself. Many of the immortals were masters of their craft; some were artists, others were authors. Yet mediocrity was unfounded nor was it tolerated.

While Antoine and Isaiah moved towards a small desk in the center of the far wall, Pedro scanned the area and noted that the expectations of the immortals, and even more so, The Inspiriti, were specific and pronounced: they would accept nothing less than excellence.

Pedro watched as a small, stocky olive-skinned man in a tailored grey suit rushed towards Antoine, seemingly out of thin air. "Antoine, dear Antoine!" He beamed, speaking English in a thick, Italian accent.

He boomed. "They told me you would be coming! My wonderful immortal *inspirazione!*" He extended his arms and gave them both a warm and welcoming embrace.

The tiny man looked at all three of them. "You all came from America, yes?"

"The chateau in Lyon," Antoine said. "It was a long journey on the train, of course."

The man gave a knowing nod, looking back and forth at each of them. "Ah yes, I understand. The veil of secrecy, yes?" As Antoine and Isaiah traded kisses on the cheek with the small, olive-skinned man, they parted, and the man beamed.

"*Sono veremente desolato!* I am so very sorry." He turned to Pedro and extended his hand. "Flavio Esposito. Hotel Manager." Pedro nodded as Flavio grabbed Pedro's upper arms, gave him a boisterous welcome, and kissed him on each cheek. He pulled back, seemingly enthralled with Pedro. "So, you are the one! You are the one who Antoine has been keeping from me!"

Pedro smiled and nodded politely.

"Don't come on too strong, Flavio," Antoine said. "He is not transformed."

Flavio nodded slowly, looking Pedro up and down, and took a step back. "You are the one who has been studying us, yes? Our kind?" Pedro smiled wanly but said nothing. Flavio glanced over at Antoine. "So, you have brought me to him! With this seemingly insurmountable mission?"

Antoine leaned down towards his ear. "Not so much, you said."

The small man nodded hurriedly. "Yes, yes, Mr. Antoine. Indeed. That is what I told you."

Pedro watched as he noticed the difference in the aura of the lobby. The guest still wandered through the meticulously upholstered furnishings in front of the painted artwork which hung from the stucco walls, but the lobby was mostly empty. As he scanned the room, he noticed the small, wooden desks towards the check in area. And the faded terracotta which bordered the walls with artistic blue tiles. It was the hotel of choice in Florence. It wasn't the difference in the activity; it was the difference in the interaction with the man who greeted Antoine and Isaiah; it was the determination he showed while ushering them to a secret room, a private office which resided far from the public areas, behind a heavy, wooden door. The walls were lined with dark, wooden bookshelves, with a tall Grandfather clock which rose in the center of the shelves on the opposite wall. Pedro scanned the small, secret room, and took pause.

This room was not their destination, Flavio had explained. "We all must have a front," he said.

They followed him as he said they would be venturing below. Antoine turned, looking at Pedro directly, and nodded, making direct eye contact. "When I take you to Rome, you will understand," he whispered.

There was no desk; there were no chairs. But there was another door, on the far wall, and although Pedro did not know the small man, he knew he was part of The Inspiriti. He cast a glance over towards Antoine, who had remained silent until that point.

"I am sure you are already well aware of Pedro's intentions," he said.

Flavio nodded. The small, paunchy man stood in front of the mysterious door as he fished a set of golden keys from his pocket. "That is why we must descend the stairs," he said, turning his attention to Pedro. "You have never taken the journey beneath, have you?"

"I…" he stammered, and looked over at Antoine, who gave him a nod. "No, but I have read about some of the nuances of the immortals in books."

Flavio shifted his face. "Books," he said. "They are wonderful, for certain, but one must experience what is in books first-hand. The power of the imagination is magnificent, but it becomes more extraordinary when what lives on the page exists in reality."

"Or in another dimension," Isaiah said.

Flavio nodded as Antoine hooked his arm around Pedro's leaning close to his ear. "You have to understand, dear Pedro, that the books which you refer to cannot be replaced by what you will experience. You wish to be an immortal, then you will surrender your mind to what can be. And what always is."

Pedro pondered what Antoine may have meant by what he said, but his thoughts carried him back to his studies. There was the mystery which surrounded the immortals; it may have been one of the greatest enigmas of his life. He knew he desired the talent, to live forever. To be afforded the opportunity to explore, in search of the answers to the questions which he had since he was a boy, when he first discovered the immortal community. Ever since then, he so desperately wanted to be a part of it.

"I have studied the code," Pedro said. "For years. In great depth and detail."

Flavio scoffed and looked at Antoine. "He has studied the code."

And then he returned his attention to Pedro. "Come with me. If you want to be of our kind, and you desire to resurrect your dear Valentina, then you must experience more than what can be contained in books and studies."

As they filed inside, Pedro noticed the old books which lined the walls, and stairs which were old, dusty; wooden and creaked with each step they took.

They descended past portraits of Goya and Velazquez, two artists he recognized from Spain, hung elegantly in ornate, gold frames, against painted white bricks.

"They are the original canvases," Flavio added. "Many are unaware of the copies which hang in the galleries in your city."

"Copies?" Pedro asked. "You must be joking, aren't you?"

He turned and looked up at Pedro and Antoine, cracking a grin. "There's quite a bit that you don't know about The Inspiriti, young man. But look down here. It's the ideal conditions for preserving original artwork."

Pedro scanned the walls as Flavio turned and headed downwards towards the darkness, walking past works from da Vinci and Lorenzetti; there were paintings from artists of all nationalities hanging throughout the walls. Pedro noted the dim lighting from the incandescent bulb hanging overhead. Flavio was right. Antoine placed a hand on his shoulder, carrying him out of his musings. "Let's go," Antoine said. "He is getting farther from us."

Flavio's words hung in Pedro's mind, and as he followed the small man, he huddled close to Antoine.

As they walked through the darkness Pedro noticed the temperature cooled.

It wasn't the frigid chill which he had experienced in winters in Paris, but a cool, comfortable feel of a cave.

He looked down as the floor gradually felt rough, and gasped when he noted that it ceased to be a "floor", but rather earth, moss and stones, water and sand.

Antoine leaned closed to his ear. "It goes on and on," he said. "Do you feel like we are descending?"

Pedro nodded, although he imagined Antoine would not be able to see him in the darkness. "Yes. I can feel the downward slope."

"It just continues."

"Where does it lead?"

Pedro jumped as Flavio appeared directly facing them. He had small candle, bathing his face in a warm glow. Yet Flavio had a sinister look on his face, his eyes piercing and reflecting the flicker of the candle. "This will bring you to the gateway to Hell," he slowly said.

Pedro gasped and shot a glance over to Antoine.

"What the?" And then he looked back at Flavio. "Why are you taking me down here? What is this supposed to show me?"

Flavio did not answer, but turned away from them, facing forward, carrying the light with him deeper into the darkness.

As the art and sense of normalcy faded into the background, they were swallowed into the darkness, the earthen floor and stones. Pedro scanned the area and could scarcely make out Antoine and Isaiah amidst the darkness, attempting to adjust his eyes, yet failing.

The gateway to Hell…

The words pierced his mind like a stake.

The descent continued, deeper into what seemed to be a secret cave, as they felt they were heading downwards, deeper into the Earth; as he looked at Antoine in a brief flicker of light, Flavio turned.

"You must prove to them that you have the capability to endure," Flavio said. "To prevent the insanity."

Flavio turned again and they continued through the mud and the muck, until there was an orange flicker up ahead, far ahead; but as it reflected on the pools of putrid water, Antoine stopped for a moment, extending his arms, stopping the others. "The guardian," he said, slowly. "The call of the flames."

He glanced at Pedro, over at Isaiah, and back at Pedro. "Are you ready?"

"Where are we?" he asked. "What is this place?"

"There are little known entry portals in secret locations throughout the world. They must be guarded," Flavio said, turning to face them again. Pedro watched as Antoine met eyes with him, in the dim flicker of Flavio's candle. Isaiah looked ahead, towards the source of the flames. "We are getting closer," he said.

Flavio raised his eyes to the others, gestured for them to follow, and turned. "It will get inside your mind, if you let it. If it does…you will never return the same."

"If you ever return at all," Antoine said.

They continued forward, as Flavio led with his candle. They now huddled close together, as screams emanated from the distance. "The Inspiriti are the protectors of the gates. Those who join us will be tasked with extraordinary expectations and we do not take our responsibility lightly. The evil must be contained. It is our duty to see that it is."

Pedro reached out and stopped the others. "So…you are…angels?"

Flavio looked up at Pedro, staring at him directly.

"Call us what you will. Those in the mortal population have likened us to vampires, others have placed us in the order of the Baal, and some should be placed there. But there are those of us who are tasked with the greatest responsibility, and you are being brought here to see if you are worthy."

Flavio ushered for them to continue, as they approached a vast, open, dark space. They looked up as the darkness above them seemed endless, yet as Pedro looked down, he saw the simplicity of a burning bush. It was large, and the flames continued, as the bush remained intact.

"Behold, the entrance to the spirit world," Flavio said.

Pedro remembered his studies as a child, when he was in Bible -study. Was this?

"Blasphemy," Flavio said. "That is all that is contained here. Hell is the antithesis of anything you have learned. Do not let it get inside your mind, yet it already has."

Pedro took a step towards the bush. As he approached it, it appeared massive. Reaching upwards into the darkness, burning with crackling flames, burning a smokeless fire in a desolate dark landscape.

"Don't, Pedro," Antoine said, reaching out for his shoulder. "It's not what you think it is." He pulled Pedro back. "You may have learned this, but this…*here*…is not what you think it is. There is much power in what is good, but this place…this gate…is not that. It wants you to think it is. It will deceive you. Don't let it get inside your mind."

Pedro took a breath as the others surrounded him.

The bush faded as a wall of flames ignited far in the distance, beckoning them forward.

"Do not proceed," Flavio warned. "The deeper you go, the harder it will be to emerge unscathed."

Pedro studied the landscape as it was partially revealed by the flames in the distance.

He looked down, and saw they were standing in a bed of sand, and led further outwards, where there was water, tiny waves which lapped delicately at the shore. Large, flat stones in the center which reached out into the desolate sea, towards the burning fire in the distance, nestled between the calm waves, leading away from the shores, the destination concealed by a swirling, white mist.

"Do not go, however much it may beckon," Flavio said, as he stood in front of the stones. His candle had burned down, covering his hand in melted wax. "The Sea of Souls," he said. "The calm is an illusion. It will always be. Only the strongest of us can proceed into the sea."

"The eldest of our kind, Claret Atarah, was cast into the sea," Antoine said, with a sigh, looking over at Isaiah.

"She is there with the damned. If we continue with this, the resurrection, there will be a portal open. Resurrection requires retribution."

"And she will come? She is evil?"

Pedro watched as Antoine and Flavio looked at each other. Flavio raised his eyebrows and tilted his head to the side. Pedro thought that was all he needed. But Antoine turned to face him. "Those who are cast to the sea cannot travel to the next realm, which is ours."

Pedro turned and looked at the sea.

He felt his heart quicken.

The beach was eerily familiar; the same stones reached outwards, through the water, towards the swirling and concealing white mist.

Would she appear again?

Flavio brought his candle closer to the others, bringing a warm glow to their faces.

"You may see the gates," he said. "But you cannot proceed without the ritual. And the sacrifice. Once you enter, beyond your thoughts, through what your own destiny may become."

Pedro studied the image.

"Reach out," Flavio said. "Touch it."

Pedro looked at the others as they watched on.

As he turned to face the scene before them; the beach, the mist, the stones…if was as if it were the opening of a deep cave, heading outwards towards light, but a muted distinction.

It was as if the clouds were eternally circling overhead, blocking the sun, yet filtering the light. He looked back again at the others as they waited, patiently.

"Touch it," Flavio said again.

He turned and drew his hand out, reaching outwards, towards the beach, listening to the call of the waves, watching the swirl of the mist. It was as if it were a postcard on a disappointing day.

He reached further, and stopped, as he gasped.

There was resistance.

He touched it again, as the waves shimmered away from his finger. He snapped his head toward the others as his mouth dropped open.

"You cannot penetrate it," Flavio said.

Pedro turned back to look, as he watched the waves lap delicately at the shore, and the mist swirl above. "It seems like I can walk right through it!"

"But you can't," Antoine said. "And Isaiah here will concur. He has seen these before."

Isaiah nodded. "Another one in Jerusalem."

Pedro shook his head slowly, as his eyes remained transfixed on the beach and shores.

Flavio approached him, and Pedro turned his head.

The flicker of the candle reflected in Flavio's glasses. "It's the gateway to Hell. There are seven of them.

Seven gates to Hell. But these portals, located throughout the world, are heavily guarded."

Antoine placed his hand on Flavio's arm. "Do not tell him too much. Remember, he is not transformed."

Flavio appeared flustered, and slowly gained composure. "Well!" he said. "Of course, you will not be able to enter these gates in your physical state. Not without transformation. And you wouldn't want to enter them, anyway."

Pedro cast his gaze back to the beach, watching the mist. "I dreamed of this place," he said. "And I saw her there. Valentina." He met eyes with Flavio. "Why would she go to such a place?!"

Isaiah placed a hand on Pedro's shoulder, leaning close towards him. "Many things cannot be explained," he said. "But we can bring her back, Pedro. That is why we are here."

"She will approach you as long as you dream of the sea," Antoine said. "And you are getting close to us, and our kind. Learning more about the Inspiriti. Are you heading towards the darkness?"

Pedro watched as the scene before them changed, as the mist gained a crimson hue, swirling before them as the waves silenced. He felt heat emanating from the scene, as he heard the roar of flames.

Flavio reached for him. "Remember. No physical danger."

Pedro turned and watched as the flames tore through the mist, the bright orange heat burning through the sea. He could hear the screams. In the distance, wails of desperation. They were far but were getting closer. Gradually louder.

There was a darkness which emanated from below, from the center of the flames, as the vision slowly appeared. Pedro remained transfixed, watching the scene before him unfold, feeling the desperation as the wails and screams became deafening.

He watched, squinted, looking towards the distance. Was it a cross? The image he had found endearing from his younger years, the antithesis of Hell.

"A cross!" he exclaimed.

They all watched as the cross moved closer. Pedro watched as something in the center of the cross appeared to be moving.

He looked back at the others. "What is that?"

Antoine, Isaiah and Flavio exchanged knowing glances. Pedro knew. This was not something that they would narrate for him, it was something for him to experience. He turned and watched, as the cross slowly came into focus.

It looked like a person, as if it were Christ, crucified, hanging, legs clasped with nails at the ankles on the base, arms splayed outwards on the ends. The subject was a female. She was nude; her hair hung downwards, red, like a bloodstained mop covering her head. Her breasts were torn apart, as if demons assaulted her flesh. Her head hung downwards as bright red blood flowed down her body, slowly drying.

"Turn away," Flavio said. "We should return. We must go! Now!"

Their feet splashed in the water and clapped on stones as they headed back inwards towards the darkness as Flavio remained close, yet leading them, cupping his candle with his hand.

"Closer, inwards! We will go to the catacombs for you, Pedro. Away from this place."

They ran.

Through the cavernous walls, splashing in puddles of water and across mossy, Earthen floors. Pedro followed and did not question. Although in his mind, his fought with the possibility that the immortals were far more than he had imagined. And more than he once studied.

Doors formed on the sides of the rocks, as if they had a specific purpose, they called out to him. Flavio stopped at one of the doors as Antoine and Isaiah stood close to him. Pedro watched as Flavio placed his hand on a large, brass handle. He looked up. "Now, Pedro, you will learn more about us. If you want to be one of us, as you have said, then you will discover more about who we are, and what we do, in here."

They all looked over at him, their faces appeared as if waiting for an answer.

Pedro raised his fist and covered his mouth and nodded hastily as Flavio looked at the others and gave a nod. Pedro peered through the others as they headed into the mysterious room as Flavio opened the door.

Pedro slowly approached the others and stopped.

A coffin rested on a stone slab in the center of the room, and Flavio stood in front of it, caressing his hand on the top. As Pedro took cautious steps towards the others, he looked up.

The walls were stone, still as if they were in a cave.

Flames ignited around the perimeter of the room, near the floor, from an unseen source.

Antoine and Isaiah waited as Flavio slowly opened the coffin. Pedro watched as Flavio ran his hand over countless crystal vials of bright, red blood.

"These are from those who pledged their allegiance to us, Pedro." Flavio remained focused on the vials. "And your blood will rest here, with the others, if you will make the same commitment."

Antoine turned to face Pedro, joining Isaiah. "We guard the gates," Antoine said. "That is a purpose of ours. Your kind has despised us yet requires us. Without us, the world would be a vastly different place."

Flavio pulled a gleaming, silver knife which reflected the flames.

He looked up at Pedro. "Do you commit?"

Antoine and Isaiah stood next to Flavio as Pedro focused on the knife. The flames reflected in the silver as he stood, watching, casting a glance at the vials in the coffin, knowing what they were for.

"If you want to be part of the bloodline, we must keep a record of your human ancestry," Flavio said. "The humans…make a great focus on fearing us. And wanting to eliminate us."

"At least those who know about us," Isaiah added.

Antoine reached out and took the knife from Flavio and turned to face Pedro. He watched Antoine approach, holding the knife upwards, grasping the handle. Pedro stared at the pointed tip; his eyes followed downwards on the sloped blade towards a golden handle which Antoine gripped.

"Just a small amount in the vial," he said. "A slit on your chest. We must always take the blood which is closest to the heart."

"And what is the purpose of this?" Pedro asked.

"We keep a record of all those who desire transformation," Flavio said. "Your blood may save you from damnation one day. And if you *are* transformed, that day will most likely come."

"Unless you want a destiny in my museum," Isaiah said.

Pedro glanced nervously at each of them. Antoine stood just in front of him, waiting with the knife. Pedro looked again at the blade. It was more like a dagger.

One fit for a murderous Queen.

He noticed the gleaming jewels. Flavio stood next to him, as Isaiah moved forward and stood next to Flavio.

"You must do this," Flavio said. "If you desire the gift so much, as you say you do, you will submit and do this."

"Open your shirt," Antoine said.

Pedro reached up towards his collar and undid the top button, slowly, as he met eyes with Antoine.

The three of them stood close to one another, watching him undo his shirt, standing before them, revealing his chest. Antoine moved closer.

"The humans do not know how much they rely on our population," Flavio said as Antoine moved closer, pointing the knife towards the center of

Pedro's chest. His heart raced as he focused on the blade, as it neared his heart.

"We protect them from much evil," Flavio said. "That is one of the purposes of the Inspiriti. We are the guardians who humans do not realize they have or need. It is this time, that you will take the oath. If you truly desire the gift."

Pedro winced as he felt the point of the dagger in the center of his chest. He closed his eyes as he held his shirt apart.

"We are the guardians of the gates, Pedro," Antoine said. "Will you prove your loyalty?"

Pedro opened his eyes. Antoine's face was right next to his, his eyes wide, intense. His face stern.

Pedro hastily nodded.

Antoine turned and looked at the others as he plunged the dagger into Pedro's chest as he cried out.

And then, he felt nothing.

He watched, in a dreamlike state, as Flavio brought a small, crystal vial towards his chest, holding it close to his skin, underneath the blood flow. Pedro watched his bright red blood slowly fill the vial, he thought that Antoine had gone much deeper into his chest. Had it pierced his heart? But then he closed his eyes, as Antoine removed the dagger as Pedro writhed in the pleasure.

There is no pain of the flesh here, Pedro.

"The pleasures of the flesh are exquisite and full of desire," Flavio said. "And we are here to protect the sanctity of the spirit." Antoine handed the vial to Isaiah, who slowly placed the crystal stopper on top of the neck.

Pedro was breathless, bathing in the ecstasy.

The penetration of the dagger ignited a passion within him which he had never thought he contained, yet the pierce of the blade had a sensuality as if he were in a chorus of the physical.

He felts his limbs drop downwards as Isaiah rushed forward and lifted him up. As his eyelids grew heavier, he felt a numbness overtake his body that he had never felt before.

Antoine handed the vial to Flavio, and he placed it among the others in the coffin. The vials were arranged in neat rows, end to end. Flavio placed the vial in the one open location, looked up at Pedro, but he was struggling to keep his eyes open. The exhaustion was setting in.

"You will sleep now," Flavio said. "You must rest well. For your mission will begin tonight."

Pedro awakened from a dreamless sleep.

He felt the warmth and softness of a bed and felt the blankets over his body. But his eyes remained closed. He felt a twinge of relief pass through him, for he could feel his limbs again. Had that all been a terrible dream?

The clap of footsteps approached as he slowly opened his eyes.

He saw Antoine at the foot of the bed. "Did you rest well?"

Pedro groaned, brought his arms up and grabbed the sides of his head. Perhaps it *was* just a dream. The thought of Antoine, and the immortals, and the Inspiriti guarding the gates of Hell seemed extraordinary, like nothing that he had ever imagined the immortals to be. There was nothing like that in his studies, never in all of the details he explored, the discussions he'd had with professors who also had claimed to know those who were immortal.

"The sun has almost set," Antoine said. "Isaiah and I are gathering the supplies. You will want to dress in something dark. Black, preferably. The less we are noticed, the better.

Pedro propped himself up on his elbows. "Antoine?"

Antoine leaned down, over the bed, and raised his eyebrows.

"What did we do yesterday? After arriving at the hotel, I mean. I know we met Flavio, right? The hotel manager? He led us down beneath the hotel to a secret corridor and secret rooms?"

Antoine straightened his posture and nodded.

"It's a typical reaction," he said. "To the process. When you gave us a vial of your blood, this is normal,

Pedro. But don't worry, you may feel as though you have lost some of your memory, and you have, but it has been proven that you now hold a loyalty to our kind, and what we do." Pedro felt as if he were dreaming; was the memory gap something he wished to discover? Or was it best left unexplored?

They left the hotel shortly after.

Pedro had some coffee and brushed off the fuzziness as they headed down the small elevator. As the doors opened and revealed the lobby, bustling with a group of new arrivals, they watched as Flavio was with the hotel staff, directing them and attending to the new guests. After a moment, he looked up and noticed them, heading towards the front doors. He approached them swiftly.

His voice was hushed as he approached Antoine. "Do you need me to arrange a car for you?"

"Only to be there when we are finished. And I need to drive it back to France. I don't know if I will ever be able to return it, so invoice me if you must."

Flavio nodded and turned back towards the registration area. "I will have my staff take care of it. And the car will be there, Master Antoine."

He made eye contact with Isaiah and then Pedro.

"The car will be there; you can rest assured. I know that you are embarking on an unprecedented mission. But if this is what it takes to rebuild our forces, and our presence, then I am in full support. And so is Rome."

Antoine glanced at Flavio as they headed out towards the sidewalk in the darkness. "Rome approves? Usually, they question my judgement. My actions. It's rare for Monsignor Harrison to do this."

Flavio took a few steps back towards the boisterous lobby. "He understands the importance, Antione." He cast a glance to Pedro and Isaiah. "Good luck, gentlemen."

He turned swiftly and headed towards the chaotic arrival of guests at registration.

In the pre-dawn darkness, the city remained asleep.

As they exited the hotel, Antoine led the way down *Via Ventisette Aprile* towards the convent.

It was not far from the hotel, a short walk. They wouldn't have much time before the sunrise, and the early risers of the city. Antoine led the way, rushing forward, but not running.

After they had walked along *Piazza della Indipendenza*, and as they approached the basilica, they stopped and stood before the remains of the convent.

It was once grand; with the onslaught of time and the assault of the elements, it had become a dark skeleton of stone against the still, dark, quiet night. Scaffolding surrounded the remains of the structure like a network of bones.

Antoine led the way down towards the remains of the convent.

Pedro walked next to Isaiah, and they watched Antoine charge forward, towards the sectioned off areas. An orange glow filtered in from the nearby avenues, but the excavation site remained in darkness. Pedro looked up at the remnants of the crumbling stone building. The moonlight reflected a pale blue on the tops the of the worn spires, but the building resembled a skeleton.

They climbed further into the excavation site through the dirt and massive stones. Columns lined the great central worship room.

Antoine dug through the sand and rocks underneath the pillar. Isaiah stood next to him, smoking a Dunhill, as Pedro held a flashlight, and watched Antoine toss sand in a pile near them with the small, dirty shovel.

"We cannot excavate," Isaiah said, shaking his head. Pedro turned and looked up, following the red, hot tip of the cigarette as Isaiah flicked it away. He blew a cloud of smoke which Pedro watched in a trance. Pedro twisted his body around, following the sounds of Antoine plunging the shovel into the sand, and the clump of dirt on the pile below; Isaiah waved the smoke away as he approached the others.

Antoine stopped digging and tossed the shovel to the side.

"The sky is lightening," Isaiah said, stooping down. Antoine sat back, drawing his arms around his knees. "Turn off the light."

Pedro snapped the light off as Antoine leapt to his feet like a cat, almost silently with no disturbance to the gravel. He waved to him and Isaiah. Perhaps listening. But what could Antoine hear that he and Isaiah could not?

"There's a guardian," Antoine said.

Pedro shifted his face. He headed forward, following Antoine, holding his flashlight. "Protecting the tomb," Pedro said.

The call of destiny fought through Pedro's mind.

It was as if there was a certain fate which waited for him at the entrance; it was said that the tomb was a small opening, carved in stone, beneath the altar of the church. But now, the building was crumbling. Long ago were the services of worship; and Lisa del Giocondo had taken the vows at the convent of Sedosera and worn the habit; yet the destiny which called to him was uncertain.

She was the Mona Lisa, at least that is what the scholars had said and speculated. A modest woman in a mysterious destiny of artistic beauty.

Her tomb was behind the altar.

He had studied the mysterious figure behind the painting, who was married to a man who worked with tapestries and was a silk merchant, yet what type of power could these bones possess? Her likeness, made into a painting.

Why were the bones rumored to be special?

They stopped in front of a pile of stone rubble, as Antoine and Isaiah shined their lights on the crumbled concrete. "This is where the altar was," Antoine said.

Pedro turned around, noticed the soaring ceilings.

Yes, it was the worshiping area, and it would be appropriate that a nun from the attached convent would be buried beneath. As the three of them started lifting the stones and tossing them in a pile further away, gradually, it came into view.

It was a shell of stone and cracked marble; a pile of rocks marked where the altar had once stood. Below, further downwards, was the entrance to the tomb: a small, round, weathered marker in the remains of the floor.

Antoine reached down into the small bag and pulled out a pickaxe. He looked up at them. "This has come in handy before in these situations," he said.

Pedro and Isaiah stood back, as Antoine slammed the pickaxe down on the round marker, towards the edge, as bright sparks reached into the air. Pedro looked at Isaiah, and nodded toward the entrance, as Isaiah shook his head. Pedro closed his eyes for a moment, listening to the clanking and the echoes against the soaring stone structure, reverberating through the night, and forced himself to remember.

"They can make their actions silent," he said, after a few moments, and opened his eyes. He looked at Isaiah, who nodded.

While Pedro did not quite understand all of the nuances of the immortals, he appreciated that gift.

Antoine reached down and tried to lift the lid. "It will take all of us," he said. Pedro and Isaiah knelt next to the round marker, as they each reached their fingers down through the floor. Antoine looked over at Pedro. "No human could ever lift this," he said. "Without mechanical assistance. But you have two immortals here, so we will enter soon. Go ahead, lift."

Pedro watched as they lifted the stone, nearly effortlessly, and placed it aside. The opening to the tomb was round, ragged, and looked of the years which it had been sealed. It was a cursory job, yet effective. The darkness, though, was what Pedro found most mysterious.

There were those buried beneath the church, in the catacombs, for centuries, that were now merely skeletons, for generations.

Yet the bones they sought were buried under the same sand, silt and rocks as the others. Pedro wondered how they would find them.

As Antoine started to light torches, they flamed upwards, and he handed two of them to Pedro and Isaiah.

They each took a torch as Antoine lowered his legs into the chamber. "There are some steps here," he said. "Leading downwards. Aim the light downwards so you can see them. They're worn and crumbled. Showing their age. But they should get us where we want to go."

Pedro watched as his flames fought their way into the darkness, reaching outwards in a desperate attempt to burn. Isaiah followed Antoine as he disappeared down into the darkness, and Pedro held his torch with one hand as he crawled to the crypt.

He looked downwards, drawing his torch towards the entrance, and lowered it slightly inside.

The cement steps were there as Antoine had said, but he and Isaiah were already further inside, enveloped by the darkness, for Pedro couldn't see the flickering light from their torches.

And then Pedro gasped, his mouth hung open.

He crouched and covered himself as the flames reached up from the catacombs and tore through the skeleton of the chapel. Antoine broke out of the catacombs, flying upwards into the air, nearly missing the flames.

Pedro grabbed the bag and held it close to his shoulder as Isaiah ran out of the burning building, his coat bursting into bright flames.

Antoine rushed towards him and dragged him outside, patting the flames out.

But Pedro stood, breathless, his chest heaving, watching as Antoine tore into Isaiah's neck, drinking his blood.

He mustered enough energy to gasp.

"You will become one with me!" Antoine said. The scaffolding crashed as Pedro took a cautious step forward.

"Antoine!" he called.

Antoine snapped his head upwards. Blood poured from his mouth down his chin and onto his shirt. "He will live!" Antoine said. "The blood is the life!"

"You said he was one of you!"

Antoine raised his eyes and glared at him with an intensity that Pedro had not seen before.

Pedro felt his heart race, and looked at Antoine, nursing Isaiah, and then slowly turned and watched as the scaffolding continued to collapse. Antoine knelt and picked up Isaiah, carrying him over his shoulder. "His heart still beats," he said. "Yes, he is one of us," Antoine said. "You will learn more in time, dear Pedro. You want to be an immortal with so much passion I can *sense it*! But you must consider the consequences. And even though we have done this for you, it's merely the first stage of the mission."

"What? You mean?"

"Yes. *We have her bones.*"

Pedro took a breath and held it for a moment, before releasing it slowly. Antoine figured it out. He kept his promise.

Antoine shifted Isaiah's body over his other shoulder as Pedro followed with the bag of bones. He looked down at the bag. In the darkness between the zipper, he could see their dirty remnants. The mission had seemed simple at first, when they had discussed it back in Lyon. But the execution had been muddled. Now, that Isaiah was burned, and near death, everything might have been for naught.

"Trust me," Antoine said, as they approached *Via degli Avelli*, which bordered the convent and monastery. The sky was lightening, and the wail of sirens approached swiftly. Pedro felt his heart pounding in his chest.

"We will never be seen," Antoine said. "That is one of our gifts."

They walked up and approached the waiting Mercedes sedan, discreetly parked on the side of the street, just as Flavio had promised. As they approached the car, the lights of the emergency vehicles flashed close to them yet passed them by.

Antoine opened the trunk as Pedro tossed his satchel inside. He grabbed the keys out of Antoine's free hand and opened the back door. They eased Isaiah into the back seat. Pedro pushed Isaiah's legs inside as Antoine dashed around to the driver's side. "Get in!" he said, slamming the door.

Pedro glided into the passenger seat and the car sped away.

He looked back.

The bright red siren lights became further in the distance as Antoine navigated the small side streets of Florence swiftly, rounding the tight corners. Pedro looked down at Isaiah, and then over at Antoine.

"What are we going to do with him?"

Antoine guided the car north, towards the border. "The blood will save him," he said. "You must trust the process. But we need to move as quickly as we can."

"Why not a train? Or better yet a plane?"

Antoine shook his head. "We cannot risk being discovered, Pedro. You have to understand. This is a journey which you chose. Remember, resurrection requires retribution."

Pedro felt a chill run through his spine as Antoine's Mercedes sped on to the Autostrada del Sol. The words rang through his mind again: *resurrection requires retribution*. He turned his head, and saw that Isaiah was spread across the back seat; the color had drained from his face. Pedro reached back and placed his hand on Isaiah's chest. "He's not breathing!" he cried. "His heart isn't beating!"

Antoine sighed. "Like I told you, trust the process."

Pedro watched as Antoine navigated the behemoth sedan into the increasing traffic. The sky had lightened, and the outskirts of Florence had livened. Antoine weaved between cars, up the hills which wound through the mountain ranges of northern Italy, speeding towards Switzerland. At this rate, Pedro thought, they would be in Lyon in record time.

"You have a ghost," Antoine said, after a few moments of silence. "And there is nothing unusual about that. We immortals are tormented. Lonely. And, at times, lost. But you will recover, Pedro. We will bring her back for you."

Pedro sighed as he felt tears well up within his eyes. "I always used to call her my Mona Lisa."

"Like the classic painting," Antoine said. "The one by da Vinci. The masterpiece which endures. Was she plain…but beautiful?"

Pedro tightened his seat belt as Antoine sped faster, flying past neighboring traffic. "Actually, Valentina was quite a gorgeous Spanish woman. I remember when we first met, I carried her a single rose. She always wore her bright, flowery sun dresses. When we met, she stood looking out over the Atlantic, miles from Madrid but close in our hearts, and our destinies collided. I remember walking up behind her, as she stood looking outwards at the waves, and America was many miles away. But she had always wanted to go. And when she turned to face me, I gave her my one single rose, the only one I could afford, and she accepted it."

Antoine slowed the car slightly and moved to the right lane.

"But she was not plain in the least," Pedro added.

"So, she was beautiful to you. Was she beautiful to all? Mona Lisa, despite her simplicity, is beautiful to all."

"She is beautiful to me, and I care nothing less."

"Isaiah and Jacob will bring her back to you," Antoine said. "The bones have power. The code has power. But you still have time to consider, before we reach Lyon. Because you will be making the same choice that I was faced with. And there will be retribution, that I promise you."

The sun was full in the sky and as Pedro lay his head back on the seat, he closed his eyes and felt the sun rays warm his face. The warmth, however, would be temporary, for that he was certain. The chill of the grave was coming for him.

Resurrection requires retribution...

THE GHOST WRITER

MADRID

THE WRITER can be a ghost.

A cascading waterfall of words, flowing through the story, leads the reader's imagination to draw its own images of thought and feeling, experience and emotion.

The artistry involved in the writing of a novel is not dissimilar to the composition of music, or the creation of a painting, or performance and dance, all in the mind of the writer.

It was the days before he had met Darius, and Antoine, and enlisted with the immortal community.

He had yet to dream of living in America, or of dancing in Paris, or of travelling to Italy to excavate the bones of one of the most mysterious artistic subjects of all time.

During the time before the promise of immortality had not yet been kept, Pedro had many days when he would dream of artistic mastery, which he also believed would lead, naturally, to notoriety and success. He longed to hang in the galleries that the great artists of the Renaissance did. But they endured posthumously, and Pedro did not desire that.

Pedro stood in his small art studio, in his Madrid flat, which overlooked the distant darkness of the *Sierra de Guadarrama* mountains towards the east, as daylight faded. He was aware of the notion of the artist. There was passion which lived within the brush, that was his motto when he sought paying work as an artist. Valentina had always been his muse; she stood behind him as his dark hair hung forward. The tip of the brush glided into a colorful pallet of oils, as Pedro hunched over, mesmerized at the mixing of the colors.

"A bit of color on the edge," he said, muttering under his breath, as he touched the bright red tip to the canvas. He slowly dragged the brush downwards, scalloped it outwards, easing it towards the lower end of the canvas.

He heard the clap of heels approach the canvas, as he turned, hooking his hair behind his ear. He knew she had been standing there, although she had remained silent. She was an artistic study, and this had been the early evening ritual.

He watched her as she studied the wisps of crimson paint at the edge as she stood behind him in a long, flowing summer dress. He looked down as he noticed the fringe on the ends of her sleeves concealing her tiny wrists as she placed her hands on her hips. He'd always thought they looked like drooping Hibiscus flowers.

She leaned forward, and her dark hair spilled downwards. He reached up, lifting it away. "Don't get it in the paint," he said.

"I'm not, I'm not," she said.

Pedro leaned back, studying her as she drew her fingers across her chin and cocked her head to the side. After a few moments of silence, she opened her mouth to speak.

"What is it?" Pedro asked. "What do you see?"

She turned towards him; her face shifted. "What is that?" she asked. Pedro raised his eyebrows as she turned and pointed to the crimson streaks he had just finished brushing onto the canvas.

"It's going to be fire," he said. "Flames."

She leaned closer towards the painting, examining it for a bit longer, slowly shaking her head. "It doesn't look like flames."

Pedro slapped his brush down on the horizontal slat of his easel and sighed as he placed his pallet on a nearby table. Valentina looked up; her eyes were wide; she seemed concerned. "Pedro, what is it?"

He paced back and forth as his heavy shoes clamped on the hardwood. His arms were crossed, as he settled on the windows across the room. He stood in front of them, watching the cityscape, studying the mountains in the distance.

"If there was anyone who I thought would understand my artistic process, I thought it would be you," he said slowly.

She approached him from behind and slowly put her arms around his waist, but his attention remained on the scene outside the window. He could see the sun was low in the sky, as the mountaintops glowed auburn in their distant and dark silhouette.

"You will get there," she said. "Continue your studies, that's what you should do. You will be great one day, Pedro. One day you will. I am certain of it."

He closed his eyes for a moment and sighed.

He had held the same brushes and worked with the same oils that the legends had; yet the bristles had remained. He remembered many days in the past, standing in central Madrid, looking up at the sun as it shone down through the *Buen Ratiro* and feeling the sense of wonder move through his mind. Madrid was a city of artists; he remembered studying the works of Goya and Velazquez which hung at the *Museo Nacional del Prado*.

The path might have been a lonely one to most, but to Pedro, he was undeniably content at times; particularly when it came to his craft.

His youth remained with him, and although he had felt a sense of flattery as the women watched him as he moved in the courtyards, and as the sun would set and paint its own crimson masterpiece across the sky, he felt a deep burning within.

A desire for something different, which he couldn't quite explain.

"I am going to retire my brushes and canvases," he said, while he wrapped his supplies in a small, brown haversack, looking downwards, taking a moment to clear his throat. He looked up. Valentina stood in front of the expansive windows which provided a vast pallet of the night lights of Madrid.

"And what will you do?" she asked.

Pedro dropped his satchel and looked up at her. She was right, but she didn't know.

There were other forms of creative expression, and to him, he thought, that the oils had become costly, and he could no longer paint for the church. There were other avenues that he desired to explore. As she stood watching him, she placed her hands on her hips, and as he noticed her, she seemed like one of the models from his own paintings.

"I was thinking about becoming a dancer," he said, as Valentina's eyes widened, and she nearly fell backwards.

"A dancer!" she said. "In Paris? That is where all the dancers are. How will you do that here? You have no experience. I have never seen you dance like the ballet dancers there. But your art is beautiful, Pedro. You cannot be a master before you practice the craft for many years."

He scoffed. "Well maybe I won't dance ballet. Maybe I will bring our culture to the theatres in Paris."

Valentina reached around and placed her hands on his shoulders. "You are such a talented painter, Pedro. Why give that up?"

Pedro's eyes fell and he shook his head. "Maybe a writer. I've always loved to write."

Valentina leaned back and smacked his shoulder, looking down at him with a scowl as he raised his head.

"Painting is your calling," she said. "You have been brushing color on canvases for years now! And your talent. Do you not see it?"

Pedro turned and studied his canvas. His face shifted and he shook his head. "I don't see it," he said. "If I have been working with these canvases for years, why am I not appreciated like Goya? Or Velazquez?"

"You have to continue to work, Pedro. Maintain your focus. That is what my papa has always said to me and my brothers. Why can't you see the talent that you have?"

Pedro hung his head. "My dream is to paint like da Vinci. Or Michelangelo. They were masters of their craft."

She scoffed. "But you are just *beginning* to paint, dear Pedro. Someone cannot be a master from the start! There needs to be a starting point. Do you think da Vinci, and Goya started where they finished? Of course, they didn't. They studied. And they practiced. And then continued to paint! You need to practice and make your work better."

He slammed his paintbrush on the ledge of the easel. "Then I don't *want* to work! I have been painting for years and no one except *you* can see my talent! I am wasting my time!"

He heard Valentina's footsteps shuffle back towards the kitchen. "You could be appreciated like da Vinci…if you believe in yourself and your own talent. But I don't like when you get like this. I am going to bed early tonight."

Pedro raised his head and looked back, and Valentina was already gone, disappeared into the bedroom, and the door was closed. There, he had done it. A sinking feeling washed through him, and he looked down at the ledge and the paintbrush which he'd slammed down just moments before. It had left splatters of red paint on his canvas; a stain in the area where that color hadn't meant to be, and then he sighed. If he could take back the last few moments, he wished he could, but what would it prove?

That he could control his frustration.

Pedro paced the living room floor, looking back at the canvas at the far end of the room, nestled in front of a line of soaring windows which provided a captivating view of the buildings and the mountains in the distance.

And then he looked towards the opposite side of the room, to the bedroom door, still shut. He sighed, and wished Valentina would emerge, but she did not, and as the sun sank below the horizon and the darkness permeated their small apartment, he sank down on the sofa.

She was the perfect Mona Lisa, he thought. Just like da Vinci's painting, just like she had inspired him.

Her eyes were wide and inviting, just as he had always remembered. Long dark brown hair, plain, yet exquisite at the same time. There was a glistening to her eyes which he never experienced in his days as a student, yet, that night, in his flat as the city lights glistened below through the expansive glass windows, there was a different look on her face.

There was a sadness, yet a look of contentedness.

As he lay on the sofa, his eyes closed, his thoughts remaining with the day, he recalled as she sat on the stool and looked up at him, crossing her arms and slowly shaking her head.

"You must focus on *something*. You have the painting, the writing, the dancing. Which do you want Pedro? What do you want for *you*?"

He had embraced a childhood of passionately supporting the arts, and when he watched the dancers on stage in tights and makeup, he dreamed of being an artist himself. For years, he wandered through his destiny, searching for his true calling. There were the sultry Madrid nights when he would stare through the expansive windows, in the flat which Valentina had owned through her parents, high above the city as if they were luxuriant stars.

But he had contributed nothing to their comfortable surroundings. And Pedro reminded himself of it every day. He knew, deep within his soul, that the inspiration had to be out there. As he watched the sun sink and as the tiny white stars slowly lightened and dotted themselves across a darkened sky, there was a sense of reckoning.

He looked up and scanned the room, and assumed Valentina had permanently retired to the bedroom, as she was accustomed to his deep musings for hours next to the canvas, as he would stare out the window frequently. But this time was different.

He didn't know how long he had been lying there, but the lights on the streets below were burning, the city had settled and quieted, and it felt late. The sky was dark, and the stars shone brightly.

He sighed.

Later that night, Pedro tossed and turned as Valentina slept soundly next to him.

She probably thought he had little direction, but he knew he did. There was a burning within. Something different that he needed to do. Was he truly the talented artist that she thought he was?

Pedro knew that he was destined for something more. A different form of creative expression. He remembered days at the *Museo Nacional* and staring at paintings of the great artists of Spain's past. He would stand until the closing announcements came over the loudspeaker, shifting on his feet, ignoring the tourists which surrounded him.

If only I could paint like that.

There was a certain admiration for the great painters, whose talent seemed to be at a level which Pedro felt he could only dream of attaining. But there were the gifts of the immortals which he had heard of; they all seemed to be extraordinary in their success. But he had only heard of them; it was as if the immortal community were that of fiction and legends, as if they only existed in the stories and the books he would find while browsing the local shops.

If only I could become an immortal.

If only.

The artists in the museums were immortalized through their art, yet could they have been immortals in their lives? If so, why were they gone? But they had been dead for years, and Pedro had feelings that the truly great interpretations had died along with them.

He shifted to his other side, grabbing the pillow and forming it around his head. Sleep would not find him tonight, it seemed. There were too many racing thoughts. Something was igniting his mind to think of what might be, rather than what his situation currently was.

Paris was certainly calling.

But why?

Was he meant to be the artist that Valentina envisioned him to be?

The thoughts pierced his mind, as if they were meant to be a penetrative sword.

As he listened to Valentina sleeping soundly next to him, he gingerly pulled the sheet away and lowered his legs to the floor, wincing at the chill of the stone.

He turned and heard her steady breathing, and she shifted under the sheet. Valentina remained asleep.

He eased himself up from the pillows and draped the sheet back over her.

She turned and faced away from him, nestling the sheet under her neck, and he caught his breath in his throat for a moment.

He paused, leaning up on his elbows, staring at the door. It was slightly ajar, opening to the living room, but he knew the hour was still quite early, well before sunrise. Even so, the curtains were drawn tight, the heavy, light blocking drapes which Valentina had insisted upon. He craned his neck in an attempt to listen.

I can give you talent.

It was merely a whisper, and not even that. But he had heard it. He looked back down at Valentina, and her deep, regulated breathing had indicated that he was experiencing this alone.

So much talent that your artistic dreams will come true...

He caught his breath and waited. He had heard it this time.

There *was* a voice, emanating from somewhere beyond the living room.

Yet he could not determine its origin, or even if the voice was real.

He waited for a few moments; the minutes passed like hours as he strained to listen. What would the voice say next? Was it even real?

He slowly lay back down, grabbed the pillow and held it close to his chest.

He must be deliriously tired. Yes, that had to be it. He had grown accustomed to sleepless nights with racing thoughts, but tonight, it seemed sleep would evade him entirely.

Thoughts of the immortals charged through his mind.

During the days when he was at *Universidad Complutense de Madrid* he had studied their ways and culture in detail.

They were known to be extraordinary in whatever they chose to do.

And then the voice became audible as Pedro noticed that he had left the warmth and comfort of his bed, and was now standing on the street below, in the dark of night.

"I am meant to be heard by you and only you."

Pedro stopped, and peered into the darkness, away from the streets and the city. The shadows dominated as the faint light from the streetlamps scarcely reached between the nestled stone buildings. They reached upwards towards the darkened sky, keeping the shadows as the sky threatened daylight in the distance.

"I have been listening to you," the voice said, slowly, quietly, yet determined.

Pedro heard the grit of footsteps approaching on stone, and he caught his breath in his throat.

Should he listen?

Remain with the mysterious man in the shadows?

In a brief attempt to turn, his legs would not allow him to move. With great effort, Pedro managed to speak. "Listening?" he croaked. He cleared his throat. "To me?"

Pedro focused on the darkness.

He could see an outline of his figure, a few feet away, yet close enough to receive a minute bit of the spilled light from the streetlamps. He turned for a moment, noticing the sky starting to lighten in the east.

There wouldn't be much more time for the mysterious visitor to emerge from the shadows. Pedro noticed him as he stood in the darkness; his hair was clearly long, his frame muscular, yet slim. He thought he must wear his clothes well.

Pedro took a breath as he slowly emerged.

The mysterious man, he knew, was not really a man. At some point he thought that the mysterious visitor, was, for certain, not *one of them*.

Was he an immortal?

Pedro could tell, by the angelic bone structure and delicate skin, not seen in mere mortals, that the mysterious visitor was now indeed one of them. The visitor wore fitted pants and a long, flowing jacket; he appeared young yet still had the look of wisdom and experience. He stood under the streetlamp in a sphere of warm light, leaning against the steel as he drew one foot upwards.

"I can make you talented. Is that what you are seeking?"

Pedro caught his breath in his throat.

He had to be an immortal.

No one beyond Valentina knew of his creative struggles; Pedro remembered from his study of the immortals that one of the gifts was the knowing gift; most had it. If this mysterious visitor could read his thoughts, then he certainly must be an immortal.

"I have a limited time to speak with you," he said. "But as I listened to your thoughts, your destiny became quite clear to me."

"Clear? How is that so?"

He shifted himself off the lamp post and took a few steps forward, taking one step directly in front of the next, as if he were on a fashion runway. Pedro seemed completely unaware of his own steps that he was taking, moving backwards, until he bumped into the cold bricks.

"Everything you have read about us is true," he said. "We are not just painters; our work hangs in the *Louvre*. We are not just writers; our books win the Pulitzer. Everything we do is extraordinary." He moved closer, his eyes piercing, and Pedro could feel his heart quicken as he had nowhere to go.

The visitor stopped as his face nearly touched Pedro's. He could feel the chill of his breath. The visitor turned his head, so his mouth was next to Pedro's ear.

"Is that what you desire?" he whispered.

Pedro felt his guard fall as his heart steadied its pacing. He thought of his myriad directions of which Valentina had so frequently reminded him. Could this strange visitor have the ability to predict his future? "I can tell you are one of them," he said. "Your one of them, right? One of the immortals they speak of, aren't you?"

The mysterious visitor approached slowly, as he ascended closer to the streetlamp. Pedro watched as he leaned against the steel pole, resting his head against it.

Pedro spoke with more confidence. "You are one of them. I can sense it. You are one of the immortals." Pedro knew he was one of them, it was apparent. His clothes were tight and formed to his body; even the top hat he wore cultivated thoughts of a different time period.

The moment lasted for ages, it seemed, as Pedro watched the visitor lean against the pole, and draw his leg up, bending at the knee. But it wasn't merely the visitor's clothes, rather his aura and the charisma he exuded.

"I know you have your dreams, your destiny," the visitor said, looking directly at Pedro. "And if you know our kind, which you claim to, then you know I can listen to your thoughts, even if they are towards the distant realms of the world. You know, don't you?"

Pedro watched the mysterious visitor as he waited, patiently, it seemed, leaning on the lamp post, watching him with the pierce of his eyes. "I felt as though I was drawn out here to you," he said. "As if somehow, I would discover the answers to my questions here with you."

"If I transform you," the visitor added. "If I transform you, we will be eternally connected. You can be far from me in distance, yet our minds will be linked as if we were standing next to each other."

Pedro craned his neck and looked back up at the darkened windows of his flat.

Valentina would certainly still be sleeping in the back room in the infancy of the morning. The light had scarcely lifted its delicate pastel wisps from the east.

"My name is Darius," he said, approaching Pedro slowly. As Darius moved closer, Pedro took a cautious step back, looking down for a moment, wishing he would not tumble on the curb. "Darius Sauvage," he continued. Pedro noticed Darius noticing him moving backwards, and Darius reached outwards to gently take his arm.

"I've heard of you," Pedro said.

"Oh, you have. I know. You must tell me more."

Pedro nodded.

Darius glared, but not in a sinister way. His stare was intense, beckoning, yet mysterious. Pedro thought it prudent to take a step backwards, but he knew the stone walls would prevent him from escaping. "Yes, I've learned about you," he stammered. "And Antoine. And those in America, and Rome. Paris. Yes. Paris."

Darius took a step closer towards him. "And where did you learn these things, Pedro? How did you discover us?" Darius reached out and touched Pedro's shoulder. Pedro looked down at his long, slender fingers; the nails were long and manicured perfectly. He felt his heartbeat as it became faster. He felt a closeness to Darius, an attraction he could not further explain. Or ignore.

There was something about Darius. This mysterious immortal who visited him in the infancy of the morning.

Darius leaned in close to Pedro's ear. He could feel the heat from his breath as he whispered. "I can tear your heart out if I choose."

Pedro watched the glare in his eyes. There was something sinister…yet mysterious…about Darius. Pedro didn't doubt that Darius would carry his threat out if he made an incorrect move. It was as though Pedro was a prisoner to his own infatuation and curiosity, yet it did not upset him. There seemed to be a difference in the philosophy of his own mind.

Darius was not a criminal; at least Pedro didn't think that he appeared to be. Darius was undeniably well dressed; impeccably groomed. But Pedro knew who Darius was, and where he originated from, even if there were no records to study which covered the years when Darius had originally been a mortal, before he was transformed with the gift.

Pedro gasped and looked at Darius as he grinned, biting his lower lip, his arms flailing as he released his grip. Pedro took a slow step backwards, wincing as he bumped into the stone wall behind him.

"You must not keep heading backwards," Darius said. "You will fall. Everyone who moves backwards eventually falls. You should always head forward, even if what you see isn't what you're familiar with."

Pedro hung his head and sighed.

Darius knew of his shortcomings, it seemed. But of course, he would know. And so did Valentina. She knew as well. "Pedro, you must find your destiny," she would say. "You must choose what most compels you. Do you desire the talent that comes with the gift?

Pedro paused for a moment and considered what Darius was asking. There had been too many days in the art studio when he didn't believe that he'd had the ability to paint like da Vinci or Boticelli.

"Do you desire the talent of da Vinci? I can give you that."

"Why would you want to do that?" Pedro asked as Darius leaned on the brick wall next to him and crossed his arms. He had a grin on his face, and his eyes were beckoning. Hypnotic.

"I transform you," he said. "Give you the gift. And you will find the world waiting for you, Pedro. You will possess all the talent which your heart will desire."

Pedro took a slow step away from Darius. "At what cost?"

Darius took a step closer to Pedro. "There will be no cost! What type of cost could there be to living forever? For immortality?" He scoffed. "As if you are even ready. Are you Pedro? Are you ready for such a bestowment?"

Pedro's thoughts were cast back to the present. He looked over at Darius, who had moved closer. "And how will you help me with that?"

Darius stood before him, his face had warmed slightly, and while the mysteriousness of his character remained, there was the constant reminder: Darius was an immortal, he was part of those shunned by society; he was involved with those who were in Paris, and Rome, and somehow, they had infiltrated Madrid also. But now, Pedro knew, the immortals were present, standing right before him.

Darius leaned in closer again, speaking slowly and coyly. "So, do you want to paint…or do you want to write? What destiny do you want to take shape for you?"

Darius took a step back and extended his hand. "No matter which you choose, no matter what you feel will become your destiny, if you choose the gift, you will experience extraordinary success which you could only dream of. It is part of our talents, our unnatural ability. But for that you must come with me, right now, at this moment."

Darius was waiting for him.

Pedro craned his neck and looked up at his flat. The sun would be rising soon, and Valentina would certainly rise with the light. Darius waited patiently.

As Pedro watched the visitor approach him and place his arm gently around his shoulders, he looked up and they made eye contact. Darius knew, it seemed. There was a shared destiny. And although the trepidation that Pedro felt as they walked away from the flat, arm in arm, he knew that there would be something awaiting him in Paris.

The sun shone through the slit between the heavy drapes, as Pedro awakened with a fuzzy feeling in head.

His eyes were bleary, and his vision blurred. What had he done last night? As his head slowly cleared and his vision started to return, he scanned the room.

This was not his flat.

He reached up covered his face with his hands and groaned.

Of course, it wasn't their flat.

Although he had no memory of imbibing any illicit substances, he felt as if he had. The memories of the previous night were hazy, sporadic at best. There was a large and quite ornate wooden dresser opposite the bed. It might have been of a less expensive wood than mahogany, but it didn't appear to be. And it certainly wasn't from his and Valentina's flat.

Pedro's heavy shoes clapped on the metal stairs as he charged down to the street below. There wasn't trust between them yet, he had been in the flat for hours. Earlier, Darius lay next to him in the expansive bed, motionless and drained of blood as if he were dead.

And now he was gone.

158

He cursed himself for falling back asleep.

But he knew that Darius must have been feeding on him as if he were a vampire, but vampires were a thing of storytelling and lore, he told himself. Darius was not a vampire, even Darius had told him himself.

Pedro winced as he touched his neck.

Something...or someone...had been feeding on him.

He pushed the double doors open and the chill of the winter plunged into the small foyer. He watched as the traffic charged past.

This was not Madrid.

The cars that raced past were more modern; the chill in the air was more intense than he had ever experienced; and the grey skies were cloud covered and unfamiliar.

He turned and charged back up the stairs, tearing into the flat, and started searching. He yanked the sofa pillows and flung them across the room; he lifted the couch cushions and dropped them in the center of the floor, leaning down and running his hands under the back and arms, in the small crevices.

Nothing.

He ran towards the bedroom, where he had just awakened, and looked for something. He didn't yet know quite what he was looking for, but he continued. He yanked the drawers out from the massive dresser until they crashed to the floor; he tore the covers off the bed, and threw them in a pile, yet nothing was there.

Darius was gone.

He looked up, dropped the sheet he was holding, and headed towards the bathroom. Something, it seemed, was different than it had been.

There was something that was oddly familiar, yet incredibly distant about this place. It was as if he were in a different time, that he had yet to experience. As if the world had evolved around him, without giving him the opportunity to experience and grow with it.

He snapped the bathroom light on and looked at himself in the mirror.

He was still the same Pedro; he had the same black hair, the same skin. It was as if he hadn't aged a day. Yet it seemed like the world had gone on without him. The cars and the buildings were modern.

Thoughts of Darius still permeated his mind.

Why were the immortals so infatuating? Was it the transformation, and the resultant gift of talent that Darius had promised him?

Perhaps, perhaps it was.

He got up out of the bed and trudged over to the window. The heaviness of sleep remained; he remembered the mornings when he would awaken and feel that heavy feeling, and this seemed no different. As he parted the curtains, bright sunlight filled the room. It felt like mid-afternoon, at the earliest. He looked out at the city, watching the tiny cars moving along the street below, and the people who darted along the sidewalks in crowds in front of shop fronts and cafes were miniscule.

Pedro squinted, peering at the sidewalk below.

Maybe Darius was down there; he said he wasn't affected by the sunlight like vampires were. There was something different about the immortals who followed the code, he had said. They had a complexity which vampires simply did not possess, he had said. But some bore similarities to the bloodsuckers, Pedro remembered. It was all revealed in the code.

Pedro returned to the bed and saw Darius underneath the heaping duvet. Still exhausted, he climbed back in the bed and fell, almost immediately after his head hit the pillow, into a deep and dreamless sleep.

Pedro's eyes fluttered open as he lay in the mysterious, yet undeniably comfortable bed, adorned with luxurious satin bedsheets and pillowy comforters.

The heavy curtains were drawn, and there was a body lying next to him under the heaping covers. He eased himself up on his elbows as the sheet fell from his torso. He was nude. He drew his hand up to his neck and winced.

Fresh blood.

The wounds were recent. The heavy curtains were drawn tight, allowing a mere sliver of daylight through. And he hadn't remembered anything after leaving the small thoroughfare outside of his flat. They could be outside of Madrid. At this point, they could be anywhere.

He looked over at the sleeping body. He reached out and gave the comforter a delicate tug; there was no reaction, no breathing. No upward movement of the chest. But it was the same mysterious visitor from earlier, yet his eyes were closed, his skin looked cold, clammy. Devoid of all color. He slept like the dead and had the pale and lifeless look of the dead. Much more appropriate for a coffin, it seemed, not an ornate Queen Victorian with heavy comforters and netting. But Pedro knew of the origins of this mysterious visitor, the one thing that he realized: the mysterious visitor had claimed to be an immortal.

As Pedro quietly slid from the bedsheets, he saw the peeks of the golden sunrays filtering through the break in the heavy curtains. He thought it might be late afternoon. Certainly, Darius would be awakening from his death sleep shortly?

He reached up to his neck and winced as he lightly touched the wound. It was wet, warm and still bleeding. He pulled his fingers back and saw fresh blood. If Darius wasn't a vampire, why was he feeding on him?

He looked over, but Darius was gone. Was he ever there?

The mosquito netting hung downwards over the tall, wooden bed posts, and then Pedro thought he might no longer be in Paris.

The heat was too stifling for it to be Paris.

Where had Darius taken him?

He pulled the netting aside and swung his feet on the cool, stone floor. It seemed relevant that the destiny had been unfounded. There seemed to be a fragment of his thoughts which he could not access; a point in time which he could not remember. Yet the destiny had proven itself to him, as an indescribable feeling had washed through his veins. He could feel the pulse of the blood and the beat of his heart as he placed his hand over his ribcage.

His heart was still beating.

He was still alive.

After the days in Paris, alone and searching for Darius, and never finding him, and after spending his afternoons at the *Louvre*, studying the works inside the museum, yet finding da Vinci's Mona Lisa to be captivating and inspiring, Pedro and Antoine headed to Miami.

Pedro was excited to journey to America, and swiftly forgot his yearning to find Darius and receiving the promised gift of immortality, but when he sat in his small apartment in the city's arts district, he started to feel quite alone.

Antoine had quickly dropped him off and handed him the keys to the apartment, jingling them in front of his face. "It's paid for," Antoine said. "The art of

Miami will differ greatly from that of Paris, but I think you will find a great deal of inspiration here."

Pedro slowly nodded as Antoine turned and walked back to his car, still running, with the headlights on. Pedro looked down at the small set of keys, and wondered if Antoine was being so generous, because Darius had given him the gift, and, since they shared the same blood lineage, perhaps Antoine felt an obligation to take care of a mortal that had received a promise of the gift. Pedro raised his head and saw Antoine standing behind the open driver's door.

"You'll do just fine here," Antoine said. "My estate is only minutes from here, but I procured this apartment for you because you need to be *here*. This is what you wanted. This is your chance to write, Pedro. We immortals have stories to tell. And if you have the talent for words as much as you appreciate art, then this is the area of the city you want to live in."

Pedro slowly nodded as Antoine got inside his small coupe and sped away. Pedro slowly placed the key in the lock, hoping that it would work. It took several attempts, and he had to wiggle it in the lock, but it worked. The door opened with a creak, and there was darkness.

A musty odor wafted towards him.

He felt for a light switch on the wall and snapped it on. A tall, wooden lamp on the side of a plain brown upholstered sofa bathed the room in an incandescent glow. This was not the type of accommodations that Antoine was used to, it seemed. Pedro knew that he was just starting out in Miami, chasing his dream, yearning for the talent which he was promised.

As he trudged inside, he removed his shoes and placed them by the door, walking across old, cream-colored carpeting, towards a small, round, wooden table. A small hallway led to two doors, which Pedro assumed were bedrooms. The accommodations where small and modest, yes, but Pedro knew that he wouldn't be spending much time here. He knew that he must receive his gift, and even though Antoine had not yet transformed him to immortality, Miami was known as a mecca of immortal activity.

Over time, as Pedro settled into the city, he spent much of his time at Antoine's estate, meeting the immortals, the coven of witches at Haddon House, and to support himself, Antoine gave him a job bartending at the nightclub *Sacrafice* on Miami Beach. Despite working at a club filled with immortals, he had yet to receive the gift, and he found himself often up at the devil's hour, in the devil's city, as those at *Sacrafice* liked to call Miami.

Pedro was initially excited to work a night job, where he made mountains of cash. At the end of each evening, he counted his tips at the end of the bar, after the lights had brightened and daylight was peeking over the horizon towards Washington Avenue on South Beach. When he was counting his tips, he heard the heavy clap of heels crossing the dance floor towards the bar.

He looked up; she was clearly not a patron of the night club. Her silver hair was tied back neatly in a bun; she wore a flowing black dress and walked with a cane. Pedro watched her as she slowly approached the bar, and sat on one of the stools, placing her cane on the bar top with a slight clank. Pedro nodded to her as he continued to count his tips.

"How can I help you?" he said after counting a stack of bills.

The woman smiled, nodded and took a slow breath. "I knew I'd find you here." She spoke with a heavy, Cajun style Southern accent. "Now if you would mix me a martini, that will help busy your mind, because I have some news to share with you."

Pedro reached for a bottle and started to pour.

"I know you have been to Haddon House," she said, watching him shake the cocktail behind his shoulder. As Pedro poured it into a chilled glass, he paused, and raised his head. "We're not supposed to serve people after closing," he said.

The woman let out a small laugh, smiled and nodded. "Oh, never you worry," she said. "Antoine won't mind."

Pedro took a breath and sighed as he poured the elixir into the glass, and he slowly placed it in front of her.

She nodded and smiled.

"Now tell me, Pedro," she said. "How long have you been here in Miami? After you left Madrid?"

"Feels like forever," he said. "A few years now, I suppose."

She took a sip and nodded. "And I suppose you know that no one has given you the gift yet, have they?

Pedro's face fell as he started placing bottles in cabinets behind the bar. He shook his head as he carried bottles back and forth.

"I see," she said. "You can call me Vivienne."

He stopped and nodded to her. "Pleased to meet you."

She leaned forward on the bar top as Pedro polished glasses and watched her. "I know much about you," she said. "You left Madrid, and you left your sweetheart there, Valentina, didn't you?"

Pedro froze. He had not heard her name for many years. He slowly placed the glass in its crate and leaned on the bar, close to Vivienne. "How did you know that?" he asked. "Have you spoken to her? How is she?"

Vivienne sighed. "Oh dear," she said. "I regret to be the bringer of bad news, dear Pedro, but she passed away several years ago."

Pedro stood up as he covered his mouth with his hand. He felt tears well up in his eyes, and through the blur, he could see Vivienne take another sip of her drink, as if nothing were wrong about her delivering such life-changing news. After a few minutes, Pedro regained his composure. "How did she die? Do you know?"

Vivienne shook her head. "I do not know the specifics. But I can assure you, we have been watching you since the immortals made you the

170

promise of immortality, and then now you are, what? Wasting away, years older? Years closer to death, and now your muse, the one who inspired you the most, is buried in Madrid?"

Pedro pursed his lips and took a breath through his nostrils. How did she know so much? Who was she affiliated with?

Pedro placed his cash box on top of his drawer and prepared to head over to the count room as Vivienne sat, sipping her martini, watching him. He cast a glance over at her nervously, and she grinned. "Of course, you don't have to be without her," she said. "Or her inspiration, for that matter."

Pedro held his cash drawer against his abdomen, and sighed, looking upwards, yet only seeing Valentina's face. "I became infatuated with the gift. The promise. And since then, I've been struggling to find my direction." He looked back down at Vivienne, who was downing the last of her cocktail. "Creatively, I mean," he added.

Vivienne stood slowly and reached for her cane, watching him the entire time. She stared at him. Her eyes were telling; she knew something profound. She was piercing, and forceful, and she balanced herself on her cane, steadying herself. "You should travel to New Orleans," she said. "And it may be an unorthodox method, but it can present a solution to your predicament."

Pedro scoffed. "What predicament is that?" He shuffled out of the bar and started to head across the expansive dance floor. Vivienne followed him as her cane thumped on the floor. "You're an artist, Pedro. A writer. A painter. The medium doesn't matter, really. But you lost your muse. And your mentor. You need inspiration, don't you? The words haven't been flowing, have they?"

Pedro stopped and turned to face her.

She appeared to be studying him, her eyebrows raised, her eyes wide. She turned her head slightly to the side as Pedro took a few steps closer to the door to the count room.

"I don't know, Vivienne," he said, shaking his head, looking downwards. He reached for the doorknob and paused as she reached out and touched his arm. He turned and faced her. "No, they haven't."

She slowly pulled her arm away and reached into her pocket, drawing out a small, rectangular black card. She reached up, handing it to him, as she turned to leave. "If you want to see her again, if you want your muse, your inspiration, then go here."

Vivienne slowly headed towards the door, he watched her cane thump against the floor and listened to her heels clap against the stone. She was moving far more slowly away from him than she had approaching him. Pedro watched her leave as he held the card. She opened the door to brilliant light, as the sun had completely risen. He stood, holding the card, watching the door close slowly, bathing the nightclub once again in artificial light. He took a moment, held the card in the palm of his hand, and drew it closer.

HOUSE OF VOODOO

New Orleans

The card said nothing else.

Pedro shoved the card in his pocket as he opened the door to the count room, desperate to end his shift. Vivienne was a wild card, and there had been other evenings when the bar closed when patrons had sat at the bar, sipping on cocktails, chatting with him as he closed up. Yet, Vivienne made the biggest impact.

As he counted a stack of cash under the harsh florescent lighting in the count room, he kept thinking of Vivienne. And the card in his pocket. And, more so, of Valentina. She hadn't fought her way into his mind for countless days, yet now, she was there, standing in the front, clamoring for his attention.

Vivienne was most definitely right.

The words most definitely were not flowing. Antoine had helped him with a tiny, modest flat in the arts district, but it was a far cry from the opulence of his estate. Not that it mattered to him, but after dropping him off at the apartment, Antoine had been rather scarce. Even at the club. While he and Darius were the proprietors, Antoine rarely made an appearance anymore.

He needed inspiration again, though.

And if Valentina could return, somehow. He placed the stack of cash in a large, manila envelope, stuffed it in his bag, and placed his drawer in the safe. As he slammed it shut and spun the lock closed, he touched his pocket. The card was still there. And the mysterious woman remained in his mind.

As he headed out the front door to the brilliant morning sun, he reached inside his pocket and pulled the card out. He looked at it again, wondering how –

or if – he should travel to New Orleans. He started to walk to the end of the block, placing the card back in his pocket, and thoughts of why Vivienne was making this proposition to him flooded his mind. But he brushed them away. As he boarded a bus to take him back across the causeway to the design district, he flopped into a seat in the center, and placed his head back on the top, closing his eyes.

And then he remembered the encounter, back in Paris. When he was at the *Louvre*, studying the Mona Lisa painting in the museum, as he had felt a hand lightly touch his shoulder.

That most definitely could be it. And there might be a connection.

There would be no sleep today.

Thoughts of the past, and desperation, washed through his mind. He remembered days in Paris, and then in Rome, and after in America. They were always on the move. Darius, the sweet, mysterious visitor. The one with a checkered past, who had become evasive shortly after he had transformed Pedro.

And after, there were moments missing. He lay on the soaked bedsheets, clutching his chest, wishing he could remember. Squeezing his eyes shut, he muttered to himself, *Our Father, thou art in Heaven. I have been on a sinful path. Can thou give me penance?*

Awash with trepidation, he lay on his bed as the pale moonlight filtered through the sheer drapes. Too many nights, it seemed. Far too many nights. It had become a common ritual of mixing a cocktail shortly before dinner, which turned into two, and then three. He would feel the warmth on his cheeks as the alcohol numbed his senses, as his eyes would grow heavy, and the hum of the television would drift off into the background.

And then he would awaken, his heart pounding in his chest, as he was breathless, drenched in sweat, and the moonlight shone through, leaving its light on the mussed sheets. He raised his knees as he tore the sheet off. The bruises were still there; they looked fresh, a deep shade of blue in small, round pools of blood under his pasty skin.

I am not a ghost.

I am still alive.

The following night, Pedro had again awakened in the early morning hours, long before sunrise. The early awakenings had increased in frequency, it seemed.

He swung his legs from the bed, wishing his racing heart would calm.

It would, he knew, but it would be hours. He winced at the chill of the tile floor as he padded to the bathroom.

He squinted as the light pierced his tired eyes; he held his arm up and covered his face as he stumbled against the low countertop. His head throbbed as he leaned down on his forearms, hanging his head down towards the sink.

He twisted the knob as the water flowed and he leaned downward, desperate for a drink.

The midnight awakenings had become commonplace in his life; he knew that his evening binge would occur, and when he was treasuring the warmth of the booze as it burned down his throat, he failed to care. And even when he awakened during the darkness of the night, as his heart would race, and the bleeding would continue under his skin, he could feel the gnaw within his abdomen as the distant call of the demons commenced.

You are dying, little Pedro.

You are on your way to us…are you ready to come down and join us?

It won't be much longer now!

He gasped as the steam from the sink fogged the mirror. He reached up and smeared a small oval in the fog, as tinny demonic laughter rang through his head. Perhaps the demons were right. The bags under his eyes were his luggage he was destined to carry for the remainder of his miserable, lonely life.

"It's the devil's hour, isn't it?" he said, as he hung his head during his weekly therapy session. The room started to spin, as he closed his eyes, and then, the spinning accelerated, as he hung his head back down towards his lap. The demons laughed in the dark distance; his head throbbed from last night's binge. There was a distant chattering as he slammed his palms against his ears, squeezing his eyes tightly. *"Leave me alone!"*

As he stood in the bathroom and screamed, his sense of reality softened, and then he opened his eyes to darkness.

The demons had stopped their teasing, at least for a moment, but he was no longer in his home. There was a distant feeling of terror, and torment and fire. He was falling downwards through the darkness, towards the thrashing pasty limbs, swallowed in a sea of regret and misfortune. It was his vision, he thought, yet he physically saw nothing.

And then he remembered where he was.

He opened his eyes, looked over to the left and saw the nameplate on the door.

The shiny rectangle reflected the light as he groaned, nursing a headache.

She sat cross-legged in a small, upholstered wooden chair across from a large, smoked glass coffee table. Her deep auburn hair hung down the sides of her grey pants suit like a red blanket, and she had her chin resting in one hand, as she was scribbling notes on a large legal pad.

He cleared his throat and looked around the office.

Her desk was as it always looked; cluttered, yet sophisticated. She was one of the best shrinks in Brickell, and Pedro knew that he was one of many patients.

"Where were you just now?"

Pedro's thoughts were cast back into the present. He faced forward, watching her. One of her legs was crossed over the other, and she held her expensive looking ball-point pen in her two fingers, flicking it on a yellow legal pad. Her long, crimson hair hung down as she adjusted her sitting position, swinging inwards and covering her breasts. Pedro attempted to force the thoughts of her breasts from his mind. They were covered by her dark grey pantsuit, anyway.

"Where did you go?" she asked again with different words. "Just now."

Pedro leaned back in his chair and tugged on his t-shirt collar, and then reached down, grasped the wooden arms, and felt the muscles in his forearm tighten. He wished the session was over, and that he could stop downstairs and relax with a drink. But now, Dr. Claire, the persistent red head, leaned forward and raised her eyebrows. "Pedro, there is a change in your demeanor this week. We've been seeing each other for a while now, and you have repeated your thoughts about Darius. And then, you were where? Back alone in Madrid? Did The Dark Ones come again? Did you see the sea of souls again?"

Pedro felt his chest tighten.

He stared at Dr. Claire, as she leaned forward and raised her eyebrows, but didn't keep asking.

She just waited.

He knew she was wanting the answer. But it was to a question that he knew she already knew the answer to.

Of course, his thoughts were back in the past.

As they seemed to do, especially once the sun went down and the sky darkened.

That was when the terror came in. Pedro always knew The Dark Ones came at night. And they were darker than the night could ever be.

He cleared his throat.

"This is how I am, Doctor. I'm an artist. I've been attempting to write, but nothing is flowing. I'm haunted by Darius, he's been appearing to me, wanting me to write his story."

"To be his ghost writer?"

Pedro nodded slowly and scoffed as he looked around the room. "So, a ghost wants to tell his story. Yet I am the ghost writer?"

Claire looked at him but said nothing.

Pedro looked down and examined his nails. "I cannot write without my muse. And Darius is not that."

"Who is your muse, Pedro?"

"Was."

Claire paused for a moment.

"I am sorry, Pedro. How did you lose your inspiration?"

He sighed.

"It all comes down to Darius. I was in Madrid with Darius; he appeared to me, promised me the world, and the gift. I would be immortal; I would have talent. And then I was in his flat in Paris. And he was gone. It was all so sudden. So unexpected."

She crossed her legs as she set her legal pad on the table. "And you still have animosity because of his broken promise?"

Pedro continued to stare blankly at Dr. Claire who sat, patiently waiting for the answer to her question. But as he watched, the hair was no longer red. The legs were no longer crossed. And then Pedro thought his eyes caught him, and he saw the long, brown hair. In an instant, he looked up, and saw Darius raise his head.

His eyes were wide and pleading.

Don't tell her.

Darius didn't have to speak, and Pedro knew it. There was the massive unresolved issue between them.

You could have so much if you would just let me in.

Pedro shot up out of his chair and clenched his fists. He glared down at him. "You left me," he said. "You promised me the gift and *you never gave it to me.*" He

183

watched as Darius leaned back in the chair, and as he drew his hand to hook his long, brown hair back around his ear, Pedro saw him turn and walk away.

Pedro gasped for breath as he squeezed the wooden arms of the chair.

Dr. Claire set her notebook down and leaned forward, her eyes wide and her face shifted with concern.

"Pedro? Are you alright?"

He continued taking deep breaths, leaned back and closed his eyes.

"You just saw Darius? Here in the office?"

Pedro opened his eyes and watched Dr. Claire get up and hand him a tissue. He held it over his mouth as he started to calm.

She returned to her chair as he took a breath and sighed.

"He's been haunting me."

"Darius was a patient of mine," she said. "About the one you claim transformed you into immortality?" Pedro scoffed, turned his head and looked out the window.

He could see the tops of the other skyscrapers in the distance, as the bright white clouds meandered across the sky like cotton balls.

"I don't think he ever did."

Claire placed her legal pad down on the table. "He never did. Are you saying that to appease me? To say you've made progress?"

Pedro shook his head while his gaze remained on the brilliant blue sky outside the windows. "No," he said. "But I see things much more clearly now. I look back to Madrid, and it feels like a lifetime ago. Or even more."

"Did Darius appear to you that night?"

Pedro shifted, leaning closer towards the table.

He picked up a cup of black coffee which had since grown cold. "I always thought he had. And then I believed that he'd taken me to Paris, and he would take me to *Pere Lachaise* and show me the secret crypts, and he always said I would be a part of it."

Claire watched him as he studied the cityscape, he knew she was watching, and could see her out of the corner of his eyes, but he did not turn his head.

"The secret crypts? Is this something that you believe truly happened?"

Pedro broke his trance and turned his head. Claire had set her legal pad on the table, and she was leaning forward in her chair. He knew she took an interest in his story because she was paid to do so, and so he thought he would entertain her. "It did," he said slowly. "But not without consequence. Darius. Yes, that was his name."

Claire paused.

He saw her mouth slowly drop open, and then she leaned back in the chair and nodded. "Another one of my patients. Certainly, he wasn't the one who claimed to transform you?"

Pedro sighed and returned his gaze to the cityscape. The sky was no longer the brilliant blue it once was as clouds had permeated the horizon; tiny raindrops started to pelt the window. "It was years ago," he said. "He always made promises, back then. Said that becoming an immortal was part of my destiny. That he could give me talent. That my life would be extraordinary."

"And now?"

"Now he is still in my life, he fights his way into it. But I don't remember many of the details of what happened after I left my flat in Madrid. That's why I'm here. I'm hoping you can help me remember."

She nodded as Pedro rose from his chair.

"What I do know," he said, while slowly making his way to the door. "Is that I remain a mortal. He has broken his promise of immortality to me. And I wallow in a pool of self-pity which I cannot seem to avoid. But I am dying, Doctor. Slowly, yes, but surely. The drink helps me cope."

Claire rose slowly, picked up her legal pad, and placed it on her desk. "I cannot discuss any details about my other patients with you," she said. "But he could never have transformed you, Pedro."

"He is not immortal. He was. But he was enamored with his own demons, it seems. And he lost the gift, apparently before he even met me."

"Yes," Claire said. "And because of that, I want you to be certain that everything he has told you is actually true."

Pedro flung his backpack over his shoulder and waited for his ride to pick him up, as he stood in the brilliant Miami sunshine, early the next morning. Despite his therapy sessions with Dr. Claire, he couldn't seem to find the support that he needed to create, which, in his heart, and his soul, was what he was destined to do.

Antoine had been evasive lately, apparently wrapped up in his own world.

Pedro had always suspected that Antoine had his own agenda when taking him to America.

Antoine quickly dumped him in a small apartment in the design district, far from the opulence of his estate in Coral Gables.

That, however, mattered less than the thoughts of Vivienne and her proposal. He reached into his pocket, drew the card out, and looked at it again.

HOUSE OF VOODOO

New Orleans

As a small black sedan pulled up in front of his apartment complex, he shoved the card back in his pocket, opened the back door, and eased himself inside the tiny car.

The air conditioning was almost deafening, but he was thankful that the driver was running it. It was an older model car, and Pedro had grown accustomed to America since he had been living there, and quickly realized that air conditioning was a necessity in Miami.

"One Andelusia Avenue," he said to the driver.

The car pulled up to Antoine's estate as the night had fallen across the city, bathing it in darkness. The homes on Andelusia avenue were a far cry from the tiny apartment that Pedro was living in across town in the design district. The opulent mansions sat far from the quiet street, behind massive oak trees with long strands of Spanish moss, which, Pedro thought, looked like webbing in the darkness as it swayed in the light evening breezes.

But the street was scarcely dark.

The wrought iron lamps which lined either side bathed the street in a warm glow, rising from elegant wrought iron benches. The yards were massive and well-tended, with tropical foliage and palm trees with lights shining upwards and highlighting their fronds.

Pedro tipped the driver and the hum of the engine quieted as the car drove away. He looked at Antoine's estate with its soaring Corinthian columns, a wraparound driveway and majestic Royal palms which lined the perimeter.

As the car sped off into the distance, the night became eerily silent. The lights emanated from the mansion, but when he started to approach the long, wraparound front porch, he stopped.

A rustling came from the bushes and a deep throated growl.

He turned and saw the glare of red eyes, staring through the shrubbery, glaring at him.

Pedro gasped and tripped over his feet as he heard the snap of twigs, the chaotic rustle of the branches, and the demonic growl and bark. The front door slowly opened as Pedro crawled up the stairs, turning around.

A dark shadow hovered behind him, glaring at him with intense red eyes, growling and barking.

Pedro snapped his head in the direction of the door as the light emanated from the mansion.

Antoine stood on the top of the steps, holding his arms outward. "Come inside, Pedro."

Pedro struggled to his feet, looking back at the growling shadow, as Antoine ushered him into the foyer.

He looked up at Antoine with wide eyes. "What was that?!"

Antoine tilted his head to the side. "Only those with darkness inside them usually experience those, Pedro. When was the last time you examined your own self? Your own soul?"

Pedro shifted his face and shook his head. "I don't understand."

"That was a hellhound, Pedro. They only appear to drag someone straight to Hell."

A shiver ran down his spine.

Back in his apartment after the meeting with Antoine, Pedro awakened again the following morning, as the sunbeams shone brilliantly through his window. Perhaps last night was a bad dream. He slowly lifted the covers, and the bruises remained. Now that Darius was gone, there was little reason to remain in Miami. The sessions with Dr. Claire had helped him little, if at all, and he knew that he longed for companionship once again. If Darius knew of Pedro's shortcomings, he didn't seem to mind, even if Darius had been evasive for years, if not what seemed like an eternity.

Pedro grabbed the remote from the mountains of comforters and sheets, and aimed it at the sleek, black flatscreen. The news ticker instantly flashed across the screen as the talking heads animated.

Local Psychiatrist Found Dead

Pedro hugged himself while still holding the remote, reading the ticker.

His eyes widened as he saw the image of the victim flash across the screen, and hastily aimed the remote at the TV, increasing the volume.

The psychiatrist was found in the bathroom of her upscale Brickell condo complex with what appeared to be a gunshot wound. Detective Martin Jenson is working with the Miami Police Department to determine a motive. The body was evaluated by the coroner and given to the care of the Waxley Mortuary and Funeral Home, in the care of its proprietor, the mortician Jacob Benjamin.

Pedro flopped down on the edge of the bed, reached up and muted the volume.

He leaned back towards the nightstand and grabbed his phone. He scrolled through the contacts list, quickly holding the small black rectangle up to his ear. After a few moments of silence, he spoke.

"Sebastian?"

"Yes Pedro. I am here."

Pedro reached for the remote and turned off the TV.

He knew that Darius was the ghost that kept on haunting him. But it did sound like Sebastian. Pedro got up and paced back and forth across the room as Sebastian continued. "She's dead. Claire. The doctor. It's all over the news."

"Of course, it is," Pedro said.

Pedro froze. The voice sounded more like Darius. "Why wouldn't it be?"

Pedro scoffed and shook his head. "Don't drag me deeper into this, Darius." He placed his hand over his eyes as his voice quivered. "You never transformed me, did you? Has this all been a lie? You are gone now, and haunting me?"

There were a few moments of silence.

Pedro could hear a shuffling on the other end of the line, so he knew Darius remained. The silence, though, gave Pedro all he needed to know. The memories of the night in Madrid were hazy, but he still remembered how Darius looked as he leaned against the lamp post, the tightness of his pants, the height of his top hat, and the length of his hair.

But he was a different Darius in those days.

Even as Pedro recalled the warmth of the light which had washed over the sidewalk in the middle of the early morning darkness, Darius had taken his arm. Pedro could remember the glimmer of light rising upwards from the mountains to the east, and turning, one last time, towards the warmth coming from the flat. The curtains were drawn. Valentina would still be asleep, but not for much longer. It didn't matter, it seemed, as he took Darius' embrace, and they walked deeper towards the darkness and remaining chill in the west.

"Pedro?" Sebastian said. "Are you there?"

Pedro blinked.

He *was* talking to Sebastian.

Pedro placed the phone back on the nightstand and walked over to the windows.

He grasped the heavy drapes and flung them open as the brilliant Miami sunshine flooded the room. A half empty bottle of whiskey sat next to a glass with the remainders of last night's tipple. Pedro looked down at the glass. Watered down and warm, most likely, as the ice had melted hours ago.

No time for relaxing today, he thought, as he yanked his boxers down to his ankles and flung them towards a small hamper.

After a quick shower, he dashed out the front door and down the corridor. The News Café would be busy this morning, as they always were. After a short ride the driver dropped him off on Miami Beach, and he stood out against the lazy tourists wandering through souvenir shops on Washington Avenue, the beach revelers in bathing suits and tanning oil, and the jogging fitness enthusiasts.

South Beach was busy, vibrant and full of life.

He was to meet Sebastian there, who was an author who lived in South Miami Beach. They were to have brunch together and discuss the craft. While Sebastian was younger than Pedro, there was a certain artistic connection between them. Pedro felt it was his only hope for a muse, beyond Valentina, who had been gone, according to Vivienne.

As Pedro turned the corner towards Ocean Drive, dodging the throngs of people which permeated the sidewalks, he thought he could see Sebastian in the distance, at one of the small tables designed for two, on the edge of the sidewalk, wearing his black slacks and shirt, which Pedro felt was necessary to match. Sebastian stood out, yet as Pedro slowly approached, he felt that it was for an undesirable reason. Sebastian sat, with his legs crossed, seemingly oblivious to the life and boisterous activity which surrounded him. As he approached, Sebastian slowly looked up.

"You look like death," he said.

Pedro scoffed, slowly nodding. Sebastian gestured for him to sit as the server approached, pouring another glass of water and offering coffee. Pedro pulled the chair out and looked back up and gasped.

Darius sat in the chair.

Don't haunt me now, Darius.

Don't come any closer. I know what you are, and I know what you are doing.

Darius reached up and flagged her closer.

The server approached the table, welcoming them.

"Two Bloody Mary's," Darius said. "One of your finest vodkas and extra olives. Oh, and make them spicy. And salt the rim. I can tell he needs it."

The server nodded to each of them and quickly left the table. Pedro pulled his napkin down and unfolded it in his lap, letting out an exasperated sigh. He looked up as Sebastian sat with a grin on his face.

"Feeding our addictions today, are we?" Pedro asked.

Sebastian sat back and crossed his arms, glancing upward at the passersby on South Beach. Although it was still morning, the city was livening. Women in bikinis and men in thongs, glistening in tanning oil headed across Ocean Avenue to the nearby beach.

Pedro waited and ignored the people around him, knowing that the drink would taste glamorous and make him feel that he was a part of the lively activity which surrounded him, if only for a few moments. The server returned with the drinks, and as Pedro took a sip, and as the bite from the spices ignited his taste buds, the silence continued until Sebastian finally spoke.

"Like I said, you look like death."

Pedro put his drink down and sat back in the chair, folding his arms. "Then we both do," he said.

"I have good reason to."

Pedro looked up from his drink.

Darius sat across from him, holding the drink, watching him, smiling.

Pedro uncrossed his arms and leaned forward, balancing his arms on the table. "You didn't have to bring me into this," he said. "You could have transformed me, given me the talent that you promised."

"But I did. And you know that I did. At least in a way. I got you pursuing your passions! But immediate transformations are now forbidden by the code, you know. I know you know that. I couldn't do it then, and I most certainly cannot do it now."

"Of course, you can't. You're *dead*! And, now what? Now what am I supposed to do? Die from liver cancer?"

Darius leaned back in his chair, laughed, picked up the drink and took a generous sip. He stared directly at him. "Your addictions will get you if you insist on constantly feeding them."

"You promised me the gift," Pedro said. "You promised me immortality."

Darius scoffed and grinned. "Your age will get you first, if not your addiction," he said. "It will quickly catch up with you. Unless you're transformed. That could have saved me. Like Delia."

"Like Delia."

Pedro knew Darius was right.

There seemed to be a pattern of immortals sinking into the throes of uncertainty and despair.

He knew Darius hadn't been alone; many others had experienced the wrath of the hooded man, countless immortals had lost their gift from drinking the blood in the decanter, rapidly aged and died a final, mortal death. But for him, he wasn't even given the gift.

Antoine always wanted the image of prosperity and productivity, for he reported directly to Rome. And even though it was now too late for Darius, Pedro understood that the plight of the immortals had been based on despair.

Darius leaned forward and stared at him directly.

"It's always those that appear the happiest, that seem to be trying to please the world, that tend to be hurting the most. Take it from me. Your ghostly advice. Don't take the same path I did."

Pedro noticed Darius watching him. "You aren't even real. You aren't even here."

Darius nodded as he took a long drink. "True," he said. "But you are. Get writing! Get to work!"

Pedro hung his head and squeezed his eyes together, shaking his head. "I cannot write without my muse. I cannot paint. Nothing."

Darius scoffed and placed the Bloody Mary down on the table with a slight clink. "What do you mean?" He balled up his hand and knocked on the table. "I am right here in front of you! What kind of ganja are you smoking, Pedro?"

He set his glass down and squeezed his eyes shut. This couldn't be. It was Sebastian, as he shook his head back and forth, he kept reminding himself. It was not Darius. Darius was dead.

He was gone.

He was simply a ghost.

Pedro heard the snap of fingers nearby and he opened his eyes. Darius remained at the other end of the table. He picked up his Bloody Mary, leaned back in his chair, took a sip, and scoffed. "I'm not dead," he said, drawing his arms outwards. "I'm right here."

It was as if Darius could still read his mind. Darius shook his head and took a large gulp from his drink. "It's too late for a resurrection now," he said. "At least from me. I'm sure Antoine will make an attempt. But I've already given instructions for him to bury me in the ancestral crypt in Lyon."

Pedro held his glass, noting the cold, wet condensation on his palm. Darius was right. It might be too late for his own transformation, which might never come for Pedro, at least not from Darius. All throughout the immortal community, it was known that Darius was really gone; it was a sentence which was handed down in only the most extreme of circumstances. Pedro did not know the reasons for the judgment and may never know.

"I call it *The Quest for Immortality*," Darius said, breaking Pedro's thoughts, and casting him back to the present.

"Call what?"

"My book," he said.

Pedro had no idea what Darius was talking about.

He fidgeted in his chair as Darius sighed. "Have you been listening to me at all?"

Pedro fidgeted.

"I know you cast your thoughts outwards frequently," he said. "But please listen to me. It's of the utmost importance."

Pedro nodded.

"We are both dying," Darius said. "You from your addiction and me from becoming mortal once again. I'd been going to Claire for months now, in the hopes that she might hold the key to me regaining my immortality."

"You're already dead. Don't you know that?"

Darius shook his head. "It's not that simple in my case," he said. "For you, there is hope. I cannot transform you, but I can see that you are transformed. I will try to keep the promise I made back in Madrid.

Pedro leaned back and scanned the crowd. Ocean Drive livened with tourists and locals alike; a line of cars spanned the avenue, nearly stopped. But the drivers didn't seem to care. Most windows were open, as those in the cars watched the crowd and the crowd watched the people in the cars.

"Ah Madrid," Pedro said, as he returned his attention to the table and Darius. They both reached down and took a sip of their morning cocktails. "So unlike Miami. Yet somehow it still feels the same to me."

He looked over at Darius who looked up as their eyes met.

"The same?" Darius asked. "How so? The two cities couldn't be more different, as far as I'm concerned."

Pedro scoffed. "It's you, Darius."

Darius leaned back in his chair. "I know what I promised you back in Madrid. I will find a way to keep my word to you. That will offer you immortality, which is what you want, isn't it?"

"I don't want to die, I know that."

"You have to desire the gift to receive it," he said.

Pedro sighed. "Why would I not desire it?"

Darius paused, looked up and appeared to study Pedro. Their drinks were finished, and Darius shook his glass, so the ice cubes clanked against the sides. But it was his eyes that captivated Pedro's attention.

They had the same intense stare which he had remembered from Madrid.

The same ferocity.

And anger.

Pedro looked down, holding his hands in his lap. Perhaps this was a mistake.

There was too much booze in his life, all the time.

Miami had not proven to be the creative fire that Antoine had said it would be, and without the promised gift, the only success he felt he experienced was that of aging. Pedro craved an accomplishment; he yearned for it.

Yet he knew that he had no focus.

Incessantly visited by the ghost of his would-be maker, the one who kept demanding that he write the story of how he lost his *own* gift, yet, when Pedro sat down with a blank page, he watched the flicker of the cursor against the white background and could feel his heartbeat.

"There is no use," he said to himself, as he rose from the small chair in the tiny bedroom. He padded over to the kitchen and reached for a bottle of whiskey on top of the refrigerator. "I need a little liquid inspiration," he said, as he fished through the cabinets for a glass. He poured the whiskey into the glass, and, for a moment, stopped and admired the amber liquid in the glass. He wasn't like the other writers, he thought. "This is the elixir of creativity."

As he returned to his small writing desk, he returned to the page, and the flashing cursor, sat back in his chair, and sipped his drink.

"You seem to be getting a lot done."

He snapped out of his musing and turned around.

Darius was in the shadows.

Pedro was surprised that he'd been sitting there for so long, as the sun was nearly below the horizon. As he looked in the corner, he could tell it was Darius. Leaning against the dresser, arms folded. He took a step into the small dome of light which emanated from Pedro's small desktop lamp, and Pedro's eyebrows raised.

Darius had grown young again.

He was not the aging mortal who had complained that his body was catching up with his soul; his vibrant and youthful appearance caused Pedro to sit back.

He placed his glass on the desk, swung the chair around to face Darius, and nodded slowly.

"So, this was you in the past?"

Darius scoffed, and sat on the bed, crossing his legs. "It's amazing what you can do when you're a ghost." He turned to face Pedro. "And you…getting a lot done, aren't you?"

Pedro nervously laughed and spun back around to face his computer screen. "I have been finding my inspiration. Your story is coming to me, I can feel it."

Darius got up from the bed and approached his workstation. He picked up the bottle of whisky and swished the amber liquid inside. "Not much left, is there?"

Pedro looked up, watched Darius playing with the bottle, but said nothing. Darius held the bottle up to his eye, and Pedro watched as he examined it through the mouth. "Nope, don't see any in there."

Pedro tilted his head to the side. "Come again?"

Darius placed the bottle back on the desk. "Not much inspiration in there, is there?"

"There's plenty. It helps me think creatively."

"The inspiration will come when you allow it. When you realize that you, and only you, can tell the story you are meant to tell, you will find your talent. And it will find you. But it's not in the bottom of the bottle."

Pedro looked at his blank screen, and the flashing cursor, and sighed. He turned, and just as quickly as he had appeared, Darius was gone.

Fleeting moments, perhaps brought on by the whiskey, he did not know. But Darius had been appearing to him regularly; he wanted his story told.

He wanted his book to be written.

Pedro knew that it was a project that he had to find the inspiration for.

As he was The Ghost Writer.

"This is a ghost story," Pedro said, as he sat at a bar in Coral Gables. The bartender was polishing glassware and looked up from his work. He appeared a bit of a silhouette against the emanating light from the backbar. "I'm sorry?" he asked.

Pedro smiled and leaned back. "The book I'm working on," he said, as the bartender turned around and picked up the bottle of scotch. He looked at Pedro and raised his eyebrows.

Pedro pointed at the glass, focusing his attention on the notepad and paper in front of him. As the bartender placed a fresh pour of scotch in his glass, he got his attention. "So you write novels?"

Pedro placed his pen down, picked up the glass of scotch and took a sip, treasuring the burn down his throat. "I don't know if I would go as far as to say it was a novel," he said as he placed his glass down. The bartender resumed cleaning the bar.

"But you said it was a ghost story? It's a story, right?"

Pedro looked back up and smiled politely. "Yes."

The bartender flung a small, white towel over his shoulder. He bent down and Pedro assumed he was washing glassware. He periodically raised his head. "I've always been fascinated with writers," he said, as he washed glasses in the sink below. "Especially authors. Are you an author?"

Pedro's face fell, and he carefully set his pen down on the bar next to his notebook. "I'm not an author, I'm afraid. I write. All the time, in fact. Never been published."

The bartender stood back up straight as he dried glassware with the towel he had placed on his shoulder. "Is that what you want to do? Have books on the shelves?"

Pedro took a sip of his scotch and nodded. "Yes. But I seem to have lost my motivation."

The bartender put the glass he was drying up on the shelf behind the bar and leaned down, his arms folded. He looked at Pedro directly. "You will find it, bud. You're sitting here taking notes and working on your craft. That is something, and that should mean something."

Pedro nodded. "Yes, I guess if you look at it that way."

The bartender straightened up and his face brightened. "Of course! I don't picture myself as a bartender forever. I have something on the side myself."

Pedro raised his head and his eyes widened, he slowly nodded.

"I'm a photographer," the bartender said.

Pedro glanced around the room. "That is art, my friend. Snapshots can be brilliant, and stunning, and tell a story."

The bartender stood back, nodded, and appeared flustered. He smiled and nodded. "Thank you, so much, thank you." His face shifted and he tilted his head to the side. "But you…are not inspired? Not by my art, I mean. But by your own?"

Pedro shook his head.

"I don't want to pry," he said. "But are you having trouble with what you are writing? Is it the plot that isn't agreeing with you? Or are you not relating to the character? They're not speaking to you, are they?"

Pedro set his glass down on the bar, held the scotch in mouth for a moment while he looked up at the bartender. He was waiting for an answer, but his face was friendly, his eyebrows raised. He leaned on the edge of the bar with his palms, his arms extended, looking at him.

"I had a muse once," Pedro finally said. "When I look back and remember her, it was her inspiration that kept my fire burning. I used to paint, she encouraged me. She died."

The bartender's face fell, and he leaned closer, propping himself up on his elbows. "I am sorry. For your loss I mean."

"I…don't even know how to process that she's gone. I was away from her for many years. But I just learned of her death recently."

The bartender walked over the other side of the bar to tend to another customer who had arrived, and Pedro examined the ice cubes in his scotch, as they are floating like tiny icebergs in a tan colored sea. He paused, for a moment, to imagine if tiny creatures would be living on those little frozen bergs, blissfully unaware that the glass walls would prevent them from venturing very far.

He found it sad, if it were true.

But he knew that his glass of scotch was not a tiny world.

Yet, when the bartender returned, and started again asking questions about his writer's block, Pedro explained to him the thoughts he just had while gazing into his scotch glass.

"You see! Most of us don't have thoughts like those. That's why you are destined for something like this, something creative."

Pedro nodded. "I was an artist, once. Back in Madrid."

"And then you came to America to write?"

Pedro scoffed and nodded as he glanced around the room. The other patron had left an empty glass on the bar. The ice cubes were still solid and not yet melted.

"We are both artists," the bartender said. "No matter which medium we craft."

"I will always remember that."

"Then why do you feel uninspired with this world around us?"

An image of Valentina flashed through Pedro's mind.

Was she his muse?

The source of his creativity?

When he was painting in Madrid, he had always thought he was inferior; that he was devoid of talent, that he would never reach the level of the great artists. And then he remembered standing in Paris, admiring the work of da Vinci. Could he ever achieve that level of craftmanship, of art?

"I sometimes wonder," Pedro said. "How my life would have progressed if I hadn't abandoned my creative muse. But I couldn't see the inspiration she brought me, day after day. I remembered sitting in my studio, hunched over my canvas. I used to hate my art. And what I created. I thought it was awful. And wouldn't ever measure up. Or even be appreciated by the world."

"Was it awful?" the bartender asked.

"Actually, she persisted in telling me that it was fantastic. That I was talented."

The bartender leaned back and extended his arms.

"Well, there you go. She was clearly your muse. I can't speak if you have the talent or not, but that is what we all need as creatives, Pedro. We all need our support. I dream of my photos hanging in galleries in New York. Am I there yet? Look around you. I'm running around behind a bar. And washing glasses. But my wife believes in me."

Pedro slowly nodded as he finished off his scotch. "She's your Mona Lisa." He raised the glass and shook the remaining ice cubes.

The bartender supported himself on the side of the bar with his palms and looked directly at him. "This is the last one, Pedro. We're getting close to closing time. Deal?"

Pedro hastily nodded and leaned back in his chair as the bartender made him one final cocktail.

The following day, Antoine was to take Pedro to meet Jacob Benjamin, the mortician from the Waxley Mortuary on the other side of town.

Pedro woke with his face buried in the pillow and the covers pulled over him as if he were in a cocoon. Someone was knocking. He didn't know what time it was when he heard rapping at the door. His head throbbed as he covered his head and cherished the darkness, squeezing his eyes shut. There couldn't possibly be someone knocking now.

Too early.

He settled back into his pillow when the raps came again, more insistent this time.

He let out an exasperated sigh as he flung the covers down the bed. He was shocked to see the daylight fighting its way behind the curtains, as he swung his legs over the side of the bed. He reached up and covered his eyes. The fuzziness would clear, he hoped.

He was working on the novel which Darius had requested that he write. But the words came fitfully, and the afternoons of writing gradually transformed into drinking.

But not in the traditional sense. As a child, he would read books that featured similar characters.

Pedro had heard of the Waxley Mortuary and its proprietor, a Mr. Jacob Benjamin. And he'd heard of Resurrection cemetery, which bordered the mortuary and, strangely, how it had no bodies.

The rumors continued to circulate among the immortal population in Miami, and Pedro was no stranger.

Jacob was in Antoine's bloodline, birthed from a night at *Sacrafice*, the nightclub with Antoine Nagevesh had built and watched burn, and then be rebuilt again.

Although active in the immortal community, Pedro carried the dark secret with him while out during the day, and interacting with the human population, he knew that he was an outsider. An outcast. He had been given the secrets that the immortals carried, but he wasn't yet an immortal.

And there were days when he wondered if he ever would be.

There were times when he wished he didn't long for the gift.

Days and nights and days again when he felt the anxiety thrash through his veins; a mystery painting on which the brush determined action, yet there was a distance about his gaze on the mortuary. For Jacob, it had become an employer; a lifeline when he truly needed it. Jacob had been transformed. Pedro had heard of Antoine's opulent lifestyle and riches yet was never able to partake in it.

"Antoine protects his bloodline," Jacob explained to him, as the clock ticked in his office. Pedro sat in a small suede chair across from the expansive dark mahogany desk, and watched as Jacob sat back in his chair, his hands together in front of him, his fingertips touching. He wore a dark grey pin stripe suit, and his hair was slicked back with a wet look.

Pedro thought that he seemed a little out of his time; also, his cherubic baby face indicated naivety, yet

Jacob spoke like a seasoned elder and astute businessman. "But if you choose to work here, you will accompany me to crime scenes, and anywhere else I may have to retrieve a body and take it back here to the mortuary."

"And there is more?"

Jacob raised his eyes and looked directly at Pedro.

Jacob's forehead wrinkled as, suddenly, he appeared older than his apparent young years.

He rose from the chair, moving towards the wall where a painting of Schubert hung. Pedro watched as he gestured his hand towards it, and then turned back to face him.

His eyes were piercing.

"You have heard about the history of this mortuary, have you not?"

Pedro shifted in his chair.

Indeed, he had.

He'd heard about Ned McCracken, who remained in a position of authority within the immortal community, who had been the proprietor of Waxley Mortuary since the 1930's, and who was rumored to have been transformed himself…but confirmation had never come.

"I know some of the history," Pedro said, as Jacob's eyes fell. He nodded and lowered his arm, sitting back in the brown, high-back smoking chair.

"Some of the history?"

Pedro nodded and shifted back to his original position. How much should he share? "I've read some of the articles about the cemetery, and the rumors that have circulated around the city that you have a special option for people who want their loved ones to return from the grave."

Jacob and Antoine both stared at Pedro.

He had gone and done it.

Brought some of his research where he hadn't confirmed the source into the equation. It was no secret that Pedro knew a great deal about the immortals and their culture.

Jacob cleared his throat.

"I will not confirm – nor deny – anything you may have read from any source, Pedro. What I will do is accompany you on your mission to return your muse from the grave, if that is what Rome wants. If they want a resurrection, then we will give it to them."

"I have the world's finest taxidermist in mind," Antoine said. "From Tel Aviv."

Jacob nodded as Pedro watched in wonderment. Antoine, and the immortals, seemed to be invested in bringing Valentina back, but at what cost?

The following day, Pedro took the Metrorail to the University of Miami. As he exited the train, he shifted his backpack from one shoulder to the other, walking briskly to the library. The sun was low in the sky, and he knew he didn't have much time before it closed. Once he headed through the doors, as the blast of cool air conditioning enveloped him, he headed back towards the reference section. There would be more articles, he was certain, on this "hooded man" that Antoine referred to so often when they spoke.

As he sat at a terminal, scanning through articles that mentioned Antoine, and Darius, he came across a headline about the fires that tore through Miami. The newspapers didn't know who was responsible for the fires at the club, Antoine's estate, and a little paranormal research society's office that called themselves "The Astral".

There was the proprietor, whose name was Sheldon Wilkes. He had been writing a book on Antoine and his life when the disaster occurred. Antoine had mentioned Sheldon's name in passing, in conversations that he and Pedro had had on several occasions. But now, Pedro was getting more of the context.

Until he felt the hand on his shoulder

"I'll write your book for you."

He looked up.

Darius hovered over him, seeming as real as he ever could be.

Pedro closed his eyes, covering them with is hands, and sighed. "You aren't real. You are simply a figment of my imagination. You are not really here." He opened his eyes and looked up. "Must you continue to haunt me?"

Darius reached upwards as he turned and glided through the stacks of books. His fingers caressed the row of spines, as Pedro stood watching him. Darius turned around and stared directly at him.

"Of course," he said. "If you cannot write it yourself. I will be your ghost writer."

Pedro scoffed and nodded. "As if you even could. You're dead, aren't you?"

And then he watched as the look on his face grew stern, and cold. Darius leaned in closer towards Pedro, and he felt a chill.

Darius grinned. "Of course, I am dead, don't you see? I would be the perfect ghost writer. No one would even suspect I am writing your novels. And you can have a glorious writing career!"

Pedro leaned his head back on the stacks and closed his eyes. "You are a literal ghost. There's a price, isn't there? Of course, there is. There's always a cost."

Resurrection requires retribution.

Pedro opened his eyes and gasped.

Darius was right in front of him, hovering face to face, staring intensely into his eyes. "I will write your books. And you will hire the taxidermist that Antoine spoke of, and you will return me to this world."

And then Darius vanished.

Pedro caught his breath, he hadn't realized he'd been holding in, and scanned the room. The lights were starting to shut down, as another announcement rang that the library was closing. Deep in the basement stacks, he saw that he remained alone. With the lights turning off, he could very easily remain in the library basement until dawn. But he chose not to.

Darius would be the perfect ghost writer, had he been alive. Pedro remembered the first moment he saw Darius, back in Madrid, now years in the past. He hadn't noticed the aura around Darius; but could he be a ghost? Could Darius have been courting him all along from the grave?

Darius leaned against the stacks and sighed as Pedro fidgeted. The library would be closing soon, and an announcement quietly reminded the visitors that the library would be closing shortly and could everyone please bring their books to the check-out area if they needed more time with them.

Darius glided past him, out towards the nest of small wooden tables which were now deserted. Pedro turned and studied him. He thought that Darius might be of the grave, but he was once an immortal, at least what he had always claimed since their night in Madrid.

As he watched Darius move forward through the tiny basement corridor of the library, his mind reverted to the same night in Madrid, when Darius had taken the same stroll, through the streets in the dark pre-dawn, when the cars slept next to the sidewalks and only a single light will illuminate one of the windows.

"I am going to take you where you will find me," Darius said as he turned.

Pedro followed as they entered a small, dusty elevator. As the hydraulics emitted a thud, the car rose towards the main floor. Darius remained speechless, as he leaned against the wall, looking over at Pedro, who stood in the center of the floor, hugging himself.

Darius leaned forward. "Do you remember that night?"

Pedro shook his head.

"Then follow me and you will find me."

Pedro sat at the kitchen table, staring at the laptop screen.

The cursor blinked, yet the page remained blank. Darius hovered, leaning on the back of the small wooden chair.

There was a luminescence about him. Something different, of which Pedro could not quite place. But a destiny he hoped he would never experience himself.

Still, Darius did not keep his promise.

Pedro wished he would not be vindictive, but he thought back to the days, now years ago, back in Madrid, when Darius had been young and vibrant and healthy and determined. Now, look at him.

Spent, used.

"The Hooded Man," Darius said slowly, easing himself back towards the table and to the opposite chair. Pedro watched him over the top of the computer as Darius hung his head in shame. "I drank," he said. "I was infatuated, I always was." He looked up. Pedro thought he might have been crying, as his eyes appeared red rimmed, and the glisten on his cheeks suggested tears.

"I'm not going to write this book," Pedro said. He sat back in the chair and folded his arms, looked up at Darius. His mouth hung open. Darius scoffed and shook his head. "Why *wouldn't* you?!"

Pedro pursed his lips together and inhaled deeply through his nose. He rose from the chair as Darius took a step back. He turned to face Darius, as he hung his head and slowly shook it back and forth. "Because you broke your promise."

"You understand that I cannot keep a promise I made to you so many years ago. Look at me!"

Pedro raised his head. Of course, Darius couldn't keep his promise of so long ago when he was no longer in a physical form. But why couldn't he have kept it when he was? Pedro sat back in the chair, reached his arm out, and punched a few random keys lightly with his index finger. "Even when I was in physical form, I didn't have the ability to keep that promise," Darius said, as Pedro raised his head from the computer.

He looked over at Darius. The shell of what he once was, he watched as Darius leaned back towards the counter. Darius was a ghost, yes, but here in physical form. At least, to a degree.

He closed his eyes and thought of Valentina, and wondered where his muse, his inspiration, was originating from. As he looked up, he glanced around the kitchen.

Darius was gone, and he wondered if he'd ever really been there.

PORTRAIT

OF A WOMAN

PARIS

THERE SHE HUNG.

Behind bulletproof security glass, between the rafters in Paris at the *Louvre*, behind the throngs of crowds that stood before him, gasping at her beauty; in awe at da Vinci's craftmanship. The art had withstood the test of time, into the hearts of man she dove with her simplistic beauty and da Vinci's delicate use of color. So simple, yet elegant; beckoning. As he stared at her, her eyes seemed to follow his movements.

She was Mona Lisa.

It was if she were living in the canvas, watching us watching her.

A smaller painting than many, yet captivating.

Pedro stood on the same night in Paris, before Antoine had ever taken him to America, when Pedro waited, folding his arms around his torso, his hands clasping his sides, staring at the masterpiece work of art.

There was a simplicity juxtaposed with elegance.

Yes, that's what it was. And he thought of his days in Madrid.

He could see Valentina approach him as he would hover over his canvas for hours, concentrating on the tiny details, with each minute stroke of the brush.

Oh, how he missed the days in Madrid.

When he walked out of his flat, down the steel stairs towards the quiet, predawn street below, towards the waiting visitor, Darius, who had leaned against the streetlamp pole in the dome of yellow light, there had been a fleeting moment, perhaps, when he thought of Valentina, who slept in the flat upstairs.

But that was the last time he thought of her; once Darius approached and cast his persuasion, Pedro had made his decision. And when they walked away, Pedro did not once turn back to see his flat windows in the distance. And later, when he stood in Paris, as the museum closed around him, he thought of Valentina once again.

Years had passed, it seemed.

232

Those he had encountered in the immortal sects had been encouraging. But the promise had never been kept. Darius had left without bestowing him the gift. And now, Pedro was in Paris alone. He had been around others, of course, but it was not the same as Darius.

They had not made the promise to him of the gift. An even though he worked as a stagehand at the Jefferson Majestic, he knew he was surrounded by immortals who had the ability to transform him and provide him with the immortality which he so desired; yet they chose not to provide him with the gift.

In those days, he had wanted to journey in a different direction.

To forage a new path of creativity in performance and dance, which Darius had introduced him to, and Pedro harbored no regrets.

Except for one.

Now, Darius was gone.

Dead, buried near Antoine's chateau in Lyon, and he had died as a mortal.

Pedro stood in front of the Mona Lisa, unaware that the buzz of activity which surrounded him had abated, lost in his thoughts. His mind cast deep in the past, dreaming of Darius, and of Antoine, and of Valentina. Long ago were the days in Miami, when he had met with Claire, and when he had written the manuscript for Darius.

Pedro remained hugging himself in front of the painting as the crowds of tourists thinned, and as the sun sank over the horizon, and the lights of Paris ignited as the sky dimmed.

He first cast his thoughts back to the present, as he felt a tap on his shoulder.

He slowly turned, and in front of him was a short, heavyset dark-skinned woman.

She spoke in a thick Haitian accent. "I can read your thoughts. And I know you want her back."

Pedro felt himself drawing in a slow, deep breath, watching her staring back at him, her hands on her hips, her mouth smug. "I can help you," she said. "I have a powder."

"A powder?"

She nodded and gestured for him to come with her, and they walked together slowly towards the atrium as security guards scurried through the museum, locking doors, and an announcement in French sounded across the public address system, indicating that the museum was now closed.

"I keep it in my crypt at *Pere Lachaise*," she said. "We must go there, if you want it."

They exited through the pyramid to the plaza outside as the sun sank below the horizon, igniting the sky with crimson and orange hues.

Pedro cast his gaze towards the sky, noticing the wisps of clouds which reached outwards from the East, and they appeared to have an auburn tint.

"The powder will raise her," she said, slowly, as they descended some small stone steps as others passed by them, unaware of the depth of their discussion. "From the coffin, you know." She looked up at Pedro as they paused for a moment where the sidewalk met the thoroughfare. "She's been dead for how long?"

Pedro shook his head and sighed. "I don't know, I just don't know."

"Well, you consider my offer," she said, as a small, black Renault pulled up to the side. She eased herself into the small front seat and drew her seatbelt around her large frame.

Pedro leaned down and picked up the edge of her flowery sundress which spilled out onto the pavement. "Thank you," she said, as she settled herself into the seat. She turned and gestured for the driver to leave.

"Wait!" Pedro said, holding the door as she reached out to close it. "You never told me what you wanted from me."

She glared at him as she yanked the door closed and slammed it shut. Pedro stumbled backwards as the tiny sedan sped away. He stood, watching the car blend into traffic, its taillights blending with the others in a sea of brightened red.

Pedro took a breath and lowered his shoulders.

That woman had approached him seemingly out of nowhere and knew exactly what he had been thinking.

Yet she claimed to have a powder.

Pedro ran towards the entrance to the Jefferson Majestic and grabbed the brass knobs of the massive glass doors which led to the front atrium. He grasped the small knob and jiggled it, but it was locked. He slapped his palms on the wood frame, stepped back, and paced back and forth. They were in there. They always were. He knew about the catacombs below where they kept coffins in rooms lined with skulls; and he knew of the inner chambers.

But no one came to the door.

He ran towards the side alley and to the back of the theater, towards the wrought iron gate, which reached upwards with brass spires, nestled between the stone walls. He stood at the gate, holding the spires, and peered inside. He saw movement in the gardens. In the distance, through the brush, he saw the flowing movement of a black dress which delicately caught a light passing breeze.

"Madame!" he called. "Madame Arsenault!"

She did not stop, disappearing into the far trees on the opposite side of the gardens. Pedro shook his head, wondering if she had heard him, and chose to ignore him. She should have sensed his presence. They always did.

It was too early for the theater to be closed, especially on a weekend evening. There should be a ballet performance, as there always was.

Pedro grabbed the gate and shook, yet it was solid in its frame, scarcely made a sound. He turned, and then stood still.

The approach of footsteps in the gravel.

So, someone *was* at the theatre.

Even if it wasn't Madame Arsenault; it did not matter.

There was no response, none of the immortals came to the gate to see him, even though Pedro knew that the immortals had keen senses and extraordinary power, and most definitely knew that he was there.

Perhaps it was useless.

Venturing down to the catacombs beneath the theater would serve no purpose, it seemed. Perhaps if Madame Aresenault would be willing to discuss the ramifications of a meeting with LaDonna Mastuer, but the Madame of the theatre was gone.

Disappeared into the trees.

He stopped and held his breath for a moment, looking downwards, concentrating on the sounds emanating from the other side of the cement wall.

Footsteps on gravel.

Someone *was* on the other side.

Possibly listening to him; perhaps waiting for him.

"Hello!" he called out.

But there was no response.

He moved closer to the wall, leaning as close as he could to the stone, and took slow, careful steps towards the wrought iron gate. He stopped at the edge of the wall, and slowly turned his head around, close to the iron gate, and saw a billowing black dress. Was it Madame?

He pulled back and didn't make a sound.

It couldn't be.

But he did not remember. There was a clatter to his thoughts, for whomever was behind the gates did not reveal themselves. He wanted inside. He wanted to see the coffins. Gain some clarity on the rumors of the immortals, and their penchant for living forever, and punishing their kind in crypts for centuries.

The small, silver Mercedes coupe pulled up in front of the theater as Pedro slowly rose from the steps. His buttocks were numb from sitting on the cement steps for so long, and he was shivering from the Paris winter. He could see Antoine's silhouette in the driver's seat, and he hesitated when he approached the car. Antoine had sounded agitated on the phone, and he knew that the drive back to the chateau would not only take a number of hours, with Antoine displeased with him the drive would seem even longer.

He slowly eased the passenger door open and looked inside. Antoine was looking out the driver's window; Pedro could feel the reassuring heat and the Beethoven wafted outwards through the speakers. Antoine slowly turned and faced him; his expression solemn.

"Darius passed," he said slowly.

Pedro slid into the passenger seat and sat with Antoine in silence for a moment. "I am so sorry, Antoine. I know how much you both cared for each other."

Antoine reached down and slowly put the car in gear and eased the car into the evening traffic. "Yes," he said. "We did. But Darius was easily influenced by others, and by his environment. And that had a hand in his own downfall."

"He was exposed to the wrath?"

Antoine nodded as he waited in a line of cars.

Pedro noticed their bright red brake lights, and he thought of his meeting with the mysterious woman outside of the *Louvre*.

"He was. But not without his own rebelliousness. Had he not been so enamored with the blood, he may not have drunk from the decanter. He may not have become mortal again. He may not have rapidly aged. But it was Darius. And of course, he would do it."

The waiting cars accelerated as Antoine made a right turn.

"It is not much farther now. His flat was close to the Siene."

241

Pedro looked out the window and exhaled slowly, knowing this clearly was not the time that he should be bringing up his own grievances; Darius not transforming him, yet now he was dead; Valentina was gone; and the mysterious woman who had approached him while standing in front of the Mona Lisa had made an equally enigmatic offer.

"You forgot I am an immortal, didn't you?"

Pedro sighed and leaned his head back on the headrest. "Of course. You know everything I was just thinking about."

Antoine parked the car and they exited. Antoine reached into his pocket and grabbed a set of shimmery keys, and approached the double glass doors, as Pedro gazed at the Siene and the Eiffel Tower bathed in lights. "I'm notably concerned about the woman who approached you at the *Louvre*," he said.

"Her," Pedro said.

"Yes. Her."

Pedro thought of her offer. And of the powder she claimed to have as Antoine pushed the doors open and started to ascend the stairs. As he spoke, his voice reverberated against the soaring stairwell. "There are those of us — immortals, of course — who have not adhered to the code as they have been expected to."

Pedro followed as they walked up several flights of steel stairs; their shoes clapped against the metal and it echoed against the walls. "I have studied about that."

Antoine accelerated his pace. He called from the floor above. "Your studies are quite different from our realities, dear Pedro!"

Pedro watched Antoine as the lock on the door appeared to be jammed.

Antoine seemed so...human...as he struggled with the key in the door. It was that part of the immortal existence that, despite his years of studying their culture and nuances, did not make sense to him. If they were so sophisticated, why did they not live a life of opulence?

Antoine pushed the door open as it creaked against the otherwise silent corridor. Pedro peered into darkness as Antoine touched his arm. Pedro stopped. "We do live lives of opulence and grandeur," Antoine said. "But in some situations, we choose to blend in. In all actuality, we immortals are not all that different from you humans. You will see, of course. And you probably already know."

Antoine flicked a light switch and a small lamp illuminated next to a plain green sofa. There was artwork hanging on the walls, but it was not nearly as glamorous as Pedro would have expected from the flat of an immortal. "I do know, but I also know of the talent that Darius had promised me, when he visited me in Madrid."

Antoine flung the keys on a nearby table. "Yes, that part I do feel some part of responsibility for. During that time, Darius was still in his rebellious phase. But he already had lost his gift at that point. He could not have kept the promise he made to you even if he wanted to."

"He wasn't even immortal when he came to me in Madrid?"

Antoine fished a bottle of wine from one of the kitchen cabinets and placed two bulbous glasses on the counter.

"Would you care for a Beaujolais?"

Pedro placed his hand on Antoine's forearm and Antoine stopped opening the wine. "Yes, Pedro?"

"He wasn't immortal, was he? Then how did he read my thoughts?"

Antoine pulled away and continued opening the bottle of wine.

"He still had some of his gifts, which he had used for centuries before he lost the gift of immortality. So, he would still have been able to use some of his gifts. But he would never have been able to transform you, Pedro."

Pedro slapped his palm against the counter. "He lied to me! Why would he convince me to leave my life in Madrid and join him if he couldn't transform me?!"

Antoine handed Pedro a glass of wine, and Pedro looked down at the dark liquid. "Just drink it and relax," Antoine said. "We will have a solution for you. But it doesn't include LaDonna Mastuer."

Pedro lowered his glass. "LaDonna who?"

"Mastuer," Antoine said, gesturing for him to sit on the sofa. Antoine set the bottle on a small coffee table, sat, placed his glass on the table, leaned back and crossed his legs. Pedro watched him, and slowly sat down next to him. He took a sip of his wine, as Antoine watched him.

"She is a descendant of the Voodoo Queen," Antoine said. "She was buried in *Pere Lachaise* in a crypt – in what we immortals call a 'coffin sentence' – for crimes against the immortal community. But she was released."

"Crimes? What kind of crimes?"

Antoine took a breath and exhaled, placing his hands on his knees, facing forward. Pedro watched him as he picked up his glass by the stem, took a sip, closed his eyes and savored it, and turned to face him. "LaDonna Mastuer has placed spells and used potions to extinguish immortals," he said. "It's all in the code. Crimes against immortals bring a coffin sentence."

"And now she is immortal herself," Pedro added.

"Yes," Antoine said. "She is. And others like her who have a clear irreverence for the code also have received the gift. Which makes them more of a threat to our kind, Pedro."

As Antoine continued to explain the conflicts between the coven at Haddon House and the immortals, Pedro had yet to fully understand the connection between the witches and the Voodoo priestess. Even Antoine didn't completely understand it.

Pedro assumed that may have been one of the reasons why LaDonna appeared to be such a threat. Besides the history that Antoine covered, she had been buried in Paris at *Pere Lachaise*, LaDonna had been erroneously released from her coffin sentence by the Crypt Dancer.

"He is the one who released her," Antoine said. He fished through the bookshelves before pausing and pulling out one particular book. "The Crypt Dancer. Rome has been calling for him, but he went into hiding. It's rumored that he's entombed. Possibly in Paris."

Antoine returned to the sofa, carrying a large, rectangular book. "But that is another story for another day."

The next day, Pedro waited in the atrium for the lecture that Antoine suggested they attend together. Pedro was pacing back and forth in front of the heavy wooden doors. Students scurried through the corridors, bags and books in tow, as the clocks would soon sound the top of the hour. Pedro felt a twinge of relief as he saw Antoine's silhouette against the early morning sunlight which spilled into the education hall through expansive glass windows.

"We almost weren't going to be allowed in!" Pedro said, shaking his head as Antoine shuffled around him and yanked the door open. Antoine turned and looked up at Pedro. "They would always allow me," he said. "I have donated a great deal to the artistic studies here."

Pedro followed as Antoine entered the lecture hall. He immediately began descending the wide, carpeted stairs which divided the sections of hard blueback chairs. The Professor raised his head from the stage below and nodded to Antoine, who slid into a row in the center. Pedro hastily sat next to him, and looked over at Antoine, who gave him a smug look.

The lights dimmed as an image of the Mona Lisa painting filled a screen in front of the auditorium.

"They said she is one of the world's greatest mysteries," the Professor said, after raising his head from the lectern. An image of the famous painting flooded the front screens on the wall as the Professor continued.

"This is most mysterious painting of all time," he said, as the assembly of students quickly hushed, and the lights dimmed.

Pedro and Antoine focused on the lecture. "They say the painting was inspired by a plain woman from Florence, Italy. A nun, the wife of a silk merchant who sold his textiles in the nearby marketplace by the convent."

Pedro watched as photos of Florence appeared on the far wall as the professor lectured below.

For a moment, he looked over at Antoine, who was staring straight ahead, seemingly enthralled.

"Lisa Giardini del Giocondo became a nun," the professor, said, continuing to scroll through the photos, as Antoine leaned close to him, whispering.

"There's a crumbling set of stone steps that lead down to her tomb," he said. "That is where we will go."

After driving back to the chateau from Darius' flat in Paris, Antoine purchased plane tickets to Miami from Frankfurt. Pedro knew, at that point, that Antoine often opted to keep a low profile, particularly when he was in Europe.

The ride from Paris to Lyon was uneventful, as Pedro had hoped, and there was no awkward silence as he had originally feared. One thing that Pedro had noticed about Antoine was his resilience; Pedro had learned about Antoine's character and leadership in the immortal sects, but he also was highly regarded by the highest-ranking members of the Inspiriti.

Antoine stood in the front parlor of the chateau gazing out the windows as Pedro watched him. Antoine released the curtain he was holding and turned to face Pedro. "Do you have any other bags besides the small satchel you brought from Paris?"

Pedro shook his head as Giovanni scurried through the living room, placing brilliant white dust cloths on the furniture.

"How long are we staying for?" Pedro asked.

"As long as it takes." Antoine returned to gazing out the window as Giovanni continued to close the chateau. "Be ready to leave within the hour. I have a plane booked for us in Frankfurt. You will accompany me to Miami, and I will see that you are inspired. You may not have received the gift yet, but from what I have seen, you are gifted."

Pedro watched as Antoine and Giovanni finished closing up the chateau. The drive to Frankfurt would be a long one, and the flight to Miami would be even longer. But he agreed to follow Antoine, who appeared to be taking him under his wing. Pedro didn't know if he was doing it out of a sense of obligation as Darius was his maker, but Pedro appreciated it nonetheless.

Pedro had spent his entire life in Madrid, and then Paris. He had never traveled to America, and he felt a twinge of excitement as he felt the twinge in his stomach. There was something about venturing outwards, crossing the ocean, leaving the homeland.

And then he thought of LaDonna, and the offer she presented when she learned of his desire to see Valentina again, to experience her influence on his craft, which, at that point, was clearly waning.

ARRIVAL OF THE PATIENT

Mona Lisa, Becoming a Ghost
A.L. MENGEL

PEDRO STARED OUT THE WINDOW at the brilliant Miami sunshine as he sat in Claire's office.

"I've thought about Valentina," Pedro said, as she adjusted herself in the chair, scribbling notes on her yellow legal pad. Pedro hung his arms over the chair as he gazed out the window. It was a brilliant, sunny afternoon, and the sky was filled with white, clouds that looked like cotton.

He shook his head.

"What have you thought?" she asked.

After a few moments, he turned, and faced her. "I don't know where she is, where she went. She died, of course, but I don't know how. All I know is that she's gone. My muse. I look back and all I see is support and encouragement." He sighed and looked directly at Claire. She raised her head and met his eye contact.

"Why didn't I see this then?" he asked.

She cleared her throat as discreetly as she could and placed her pen and pad down on the table.

"Many times, we can't," she said, and leaned forward. "We become self-involved, and many times, it's an effort for self-improvement. But none of us can achieve greatness alone, Pedro. At least, until we take a step outside of our lives and take an introspective look at who we are as individuals."

Pedro took another breath and sighed.

He looked out the window again, as Claire leaned back in her chair, and picked up her pad and pen from the table.

"We often cannot determine who is supporting us the most until that support is gone."

He closed his eyes and saw her once again.

She was always there, he remembered that. Now. Why didn't he notice it back then? And now she was gone. Her support was gone.

For an infatuation.

"I think about her, quite a bit now," he said. "And where she might be. And what happens." He looked back over at her. "Where she's at."

Claire took a deep breath, nodded, and placed her pad and pen back on the table. She got up, walked over to Pedro's chair, and leaned down as she placed her hands on the chair back. "Where do you think she is, Pedro?"

Pedro scoffed and shook his head, looking forward. "I only know what I was raised to believe," he said. "Living in Spain. You are good you go to Heaven; you are bad you go to Hell. That was pretty much the belief system. But with her, she was good." He felt a confidence rise in his voice. "I know she was. She had a good spirit."

"Then you know where she is, based on your belief, right?"

Pedro sighed again, hunched down in his chair, and folded his arms. They sat in silence for a few minutes, until Claire returned to her chair, reached forward for her notebook and pen, and sat back, reaching up with her hand and placing her hair behind her shoulder. "So, what do you think happens, Pedro? What do you think happens after we die?"

He released his breath and shook his head. "I honestly don't know," he said. "As a good Catholic, I've been raised to believe that our soul is immortal. And our bodies die, decompose, and then our soul is reborn into a new immortal, physical body."

She nodded as she scribbled notes on her legal pad. After a moment, she raised her head and adjusted her glasses. "Do you think that Valentina is still with you, somehow, in some way?"

Pedro looked at Claire, who leaned forward, holding her pen in the ready position above her notepad. She appeared interested in his story, and eager for the answer, yet Pedro wondered if it was because she was truly interested, or if she was simply doing her job.

"I think about her," he said after a few moments of silence.

Pedro felt like he was disconnecting from the conversation, as Claire continued to ask questions, and he remembered answering them, but he did not remember what he said.

When the session was over, he paid and shook Claire's hand professionally, and as he closed the door, he did not know that it was the last time he would see her alive.

The detectives noticed movement inside the body bag when the coroner placed the bag in the living room at Claire's condo, in the Brickell section of Miami. What had gone against protocol was the release of her body to the two leading morticians in the city, Ned McCracken and Jacob Benjamin, of Waxley Mortuary and Funeral Home, which governs Resurrection Cemetery on the other side of town.

Despite how Claire was found, in her bathroom, splayed on the commode, eyes gouged out and a pistol in her hand, it was presumed, initially, that she might have committed suicide, but the two morticians who were called to the scene knew otherwise.

After she was taken to the Waxley Mortuary, Antoine learned of her death from Jacob's phone call, and drove to the funeral home. He waited as the expansive, wrought iron gates slowly parted inwards, waving to the security guard in the small booth on the side. As he pulled the car forward, he saw Waxley slowly appear into view between the thickness of the forest which surrounded it; the Queen Anne architecture was uncommon in the Miami area, better known for Spanish, Mediterranean and Caribbean styles.

But Antoine knew that Waxley was a snapshot in time; its original proprietor, Everett T. Waxley, had succumbed to a stroke in the 1930's.

Now Jacob Benjamin managed the operation, and, with the times that Antoine had visited the funeral home and mortuary, he had noted that Jacob had preserved the early twentieth century feel from the building, and Waxley had catered to the Miami elite, as it had throughout its existence.

Jacob appeared in the archway; undeniably youthful, vibrant, and eternally young. Yet exquisitely intelligent for his years at Waxley, which seemed to be everlasting.

"Nothing is eternal," Jacob told Antoine as they released their embrace.

"Indeed."

In the days when Claire, the beloved psychiatrist, was found dead in her condo bathroom, Darius was still alive. Barely, it seemed. He was one of her patients, and they found a connection together. Somehow, in some way.

But Claire wasn't really gone when they zipped up the body bag and hoisted her body into the living room. She could feel the chill of the plastic, hear the rustling, and the heaviness as they lifted and carried her away from everything she knew.

Claire remembered.

The night that James died had been like any other ordinary evening.

Claire had stood in the parlor, overlooking the dry, dusty streets of Coconut Grove, just as the sun had dipped in the skies towards the west; the coming darkness from the Atlantic had penetrated all but a small sliver of the fading light towards the horizon.

She had placed one of her favorite records on her cherished antique phonograph, and as the piano filled the room, she turned away from the window, and looked over at the closed door. James was lying downstairs. There was absolutely nothing she could do about it. She couldn't turn back the hands of time, nor did she care to.

The police would be arriving shortly, along with the coroner, and they would come in, head down to the basement, and remove his body. They would ask her questions, try to comfort her. But mainly ask her questions. How did this happen?

But she had been through this procedure before.

And there was little she could do or say to change anything, and she knew that she had nothing to do with his death.

"I had nothing to do with it," she said to herself, as she slowly padded her way to the sofa. She sat and hung her head down, as her crimson red hair hung downwards, concealing her face. "Another one lost," she said.

Not long after the police came to investigate James' death, and after the funeral, and the burial, and the days that Claire chose to mope around the house, looking out at the swaying palm trees amidst the grandiose old oaks with Spanish moss which caught the wind in the cooling afternoon breezes, Claire chose to return to work.

She never understood why she spent each day, every day, listening to others' problems, and prescribing medication for them.

Which she sometimes took herself.

Losing James was a shock, but it didn't really upset her.

Too many times, it had happened. As she pulled her sleek black luxury sedan into the Miami parking garage, she flung the gearshift into park and cut the engine.

She examined her appearance in the rearview mirror and sighed. There were still bags under her eyes. But she had to shake it off. She had to get back to work. James was one of many. She shook her head and flung the door open, grabbing her bag.

Her heels clicked on the cement as she walked out into the brilliant Miami sunshine. Her first day back, and this was professional Claire, at least as best as it could be, considering she was again a widow. She crossed the side street towards a soaring glass skyscraper and wondered if this was premature.

She passed the giant gold letters BRICKELL ONE on the side of the marble exterior and headed through the soaring glass doors. A blast of cool air hit her as she removed her sunglasses and let her eyes adjust to the lobby.

She rummaged through her purse for her elevator pass, and nodded to the security guard who sat at a desk in the shape of a U. There was nothing to be afraid of, she thought, as she pressed the elevator call button. I've had clients before who were part of the immortal community.

But this client, who she was called in to speak with today, was different.

"His name is Darius Sauvage," her receptionist said when she arrived in her office, as she handed her a heavy manila folder. "One of the leaders of *Sacrafice*."

Claire nodded. "Yes, I've heard of him. *Sacrafice* is the night club on Miami Beach, right? Why does he need my services?"

"Word on the street is that he lost his dark gift," she said. "And is now mortal again. Aging rapidly. He's waiting for you in your office."

Claire nodded. "Thank you, Miranda."

Miranda placed her arm gently on Claire's arm. "There's one more thing," she said. "Darius...does not look like what you think. When I said that he aged rapidly, *he really has*. You best prepare yourself."

Claire nodded and headed towards the massive wooden double doors. As she placed her hand on the cool brass knob, she paused for a moment, trying to remember Darius. When had she seen him?

And where?

Antoine, he had something to do with Antoine.

She opened the door and saw his silhouette sitting in one of her side chairs across the office. The light from the windows shined inwards and blocked her vision, but she could tell that he was sitting still, with no acknowledgement of her presence, nor any inclination that he was going to move or greet her.

She quietly walked over to her desk and placed her bags down on the floor next to her chair. She picked up the file and carried it over to the sitting area, keeping her eyes trained on Darius the entire time.

As she approached him, the light revealed his physical state. His hair was long, unkempt, hanging down in front of his shoulders and concealed his face. It looks like he hadn't bathed in a while. There was a glass bottle of beer sitting on the coffee table.

"Hello…Darius? Is that you? Are you Darius?"

She sat down in the opposite chair and watched him, but Darius kept his head hanging low.

She crossed her legs and placed the file down on the coffee table, spread open. She cleared her throat.

"It says here that you're coming to see me because you have a condition. A physical one."

She looked up at him. She strained to hear him, but she thought she heard him mutter something under his breath. "What was that? What did you say?"

She watched as he slowly raised his head. She caught her breath in her throat and made an attempt not to gasp. Darius was horrendous

At least from what she remembered.

No longer was he young and attractive; his face was scored with deep sagging skin and heavy wrinkles, his long hair which had appeared darker from her perspective earlier now had caught the light and framed his sullen face in deep grey.

"You gasped," he said softly. "Does old age scare you Doctor?"

She let out a nervous laugh. "No, no no! Please Mr. Sauvage…please…accept my apologies for giving you the wrong impression! I just –"

"You just?"

"– just want to make sure you are comfortable, Mr. Sauvage. I see you have a beer there. Did Miranda bring that for you?"

He nodded.

"Good," she said as she stood. "My main goal – at this point – is to make sure you are comfortable here. I know you have come here because you need to talk with me. But you don't know me, although I do know about you."

He nodded. "Yes, I am sure."

"And so, at this point, we have to build some trust, don't we?"

He raised his head and looked at her as she sat back down. She looked at his tired, sunken eyes. What had happened to him? Was Antoine still alright? They were prominent immortals in Miami, quite well-known philanthropists. But here, Darius, what had happened?

"You are still scared of me," he said. "I can tell. I can see it in your eyes."

She took a breath and held it for a few moments, looking down at the coffee table as if the answer were lying right there.

She released it.

"Darius, I'm going to level with you."

He leaned forward.

"I know all about you and Antoine. Both of you. And you both have done a lot of *good* for the city. You both seem to be great role models. But I honestly haven't seen you for a while and haven't seen Antoine either. I will be completely honest with you, Darius. I hadn't known you'd grown so old."

"I'm not really that old. Or older than you think. Take your pick."

Claire grabbed her notebook and pen, crossed her legs, and waited. After a few moments of silence, Darius started again.

"I've...lost...my gift."

"Go on, Darius."

"The immortality I once had."

He shifted in his chair, picked up the beer, and took a long swig. "Can I get any more of these? They'll help me open up to you. Honest, they will."

After his session had ended and Darius had left, she flopped against the door.

In her hand, she held a large, manila envelope marked CEMETERY, and in her other hand, she held the tiny glimmering key.

Darius had crossed a line. She knew he was troubled, and she knew she was there to help him, but she simply felt violated.

No longer was he going to be downing bottled beers in their sessions, if they would even have any future sessions at all. He clearly transformed; she didn't know if it was the effects of the alcohol or the dark torment that resided within his heart, but she had to speak to Miranda.

She sighed and looked down at her clenched fist. She could feel the metallic heat of the tiny key dig into her palm.

It wasn't that big.

And it certainly couldn't be found. Not by anyone.

She padded over to her desk and flopped the envelope on the top of a pile of papers, and turned around, opening the cabinet behind her large, black swivel chair.

A bottle of Ardbeg.

Her favorite scotch.

She kept her right hand clenched, grasping the key, as she grabbed the slender, green bottle and placed it up on her desk, as the voice in her head sounded: *a little too early to be drinking yet, don't you think? It's not even ten in the morning!*

It sounded like James.

All of his nagging.

She let out an exasperated sigh as she rummaged through the cabinets for a glass. "No ice required," she muttered under her breath. "Ah ha!" She drew the glass out from between a sea of green file folders and hoisted herself upwards, sitting in her massive chair.

As she settled into the soft seat, she drew her clenched wrist up and released it.

A small, silver key clinked against the side of the glass.

There it was.

Her heart pounded as she saw the key. Before today, she hadn't held it in her hand for years. But today was different, today her husband lay in a freezer in the morgue, and later this afternoon she would be heading to the Waxley Funeral Home to be making plans and preparations.

But this key had to remain a secret.

She poured herself a generous amount of scotch and looked at the amber liquid in the gleaming crystal glass.

It had to reach the halfway point; and she knew that this was a slippery slope.

But she didn't care.

The brown liquid tantalized her.

She missed the warm fuzziness, the earthy taste, and the burn down her throat.

She grabbed the glass and downed it, covering her mouth with the back of her wrist as the fuzziness warmed her body almost instantly.

Where have you been, you old friend?

Why have you been gone so long? Why didn't you write?

She slammed the glass down on the desk with a clank and poured herself another.

It was just as generous as the first, and then the shimmer of the silver key caught her mind.

"Oh, save me," she muttered under her breath. That damn key. Always coming back to haunt her. And that damn mausoleum. Can't they just demolish the horrid thing?

She grabbed the glass with her left, and picked up the key with her right, and looked down at them both, looking back and forth, and settled on the scotch. *You're heading down a slippery slope, girly girl. You remember what happened when you downed the entire bottle last time?*

She closed her eyes.

There was a chill to the air, she remembered. It was a rare cold front in the Miami area; and for her, being a native, she had worn a jacket for the first time in months. She reached up above her breasts and felt the chain, gliding her fingertips downwards until she felt the cool metal key. Ascension Avenue was desolate, and Waxley was shut down for the evening. She knew that visiting hours were over, but she wasn't there to visit.

She had to get into the mausoleum.

She looked towards the right, under the blue tint of the clear moonlit sky, and noticed the pale reflection on the treetops. The dark foliage swayed in a passing breeze as she approached the dark spires of the wrought iron fence, and wrapped her hands around them, looking into the cemetery.

The mounds of dirt looked like a small mountain range underneath the pale blue moonlight. But there would be no entry tonight; the bodies would be locked up. For only she held the key.

"The bodies are gone," she said, looking outwards and scanning the cemetery. And then looked over at Waxley. "Yet they continue to operate."

She held the key out from her chest, and watched as the silver glimmered in the moonlight, and was carried back to her desk, sitting there, examining the key, holding her glass of scotch.

She set them both down for a moment. "Waxley will get no more bodies," she said. "And I am done providing them."

She picked up the glass of scotch with her left hand, and the key with her right, and slowly placed the small key on her tongue. She drew the scotch up to her lips and downed it all.

There was a distance to the light when its auburn fingers soared across the sky; as if the angel's wings were aflame, in an unreachable cosmos. As if the dimension were somehow married, both in time and principle; that life must always be respected and preserved.

The clouds raced across the skies as the sunset faded and drew the darkness. Claire stumbled through her office as the sun sank beneath the horizon in a fiery display of pink and orange. Her head throbbed and her throat was scratchy. The fuzziness remained with her as she glanced over at the desk. The bottle was nearly empty.

What did I tell you girly girl?

275

She drew her palm up against her face and shook her head. *Bottle takes me, every time.* She staggered sideways as she caught her balance.

The coffee table.

Now that would have been a smart.

But she regained her composure.

"Get me the hell out of here," she mumbled, as she stumbled towards her desk, grabbing her bag. She flung herself towards the door and tossed it open and looked at Miranda's desk.

Empty.

Of course, it was late.

She was passed out on the floor in her office in a scotch induced stupor.

And then she blacked out.

She didn't remember leaving the office, walking down to her condo on Brickell, just mere blocks from her office. A casual observer would have noted her walking down the side of BRICKELL ONE and suspected she had just left happy hour. Her steps had been methodical, but her route had transitioned from left…to right…and back again.

The traffic, fortunately, was light, but she was in blackout. She fumbled in the pocket for her keys, drew her card through the slot, as the doors slid open to a foyer with marble and tall potted plants.

A security guard sat silently behind a desk and didn't even look up as she staggered by.

But she didn't remember anything.

Until she reached her condo door. She gasped as she felt a hand on her shoulder. "Oh!" she said. "I forgot you were following me."

"Don't worry. You're a bit intoxicated right now."

The voice was male.

Deep and calm. Something she might have heard on the radio. But she couldn't place it. As she opened the door and flung herself inwards, a blast of cool air spilled into the corridor. "Damn it!" Claire said. "They should have set that to eighty degrees!"

"I don't understand," the deep voice said.

Claire flopped her bag on the counter as she adjusted the thermostat. "It's a crash pad," she said. "For late nights at the office. Stays empty most of the time. Apparently, the cleaning service put the temperature down below seventy!" She shivered but stopped as she felt a pair of strong hands grasp her upper arms.

"I will keep you warm."

Her throat tightened and she drew a breath inward.

"Wait a minute," she said softly. "Forgive me. I've had a lot to drink. But how did we meet?"

"Go sit down," he said. "And I will tell you."

Claire could feel her heart pound in her chest as the gradual wear off of the liquor had been slow coming. While some of the fuzziness remained, she sat slowly on her sofa and watched the shadow of the man on the opposite side of her condo living room. She squinted her eyes against the darkness as the shadow took one of the side chairs across from the expansive coffee table.

The light emanating from the foyer did nothing to reveal him, and her heightened sense of alarm overtook her dulled senses from the alcohol.

Where did she meet up with him? How had she invited him into her condo?

"I…" she said softly. "I'm sorry. I honestly don't –"

"Remember."

She scoffed and nodded, closing her eyes and dropping her face into her hands. "Yes…I don't remember."

"I didn't think you would."

In an instant, her mind flashed with an image of him reaching up and grabbing her, plunging his fangs into her throat, drinking from her till near death.

But she took a breath and exhaled.

"I've been watching you," he said.

She gasped. "Watching me?"

"Yes. Your new client. Darius. He is under investigation with our kind. And I know you don't remember. But I approached you after you left your office building."

She felt a twinge of relief wash over her. "So…you are an immortal?"

"Yes."

She shook her head. "Why did I invite you up to my condo?"

Claire leaned forward and studied the shadow.

She saw him move, adjust his posture, but she couldn't tell which immortal it was. He certainly couldn't be Antoine. Darius said he was buried in a coffin sentence. And those coffin sentences that Darius spoke of. What were those? So foreign to her, it seemed.

The immortals were a different kind, a peculiar species. Something she had always known about during her time in the world; they were always there.

But now, an immortal sat across from her in the shadows.

A mysterious one.

Who had not identified himself, yet one who she had clearly met, and invited into her condo, with no recollection of what he looked like or who he could be.

You wonder, but what if you knew?

Her thoughts stopped.

It was the voice. His voice. Her mind was open, inviting, a blank canvas on which he could paint. She knew her power was weak, and she didn't mind. There wasn't anything more mysterious than an immortal in the shadows; the humans, she knew very well, had always been fascinated with them.

For she, like countless others, had always wondered what it might be like to live forever.

Do you want to live forever?

"It's a curse, you know."

She gasped. "What is?"

"Living forever. It's a curse. Something we immortals all must endure."

So, he had been reading her thoughts. That wasn't much of a surprise, yet it still caught her off guard.

But she had always thought that they had a gift. It was a gift, immortality, wasn't it?

"They call it a gift," he said. She saw his dark shadow shift in the chair, and he leaned forward, yet his face remained shrouded in darkness. "But we really are tormented," he said.

"When we receive this gift, we become dead to the mortal world. No one recognizes us, or even seems to care. Life starts to pass us by. The living either are enamored with us, become infatuated or obsessed with us...or fear us. There is little solace other than our own kind."

She paused, looking at the visitor.

Her mind still drew a blank, even though she knew that there had been a gap in time after when she left her office, until when she arrived at her condo, that appeared to be unaccounted for. She strained her eyes to see the visitor, but as he sat across the living room, he remained a silhouette, despite the light from the stove which filtered outwards into the darkness. "What...what did we do last night?"

She watched as the visitor leaned forward, yet his face remained in darkness. "You brought the key with you," he said. "To the crypt door. At Resurrection."

She covered her mouth with her hand. Yes. She was starting to remember. The fog in her mind just needed a little help lifting. But she remembered the key. And the Ardbeg. She couldn't remember what had possessed her to drink so much, especially at the office, and then an image of Darius, her long-time patient, flashed through her mind. She remembered him sitting in the chair, downing bottles of beer, tossing them in the trash as the bottles clanked.

"You've been so allegiant to our kind," he said. "Certainly, there is a reward for you if you so desire."

"How can it be a reward if you told me, it was a curse? Why would I want to be tormented if you say that you are?"

She studied his silhouette, but he said nothing.

She felt her heart beating in her chest as she was waiting for something to happen. There was too much missing; a blackout, it seemed.

But he was an immortal. Yes, he was. His voice didn't sound familiar. She didn't feel that he would harm her, for she knew some of the characteristics of the immortals, particularly those who lived in Miami.

"I have a proposition for you."

She listened to him, as her thoughts ceased. She saw his silhouette grow larger as he slowly approached; his fingers were cold against her cheek. Her eyes closed, and then.

Darkness.

"I am meant to be heard by you, and only you."

The visitor approached the couch and sat next to her, placing his arms around her shoulders. "You will feel nothing," he said. "And then you will awaken, and your life will be eternal…"

After Claire had a breath of an eternal embrace, Pedro rang the chime at the Waxley Mortuary. As he waited for the door to be answered, he glanced up at the building. It was a wooden structure, with decorative trim, and a large, open front porch. A rounded tower rose from the side, and Pedro though he saw someone looking down through the sheer curtains above.

The architecture was certainly out of place in Miami. He remembered Antoine telling him about Waxley, that the building had been in existence for over a century, and the proprietors were in contract with the immortal community. As Pedro looked outwards, through the trees towards Resurrection Cemetery, while he noticed the rising and weathered stone monuments, he didn't have time to notice the mounds of dirt next to the graves. He thought a contract between a mortuary and the immortals was bizarre, but then the door opened.

He turned around.

A middle-aged Hispanic woman smiled warmly. "Are you Pedro?"

He nodded.

"Then do come in, please," she said. "You've been expected."

She turned and gestured for him to follow her.

As he stepped up and crossed the threshold, he made every effort to contain his wonderment, yet his mouth dropped open when saw the massive stained-glass gates towards the right of the soaring foyer. A large chandelier hung above them, and he noticed a massive mirror hanging on the opposite wall. But he returned to the colorful gates. Something he had never imagined in a funeral home before.

"Those gates lead to our viewing rooms," she said. "But please, come with me. Over to the office. Mr. Benjamin is waiting for you."

Pedro followed her to the double wooden doors.

He watched as she drew her ear close, holding the shiny brass knob.

While Pedro heard nothing, after a moment, she slowly opened the door inwards. Pedro craned his neck to see.

As she gestured for him to enter, he saw Jacob in a black pinstripe suit behind his desk, although the jacket hung on the back of the tall, brown leather chair, revealing a starched white shirt and a bright yellow pair of suspenders.

"Welcome!" he said, standing up, extending his hand outwards. "You must be Jacob?"

He nodded. "Yes. And I know why you're here."

286

Pedro froze.

There were few in Miami who knew of Pedro's desire to resurrect his muse, his long-lost Valentina. But the staff at the Waxley Mortuary and Funeral Home was briefed by their head mortician, Jacob Benjamin. He placed a hand on Pedro's shoulder and leaned close to him. "We have a new arrival," he said. "A new transformation. She will become your Valentina."

Pedro followed as they headed towards the long corridor that spanned the rear of the building.

As they approached the last door in the corridor, Jacob pulled a set of silver keys from his pocket. Jacob noticed how they caught the light from the nearby wall sconce candelabra.

"She's just inside," Jacob said. The door creaked as he slowly pushed it open. Pedro peered through as the white sheet came into view.

He took a few cautious steps into the receiving room, as her body was next to a casket.

"We have to have a funeral for her, of course," Jacob said. "And the casket will be buried. But there will be no body inside. She is here for you, Jacob. Locked in an eternal embrace. Immortal, and will never die."

Pedro placed his hand on the sheet gently.

Claire's body was covered, but he remembered his therapy sessions with her. It was an assumption that she was transformed, she received the gift.

"It's all skin, bones and body, Pedro. The ritual states that several elements must be present, and, as Valentina has been dead for too long, I imagine all we will be able to harvest from her grave is her heart. If she truly is your muse, and your inspiration, her heart will be there. The bones must come from an influential figure. And the body of an immortal will allow you to be assured that she will never, ever die on you again."

Antoine dropped Pedro off at his apartment building after his meeting at Waxley. Pedro trudged to the door and fished for his keys in his pants pocket.

"Hey, Pedro," Antoine said from behind him.

Pedro turned, his hand holding his key in the door, and saw Antoine had emerged from his car. He held his hands on the crest of the door. "Don't do it, Pedro. LaDonna Mastuer does not offer this solution for you from the kindness of her heart. Her heart is made of ice, if not stone."

Pedro looked at Antoine's face, it had softened. He was pleading. He entered the darkness of his tiny abode, and left Antoine standing in the parking space, behind his door, watching him. Pedro could feel the pierce of his stare as he slowly closed the door. He closed his eyes and leaned his head against the wall, and listened, until he heard Antoine's car pull away into the distance.

In the days after Antoine had first taken Pedro to America, before he had been provided a modest apartment in the city's design district, and when they had first arrived from Europe and opened Antoine's estate in Coral Gables, there was a certain desolation to the mansion. As they entered the expansive foyer, the smell of soot still lingered in the air. Pedro noted the plywood which covered the winding staircase, blocking access to the second floor.

Antoine tossed his keys on a large, round mahogany table in the center of the marble floor, as Giovanni scurried through the rooms, turning on light switches, adjusting the thermostat, and then carefully lifting dust cloths, while Antoine went into the front parlor and retrieved a bottle of wine.

Pedro watched as Antoine appeared to be fully engrossed in opening the bottle. "We have several guest rooms on this level," Antoine said without looking up.

Pedro approached the small bar in the corner of the room. "What happened, Antoine?"

Antoine raised his head. He looked defeated. "I knew that I was returning to this mess," he said, slowly and quietly. "But now, seeing it in person, I have a better understanding that we have a bigger problem in this sector than I had originally thought. The entire second floor is under renovation, as there was a devastating fire recently."

Pedro sat in one of the leather stools as Antoine leaned down and fished two large glasses from beneath the bar. "We don't know who caused the fires, but we have a suspect."

"Who?" Pedro asked, while picking up his glass of Beaujolais by the stem.

"There's a coven of witches in this area," Antoine said. "And that's what has me concerned about your interactions with LaDonna Mastuer back in Paris."

Pedro let out a nervous laugh as he took a slow sip of wine. "That was nothing, I honestly think. She came to me...so unexpectedly. But I don't think she is of any importance."

Antoine scoffed and meandered over towards one of the sofas across from the fireplace.

Giovanni was preparing a fire, and Pedro swiveled his chair to see Antoine from across the ornate parlor. "That is what I am afraid of," Antoine said, as he leaned back into the sofa, draping his arm over the back, examining his glass, lifting it towards his nose, closing his eyes. After a moment, Antoine lowered the glass and looked directly over at Pedro. "If you are as infatuated with our kind as you claim to be, then you need to hold a basic awareness of where our threats originate," Antoine said.

Pedro slowly rose from the barstool and joined Antoine, sitting on the opposite sofa.

He set his wine glass on the table between the sofas gently, as the new fire roared the in the fireplace. Giovanni had indicated that he was going to venture out to the market.

Antoine leaned back, crossed his arms, and stared directly at Pedro. "You've studied so much about us," he said. "Do you know who she is, or why I am concerned?"

Pedro leaned forward, placing his elbows on his knees, hung his head down. "No, Antoine. I do not."

"I had a feeling you didn't. But I don't fault you for that. Ms. Mastuer can be very persuasive. And she has abilities which some immortals cannot even fathom. And you, still as a mortal, would have no perception of what she would be doing while in close proximity to you."

Pedro looked up. Antoine was taking another sip of his wine, closing his eyes and apparently relishing the taste. "What is it, Antoine?"

"She is from Port-au-Prince," Antoine said. "A direct descendant of Madame Laveau, who is serving coffin sentence in New Orleans."

"You mean…the Voodoo Queen is an immortal?"

Antoine let out a chuckle and rose to stoke the fire. It roared once again, filling the room with its warmth and light "Oh yes," Antoine said. "Many of them are. The witches as well. But you have to understand. Like the coven of witches here in Miami, LaDonna Mastuer is a direct threat to the immortal kind. She was serving a coffin sentence in *Pere Lachaise* in Paris when she was inadvertently released. And that is how she found you."

"Why would she take an interest in me?"

"Because you were staring at the one masterpiece that has engrossed your thoughts for as long as I can remember," Antoine said. "You were standing in the *Louvre*, dreaming of becoming an artist as great as da Vinci, and those type of thoughts find their way to her."

"Why would she care?"

"Because you also have been quite open about two things. You have expressed an interest in receiving the gift of immortality, and you also have a deep desire to find your muse again. Valentina. We all are keenly aware of it, Pedro. Your desire provides her with the means to approach you and use you to take control over the immortals."

Pedro leaned back, took a breath, and sighed. Antoine appeared to know everything; his thoughts were not protected when it came to immortals, and it seemed as though LaDonna was no different. How long she may have been standing behind him in the museum in Paris he may never be able to determine, but did she get to him? Possibly.

She had offered him a solution to his troubles; a guaranteed way to resurrect his beloved Valentina, his beloved muse and inspiration. But Antoine appeared to be leading him away from her.

"I know how dearly you want to be transformed with the gift of immortality," Antoine said. "And I know Darius did not keep his promise. He could not keep it. He shouldn't even have made it. But he did, and it is what it is. And I will make it right for you. I will give you the gift that Darius could never do. But I will not make you a promise. For the fate of this lies within you, Pedro. I will only transform you if you remain away from LaDonna Mastuer."

Pedro clasped his hands in his lap, pursed his lips, and stared downward, but saw nothing. His thoughts were no longer in the parlor, yet he could still hear the crackle of the fire, and Antoine's footsteps as he headed out into the foyer to take an incoming call. Antoine had given him an enormous amount to think about; and the decision would not be a light one.

As Antoine retired to his suite, Pedro remained in the parlor, watching the fire as it slowly died down. He had been sitting on the sofa for hours, pondering whether he should ignore Antoine's directive. He knew, from the point of when he was still a student, that he longed to be part of the immortal community. And still, Valentina remained in his mind; it was as if she penetrated his thoughts, long after Darius had taken him away from her. He sighed as he poured himself the remainder of the wine from the bottle he and Antoine had been sharing. He held the glass in his lap, leaned back on the couch, and sighed.

He didn't know why he continued to blame Darius.

"We have to live with the consequences of our choices," his mother would tell him when he was still a boy. Yet that night in Madrid, when he crept out the bed, to the call of immortality, to the quest for a talent which he never believed he had, he left the one person who had consistently believed in him and his work.

Was he a painter?

He was, at least then. The days when Valentina would sit on a small stool and look up, watching him hover over his canvas, gliding the brush across the palette with determination were seemingly long-lost. She was there. She always was. Watching him, encouraging him. And telling him when something needed to change.

Now he had the opportunity to resurrect her.

It was simply unheard of in the human world. LaDonna promised a powder, something powerful and magical, it seemed.

He snapped out of his musing as a pop emanated from the fireplace.

There were only burning embers; bright orange in a sea of dark ashes. He contemplated going to bed. The guest room was just down the corridor off the foyer, which Giovanni had shown him shortly after he arrived.

He thought of the small card which Vivienne had given him previously at the bar at club *Sacrafice,* but it was back in his apartment, sitting on his writing desk. Not that he needed it.

Go to see her…

He froze as a voice hissed in his head, seemingly unseen, mysterious and unable to be placed. It sounded neither masculine nor feminine yet had an otherworldly feel to its tone.

You will need her help…

Pedro ran to the window and yanked the curtains apart. The sky flashed with lightning and an approaching storm, illuminating the gardens, trees and Antoine's statues. *Go to New Orleans…and she will walk again…*

Thunder crashed overhead as the lights went dark.

Pedro ran towards the kitchen, clumsily bumping into furniture.

He saw Giovanni's frame in the shadows in the kitchen, as he rummaged through a drawer.

Giovanni gasped as Pedro tore into the kitchen.

"How do I get to New Orelans?!" Pedro whispered as Giovanni placed several candles in pewter holders and struck a match.

"If you must go, take one of the cars," Giovanni said, looking up at him. "Antoine will get you a driver."

Pedro held his hands out and shook his head. "No, no! I don't want Antoine to know I am going there. *He must not know!*"

Giovanni scoffed as he shook his head and blew out one of the matches.

The candle bathed their faces in a warm glow.

He handed Pedro one of the candles.

"Be careful with that, Pedro. We don't need another fire. Master Antoine is still overseeing the renovations."

Pedro nodded hastily. "How do I get a car?"

"There are several spare sedans in the garage," Giovanni said. "But you won't be able to keep this trip from Antoine. You know that don't you?"

Pedro placed the candle on the counter, sighed and closed his eyes. "I cannot…"

"Do not cross him, Pedro. I know that you desire the gift. But if you cross him, you will never receive it. Even if he doesn't give it to you, he has the power to ensure that no immortal will *ever* give it to you."

Pedro's face fell. "And then I won't receive the talent which Darius had promised me."

"If you betray Antoine, then you won't receive the talent, or any gift for that matter. You will be banished from the immortal community forever. Or worse, Pedro. It could be far worse."

Pedro retired to the guest room with his thoughts racing.

As he lay in bed, his arms behind his head, the candle dripping streams of wax down the base of the holder and onto the bedside table, he thought of Valentina. He cursed himself for leaving her, for following an infatuation of the immortals which seemed to be full of empty promises and strict governing. He knew that he could not betray Antoine; his help was needed far too much in the quest to regain his muse and discover the talent she had always insisted he had within. The creative fire which she told him always burned inside him.

As the sun crept over the horizon, and as the warm rays flooded his room, he saw that the storm had passed. After several hours of fitful sleep, he felt exhausted, but hopeful. Antoine was reasonable. Everything he had done for Pedro since he arrived in Miami had been for his benefit, the apartment, the bartending job. While Antoine could become evasive at times, he knew that he needed Antoine's blessing to go to New Orleans, despite the warning he gave him.

Pedro headed to the bathroom and splashed some water on his face and started rehearsing what he going to say to Antoine, how to seek his permission.

He stopped when there was a knock on the door. It slowly opened and Antoine took a few steps in the room. "I know you want to go for the powder,"

Antoine said. He sat on the bed, as Pedro stood in the bathroom doorway, speechless.

"And I am not going to try to stop you," he said. "In fact, I am going to help you. The powder is powerful, Pedro. And it works. It can take the living and given them an experience of alternate dimension, and it can resurrect the dead. But I know how allegiant you have been to our kind, and over many years. I am going to give you the power. It is your decision. I strongly recommend *against* using the powder. We know too little about it, and its power, and what it can do. And we know too little of the witches and the Voodoo priestesses. I've talked to Jacob, and he is going to accompany you to New Orleans. I am giving you the freedom to investigate it for yourself, but always remember, resurrection requires retribution."

Antoine got up and approached him, standing close to him.

"I am going to leave you to your own devices, Pedro. If you use the powder, you will not know what type of gates you may be opening. You have my permission to research it but be sure to heed my warning."

"You must return to Spain," La Donna said. "To the grave where she rests. You will go under the shroud of darkness and there you will find them. The shadows will sense you. And the powder. But this will bring her back."

Pedro thought of Darius as she reached up towards the dusty wooden shelves and pulled the small ceramic jar from the contents. His proposition was weighing heavily on Pedro's mind. If Darius returned from the grave, he could write his books, but would that bring Pedro the talent he sought? He had his doubts.

Pedro watched as she held the jar in her hand gingerly, caressing the cork with her open palm, her head lowered, as if she were deep in thought or in prayer. She slowly approached the table where he sat.

"Draw the curtains," she said.

Pedro hastily reached up and tugged at the light fabric, yanking the drapes together on the small, tinny brass rod. It did little to filter the light, although the throngs of tourists crowing Bourbon Street would no longer be able to stop and peer inside the curious front windows of the House of Voodoo.

She placed the jar on the table, took a breath, and raised her eyes towards Pedro.

He waited patiently as they sat in silence, knowing that this conversation could never be rushed. "There will be no return," she said. He looked down and she wrapped her palms around the small ceramic jar. He watched her fingers tremble as she spoke. "Once you use this powder you will have the power of the gift," she said, slowly. "You will have the power of resurrection. But there will be *no return.*"

Thunder crashed outside as LaDonna cast her gaze out towards the curtains.

"Storm's coming," she said. She looked back at Pedro. Her eyes were intense, wide, staring directly into his. "Now a warning," she said.

Pedro stared at the small jar. "What type of warning?"

"Once you use this powder there will be no return," she said again. "Resurrection requires retribution."

Pedro gasped.

303

The night in the chateau flashed through his mind, when he was with Antoine and Isaiah, discussing the ramifications of the path he had chosen. And as he shut the rickety wooden door and stepped out onto Bourbon Street, the rain fell in torrents, as the thunder crashed above again. As tourists huddled under awnings next to boisterous bars, holding plastic cups of elixirs and cocktails, he pulled his jacket close to his chest, holding the small, glass jar in his pocket, protecting it with a cupped hand.

He could not reveal to Antoine what he discussed with LaDonna.

As he ran under the awnings, the winds blasted the street as sheets of rain fell. Wrought iron lamps swung in the winds as tourists crowded closer to the buildings; Pedro darted through the crowds, reaching his arm outwards as he spotted the waiting sedan. He opened the back door and slid into the back seat.

He leaned his head back, took a quick breath, and exhaled.

"Did you get it?"

Pedro looked forward. Jacob turned around to face him, raising his eyebrows. Pedro slowly pulled the glass jar out of his pocket, holding it up for Jacob. He gasped. "So that will bring her back," Jacob said, as he turned to face forward, put the car in gear, and turned the wipers on as fast as they would go. He navigated the French Quarter traffic as Pedro let his breath out, settling into the back seat. He held the jar in his laps, cupping it with his hands to protect it.

"I don't know…what…is going to become of this," Pedro said, slowly, as Jacob navigated the dilapidated streets of New Orleans, heading towards the interstate. The drive back to Miami would take all night, at the very least. Jacob would keep the powder in the safe at Waxley while he and Antoine traveled back to Madrid, to exhume Valentina and bring her remains to America. But the powder was the wild card. He had placed trust in LaDonna that the powder truly does have the power of resurrection, but Antoine had insisted that the power lies within the bones.

Either way, Pedro was not completely confident that it would work, but he opted to try. "It's going to be my biggest project," he said as his eyes remained focused on the tiny jar with the yellow powder.

Jacob eased the sedan into the traffic approaching the outskirts of New Orleans. "What did you say, Pedro?"

Pedro looked up, watching the cars pass, looking through the windshield.

"I said that this is going to be my biggest project," he said. "My ultimate artistic masterpiece. Bringing back Valentina."

Jacob nodded. "I know. This is important to you. A promise was broken. So, I understand. But like I was saying earlier, I'll hold the jar. I'll keep it safe. You bring back the remains, and we will all meet at Waxley to plan a course of action. But you have my assurance, the powder will be safe."

Pedro looked back down at the tiny jar his was holding. "Yes," he said. "This power has incredible power. If it were to fall in the wrong hands...I don't even want to think about what could happen."

"Why don't you get some rest?" Jacob asked. "We will be on the road for hours. And I'm good for the drive. But you still haven't received the gift yet. So, you need your rest."

Pedro nodded without saying anything, even though Jacob cast a glance towards the rear-view mirror. Pedro leaned back, closed his eyes, and listened to the road vibrations, as his thoughts carried him towards the deep, dark realm of dreams...

THE WIDOW AND THE TAXIDERMIST

Mona Lisa, Becoming a Ghost
A.L. MENGEL

TEL AVIV

THE DAWN APPROACHED as Isaiah continued delicately pulling the skin from the rotting corpse; he remained careful not to disturb the fur, or the teeth.

Despite his trepidation, there was an undeniable invigoration with the destiny of an artist. Without argument, whichever medium that artist chose, the muse would always visit.

In the days when she would seldom visit, he would experience the same trepidation as artists who worked with canvas and paint, sculptors and musicians. But Isaiah knew what his canvas was.

And what it would be.

And there was a certain panache, he felt, of being a member of the select few. He knew it when he had first entered taxidermy. It was something that wasn't supposed to be, they said. You are heading down a dark path, they said.

But he paid them no mind.

With perseverance came time, and dedication, and with that, the next revelation was his discovering his own talent.

There were days when he thought that he had no destiny in life, no calling. And other times when he would feel discouraged, as many artists do. But years ago, when he was still a boy, as he walked back home from school, in the dry and dusty desert heat, he trudged through the sand and tiny stones. His sandals gritted as he slid them across the gravel, holding his small satchel of books on his back.

The sun was low in the sky, shining directly in his eyes. He lifted his arm up across his forehead. There was something there. He saw it. A small dark shadow.

Isaiah!

A voice hissed from the darkness.

And then there was nothing.

His thoughts cast back into the present, when he walked after the museum had closed; he stopped and switched his satchel from one shoulder to the other. He scanned the area, yet he was alone in the alley beside the museum. As the sun sank beneath the horizon, and the darkness permeated the city, he froze as he heard footsteps approaching.

They were determined, displacing the gravel, coming closer, as Isaiah watched the shadows elongate. Despite the darkness they remained, darker than anything that he could have imagined, and there seemed to be a whining emanating from them. But then the footsteps stopped. He raised his head.

"Antoine!" he said. He turned his head for a moment, noticing the dark shadows had retreated.

"They follow me," Antoine said.

Isaiah turned and looked back at Antoine, raising his eyebrows. "They are nothing new to me. It seems they watch me."

"It's a long story," he said. "But we have a mission from Rome that we need your services for. Is there somewhere we can go to talk?"

"My house is just a few blocks away."

Antoine shook his head. "No. That won't do. Somewhere where no one will hear us. No eavesdropping."

Isaiah looked downwards; his face shifted in thought. After a few moments, his eyes brightened, and he looked up. Antoine was patiently waiting, leaning against a nearby dumpster.

"Inside the museum!"

Antoine straightened his posture, approached him, interested. "We can talk there?"

"Yes! My office. I just left there moments ago. The museum is closed. There will be no concerns of tourists. The staff will still be there closing and securing the building, but my office is secure. We can close the door and you can tell me what you need to tell me."

Antoine nodded, and they proceeded towards the entrance to the Tel Aviv Museum of Art.

The palm tree fronds swayed in a passing breeze, and the temperature remained balmy. Isaiah reached into his pocket and fished out a set of keys, the lock opened with a click, and he ushered Antoine into the dark atrium lobby.

"Follow me," Isaiah said in a hushed tone. "We can go back to my office and talk."

They rushed through the museum, walking silently, as the security staff continued turning off lights and executing the nightly shut down of the museum.

"What is it, Antoine?" Isaiah asked as they shuffled into his office. He snapped the light on as Antoine sat in the chair across from the desk.

"We need your assistance," Antoine said, as Isaiah moved a stack of papers and books to the side so they could see one another. "We have a potential candidate for the gift. He has a great deal of proven loyalty to our kind and has been studying us since his youth."

Isaiah slowly nodded and gestured towards the door.

Antoine rose from his chair and closed the door quietly.

"Of course, he is still being vetted for transformation," Antoine said, as he returned to his chair. "But he is highly likely to be approved."

"By Rome?"

Antoine nodded.

"And then where do I fit into all of this?" Isaiah asked.

"We need your skills," Antoine said. "Pedro is the candidate. He has a tremendous talent for art and writing, he could bring much notoriety to our kind if he were to develop a bloodline with his creativity. Our population has waned since the hooded man. And Rome has ordered a repopulation. In different times, we may not take on this sort of mission."

"What mission is that, Antoine?"

Antoine took a breath and released it. "Well, Isaiah, that is where you fit in," he said. "You are the taxidermist that the Inspiriti employs as needed for these types of projects."

"True."

"And, in this particular case, Pedro seems to have lost his muse. He seeks talent. He was promised transformation. But has received nothing."

Isaiah scoffed as his mouth dropped open. He unfolded his arms and leaned back in his chair. "Come again?"

Antoine shrugged. "He's an artist, Isaiah. He needs to be inspired. And encouraged. He lost that when he followed the promise of the gift, which Darius made to him."

"So why can't he be inspired by his environment? Or other artists?"

Antoine sighed. "I tried that. I brought him to Miami and set him up in a small apartment I own in the design district. I got him a job at the club. But he still seems to be haunted by Darius, and desperately craving the gift, and he just seems to be sinking into a world filled with alcohol."

Isaiah flung his arms apart. "So just transform him, Antoine. Isn't it that simple?"

"No, it isn't. He needs to produce and prove to Rome that he has the talent that we believe he does before he is finally approved for transformation. Come on, Isaiah, you know why we are doing this now. Back in the past, we were too lenient on transformations and look where it got us."

"Yes, I understand. We lost so many of our population to the hooded man's wrath. So how can I help, Antoine?"

"I need you to come with me to my chateau. I will have Pedro travel to Lyon to meet you and we will discuss his predicament. But you, as the most talented taxidermist in the world, can help us, Isaiah. His beloved Valentina, he says, was the source of his talent before Darius visited him. She passed away while Pedro was searching for Darius. We need her back so his talent can reveal itself."

"Skin, bones and body," Isaiah said, looking up, nodding, musing. He looked back down at Antoine. "And so, we will head to Miami? To your mortician?"

Antoine nodded. "Yes. After we meet in Lyon and procure the bones from the convent in Florence. The mortician is already in support and will have all the necessary tools at your disposal."

"Okay then," Isaiah said. "I know I told you that I would do anything for you. So, of course, Antoine. I will help you."

MIAMI

Just after Club *Sacrafice* opened for the evening, Pedro was polishing glassware at the bar when he heard the clap of heels on the concrete floor. Whomever was approaching was entering through the vestibule. He thought it was early, but the bar was open. "I see you got your powder."

He looked up.

She looked the look same as she did when he first met her, when she handed him the card for the House of Voodoo. She sat slowly at the bar, and when he offered to make her a cocktail, she declined. "No, I am here for other purposes," she said. "But don't worry. My visit will be brief."

Pedro nodded and returned to his setup duties.

"And now that you have the powder, you hold the power to resurrect." She rose form the barstool and started to walk back and forth in front of the bar, as Pedro watched her, half concentrating on his setup work. "Of course, wielding this type of power comes with a great deal of responsibility. And loyalty."

She stopped and looked at him directly in the eyes. Pedro carefully set his glass down, locking eyes with her. She stared at him with an intensity that he had not experienced before; her lips were tight and pursed, her hair tied back neatly in a bun. "And if you choose to use the power, even more so."

"And what if I do not?"

Her face softened as she let out a small laugh. "Well, then you will still have to repay me, Pedro. And the coven. You see, we have given you a choice, Pedro. You now have another option. A guaranteed option that will not summon demons. A powder that works without equivocation. But for those types of parameters, there are costs. We will not forget, Pedro. Haddon House has a very long memory. But when we deem the time to be appropriate for us, we do collect on our favors."

She balanced herself on her cane. "When you go to Haddon House, you can ask for me. They call me the widow."

Her heels clapped as she walked out of the nightclub, and Pedro stood behind the bar as the music livened, watching her leave and exit through the front door. New Orleans was his choice. Writing was important to him and developing his talent as an artist was his passion, but he started to wonder if his longing to be reunited with Valentina was for little more than seeking the inspiration which she provided when they were living together in their Madrid flat. Was he proceeding with this mission to resurrect her for selfish reasons, or was it a true pursuit of a long-lost love?

He chose to leave what they had behind without warning, and he quickly forgot about her, infatuated with the promise of the gift and the talent that came with it. While he frequently had bouts of depression and believed he was talentless, Valentina had always encouraged him, and reminded him that he already possessed the talent for which he was on an eternal journey to find.

Pedro awakened with a start.

He groaned and glanced at the clock.

Nearly mid-day.

The sunlight poured in through the blinds, and he winced at the brightness as he pulled the covers back over his head.

The knocking continued.

He groaned, swung his legs over the bed, and trudged over to the door. Who could be knocking? He scarcely knew anyone in the city.

He opened the door and Antoine was peering over the side of the railing. He turned and removed his dark sunglasses. "Well, it seems that your mission has been approved," he said, proceeding into the apartment. Pedro stood aside as Antoine walked through the living room, his face shifted in disgust. Pedro hastily cleaned up the empty pizza boxes and beer cans.

Antoine turned to face him. "Is this how you respect my apartment I gave you?"

Pedro stammered. "I…uh, no, Antoine. Things got a little messy last night."

Antoine glared at him and nodded as he entered. "Indeed, they did."

He turned to face Pedro. "So. I've been contacted by Rome. They have granted me permission to assist you with your resurrection."

Pedro's eyes widened. "Really! So, The Inspiriti will be involved?"

Antoine nodded. "Yes. Your case has been reviewed and discussed and it has been determined that your induction into the immortal community is more important than ignoring it, and for that the immortal rituals and practices will be at your disposal for your resurrection."

Pedro shook his head. "That's…unbelievable. And amazing!"

"It's time to get yourself together, Pedro. Take a shower, get dressed, take out the trash and let's clean up this mess. A plane is booked to take us to Madrid as soon as we arrive to Miami International. I've already had management arrange to cover your shifts at the club."

Pedro tore off his shirt and ran towards the bathroom as Antoine stood in the living room, his hands on his hips, shaking his head. Pedro didn't pay it any mind. Things were starting to happen! He turned on the water and shimmied out of his underwear, treasuring the warmth of the water as the fuzziness seemed to wash away and flow down the drain. For the first time in a long time, he felt hopeful. This was a positive thing, for certain.

As he massaged the foaming shampoo into this thick, dark hair, he could hear Antoine in the living room, shaking open a garbage bag.

He wished he'd not trashed the apartment like he did. But the late nights bartending at the club, and then finding every spare moment to attempt to get some writing done, there just plain and simply wasn't time to clean.

Pedro grabbed the handle and turned it to off, reached up and grabbed a towel, pulled it down and wrapped it around his waist. As he opened the shower door, Antoine appeared from the hallway. "You didn't have anything in the refrigerator," he said. "I was going to clean it out but there was nothing there. How do you survive if you don't eat anything?"

Pedro eased himself around him, skipping over towards the bedroom. "I wouldn't need to eat if you would just *transform* me and give me the gift I was promised!"

"Touché. But, of course, you could eat if you wanted. There are those of us who partake in the blood life, and others who do not."

Pedro pulled up his pants. "Yes. I have studied it all."

Antoine nodded. "Let's get finished getting this place closed up so we can meet Jacob. He is accompanying us to Madrid."

Pedro raised his eyebrows and nodded as Antoine returned to the living room, hoisted up a large bag of trash, and headed out the front door. Pedro knew Jacob had agreed to hold LaDonna's powder at Waxley, and he could feel the anxiety building as he hoped that it was in a safe and secure location.

Pedro hastily tossed some clothes in a small backpack and disconnected the small laptop computer which Antoine had given him, in an effort to inspire him.

Unfortunately, it hadn't worked. But he did feel a twinge of inspiration, knowing that soon, Valentina would be in his arms again, providing the encouragement and inspiration which he never knew he had when he painted.

Antoine appeared in the front door. "Ready to leave?"

Pedro nodded as Antoine walked through the apartment, turning off lights, making sure windows were locked, and nothing was left running. "You are going to be gone for a while," he said, as they headed out the front door. When they were in the car, Antoine started the engine and it roared to life. As they pulled on the boulevard, Antoine explained. "Jacob is coming with us, and he will get Valentina's remains prepped and casketed so we can return to Miami. Then he will take them to Waxley. But right afterwards, we must return to Europe, to the chateau. But we will return separately. As I have to travel first to Tel Aviv. There is someone that I will want you to meet when we finally make it to Lyon."

Pedro listened as they neared the airport, staring out the window. Now that things were in motion, he started to question Antoine's motives. Why was he helping him so much? And more importantly, why was The Inspiriti now so involved? As the shadow of doubt crept closer to him, he realized that he had difficulty accepting a turn of events in his favor. As they headed towards the special entrance for private flights, he watched as Antoine maintained his commanding presence.

When he left the car for the valet, Pedro watched as Antoine gave a simple nod. They all knew him. How could he be so charismatic?

The doors were held open for them as they proceeded through a corridor to a waiting limousine, which would transport them to the jet that would take them to Madrid. Antoine mastered the art of charisma. Pedro watched Antoine and wished he could command the same presence. As the guilt for getting the powder started to eat at him, Jacob appeared, waiting at the base of the stairs leading up to the plane. He waved at them as the limo pulled around, and Pedro stared at the plane in awe.

The jet started its descent as Pedro woke from a deep sleep.

He saw the sun was shining as he looked out the window, stretching upwards in his seat. He turned and saw Antoine watching the news on a flat screen television mounted on the bulkhead. Jacob was sitting next to him, appearing to be nursing a Bloody Mary. He turned to face Pedro. "Well, good morning, sleeping beauty. Did you rest well?"

Pedro yawned and nodded.

Antoine leaned over and looked at Pedro. "The captain told me that we should be on the ground in just a few minutes. We will have plenty of time to relax and check into the hotel before we head to Almudena."

Pedro looked out the window and felt a twinge of nostalgia as he feasted his eyes on his beloved city for the first time in a number of years. He remembered the Almudena cemetery. The adjoining cathedral rose towards the heavens from the city buildings below.

She would be buried just beneath the stones.

He hadn't remembered returning to Madrid since Darius took him away from the city, but he now realized how much he loved and missed his homeland.

As the buildings grew larger and the landscape was closer, he felt the rumble of the touchdown and the jet wheels on the tarmac.

He sighed and turned back towards the cabin. It had been a long flight, but a comfortable and relaxing one. Amazingly, he felt rested.

A twinge of excitement coursed through his body, he felt as if the blood in his veins was flowing more rapidly.

He was finally going to see his Valentina once again, after so many years.

His muse would be in his arms, and he would create once again, after so many years.

But she was dead and buried for nearly as long as he was gone.

As the jet pulled up to a gleaming steel stairway, he looked over at Antoine who was speaking with the flight crew. The seed of doubt had been cast. Valentina had been dead for a long time. Pedro didn't know what to expect when they opened her coffin.

Would she be able to be resurrected?

He followed Antoine and nodded to the crew, as they emerged and descended the stairs to a waiting Mercedes sedan. As they headed into a dark, discreet interior, he thought he should place more trust in Antoine. He had assured Pedro numerous times that the immortals had a ritual of resurrection that was certain to bring Valentina back in all her glory.

Madrid seemed like home, yet now, still unfamiliar.

It was as if he were a different person when he was living there, now returning to a somewhat unfamiliar world. As the car drove them to the hotel, they passed Pedro's old neighborhood.

He could still remember the family gatherings on Sundays after church. And the cathedral, he saw wasn't far; he could see the spires rising into the sky.

He wondered what his parents were doing. Or even if they were still alive.

It was many years since he had been a young boy running around *Ribero de Curtidores*, the street which was always filled with tiny tents and flea market vendors selling wares and crafts. It was in those days when papa learned that his boy wanted to be an artist, it was then that the connection had been lost. Mama always loved him, no matter which path he chose, but papa wanted his son to be a successful businessman, and Pedro knew that was never in his destiny.

Mama encouraged his talent and signed him up for the art classes where he discovered his passion for painting, but it was Valentina who helped him develop his creativity. And when Darius arrived, the unscheduled visitor in his life, a new excitement was awakened as Pedro pursued the journey to become an immortal and discover the talent with which the immortals were gifted.

He wanted to be extraordinary.

And the immortals, Pedro thought, were just that. He would settle for nothing less.

The car pulled up to a small, nameless hotel.

Pedro looked up at the brown masonry against blue and pastel yellows and pinks. The cream-colored drapes were closed in all the windows, and as they exited the car, Jacob remembered the buildings which rose from the tiny sidewalks and narrow streets.

The driver assisted Antoine and Jacob with the bags from the trunk as Jacob got out and wondered why he hadn't seen this building before. They were clearly in *barrio de La Latina*, the oldest part of the city, with its narrow streets and large squares.

"We won't be here for long," Antoine said. "There's some time for you to rest while we wait for darkness. And then we will head over to Almudena. The Inspiriti have locations throughout the world for respite from missions like these."

Pedro nodded and looked up at the small, scalloped awning above the small, glass double doors. They creaked open as they entered a cozy, dimly lit lobby, with dark wood furniture and desks. Antoine had said that this would be a temporary stop over, simply for some rest before heading out.

And it was there, at the cemetery, Almudena, where she was buried. So long ago, it seemed. Many years ago, when he had left the bedroom where she had slept so soundly.

Never to hear her voice again.

Pedro awoke from a deep sleep.

He scarcely remembered heading up to the hotel room, and his head was throbbing. Jacob emerged from a tiny balcony in the master suite, smoking a cigarillo.

Pedro watched as the smoke clouded above his head, but as the sweet smell of the smoke wafted towards him, he leaned back on the pillow, covering his eyes with his arm. "That's giving me a headache," he said.

"Your headache is from your tension, Pedro. And the stress. Antoine told you to rest, and you did not."

Pedro lowered his arm and looked up at Jacob. He sat in a small side chair.

"What did I do?"

Jacob took another draw on his cigarillo as the ember brightened against the dark room.

"You thought that Antoine's absinthe would give you the courage to go through with your mission. Or at least that is how I remember you saying it, I think. Once the first sugar cube was dissolved, there was no telling."

Pedro closed his eyes and sighed.

Of course, Jacob was right.

Scattered memories flooded into his mind, but it was like a puzzle that was yet to be assembled.

He swung his legs over the bed and looked over at Jacob. He sat, smoking, and watching him.

Jacob knew better than him.

Pedro got up and trudged over to the doors and parted the curtains. Antoine was there, leaning on the wrought iron railing, looking outwards into the city lights. It seemed late, and the city was quiet.

Pedro emerged from the suite and joined Antoine, leaning on the railing next to him.

"We still have some time to wait," Antoine said. "It's not quite late enough."

Pedro nodded, peering out towards the cathedral.

The spires rose into the night sky as it was illuminated by the pale moonlight.

It was time to bring her back. The image of her smile flooded his mind as they walked in the still, quiet night. It was only mere blocks away, where their flat had been, where Pedro had furiously huddled over his canvas, on his tiny stool, as she would stand behind him, placing her small, delicate hands on his shoulders, watching him.

Yet in that dark night, when they were taking the long, last journey to the cemetery, as the tools clanked together in the small satchel, Pedro knew that there would be no retribution for his infatuation, only if she were to truly return. And bring him the inspiration which he so desired.

He shook his head, a selfish fool. Was that all he was?

"We have arrived," Antoine said.

Pedro looked up and saw the gates to Almudena.

The gates were as grand as Valentina would have ever been, when she was alive.

Columns rose towards a covered wall, yet the center, the entrance, reached with columns and spires towards the heavens. It was the grand stone and masonry juxtaposed with an elegance befitting a Queen.

Despite the elegance, the aura of Almudena was filled with darkness.

The stones and monuments stood up from the ground like an army of stones, each telling its own story, experiencing a singular history.

They headed inwards, towards the rear of the graveyard, where Valentina was reported to be buried.

Pedro cast his glance up towards the sky, as he admired the moon and the stars. There was so much mystery which expanded far beyond the planet.

So many different philosophers whom Pedro had studied, and their theories about life and death. And what happens when we close our eyes for the last time.

But Valentina was somewhere, further back in the sea of crypts and vaults which lined next to each other in a seemingly endless journey through legacies and lives already lived.

We are coming for you, Valentina. We will rescue you from the grave...

He knew that much.

She had left the physical world and left physical remains, sealed in her coffin. But those remains would be something that would only be a factor in her resurrection, and as they headed through the cemetery. They walked past monuments and rising mausoleums, towards the tree where they had said she was buried, deep within the protection of the earth, and he wondered if it would really be her.

Would her soul return?

Or would it simply be her body?

He remembered the small, glass jar.

LaDonna had promised that the powder would work, but he didn't ask an important question. Yes, the powder would bring Valentina back, as the promise that was made in New Orleans insisted, but the question now cast a seed of doubt as they approached Valentina's marker.

"Will her soul return?" Pedro asked, as Antoine flung the bag down. The tools clanked inside.

"Only if it wants to," Antoine said. "But if you have the deep connection that you believe you do, then her soul will return to you."

Pedro turned away from Antoine and thought of the jar in his pocket, when he had left New Orleans.

He could still feel the cool glass, and La Donna's words once again tore through his mind. *"There will be no return."*

He grabbed a shovel from Antoine as they started digging.

The ground was tough, rocky.

Not what he expected.

But as they continued digging, and as the mound of dirt grew next to them, he looked down at the earth, as they got deeper, and closer to her. He took a deep breath and held it as their shovels clapped the concrete vault. Just inside, she was. Memories of her flashed through his mind, as Antoine reached downwards to break the seal.

There was something about Antoine which Pedro did not fully understand. A superhuman strength, a supernatural presence. Was he angel, or was he demon? Antoine was assisting Pedro, he took him under his wing, and provided encouragement for his writing, and a place to stay in America. The apartment was small, modest, not the same.

He watched Antoine lift the vault cover, seemingly without effort, and he watched as a crumbling coffin slowly came into view. He turned and closed his eyes.

It felt like a betrayal.

Antoine had said not to go to New Orleans, he had warned about LaDonna.

But Pedro went regardless. And then he thought of Darius, and what he had offered. He had offered to write for him, to be his ghost writer, to allow him to walk the Earth once again.

Antoine hoisted the cover and placed it on the ground with a thud. He was doing all of this for Pedro, without asking for help, or giving any indication that he was sensing Pedro's thoughts. Antoine knew that he had the powder, but he never mentioned it.

He touched Pedro's arm. "Are you ready?"

Pedro sighed. "Yes," he said. "We need to release her from the chains of the coffin."

The coffin was dirty, caked with soil. They worked together to lift it out of the vault, as water dripped and puddled at the bottom.

They placed it on the ground, next to the mound of dirt, and Antoine started to tear away the lid. The wood broke easily from the years of being waterlogged.

As Antoine tore away a large piece of her coffin, Pedro shut his eyes tight and turned away.

He listened as the wood cracked and splintered. He could not see her in this state of decay.

He pictured Valentina, back in their flat, in the studio, as she would wear her summery dresses and dance through their apartment, singing to him, smelling of lavender and perfume; he remembered as the back of her hand would slowly caress his cheek, delicately, as he would concentrate on the wisps and strokes of his brush.

He wished he had focused on her more.

"Pedro."

He opened his eyes but was still facing away from the grave.

He felt his heart race inside his chest, and he could smell the scent of the grave in the air. Would she be unrecognizable? Would the grave, and the assault of the water, and the onslaught of time allow her body to be preserved so he could see her face one time again?

"Turn around, Pedro."

He closed his eyes and took a breath.

This was coming.

He knew it, and Antoine knew it, and they both knew that the sky was lightening in the east, and if they were going to proceed with this, they needed the parts of the body that connect with the soul, and even then, without the ritual, Antoine said that there was no guarantee that what returned was who you believed you lost.

A body was a body, Antoine said. A physical shell to house the soul, and the soul was what was immortal.

Pedro gasped when he saw the coffin.

Valentina's skin was dark, leathery, and clinging to her bones.

Her mouth was open, as if she were screaming. He looked up at Antoine as tears welled in his eyes.

"This is not her, Pedro. Who she was is gone from this world. This is simply the body she had, it gets old, or sick, and it dies. We immortals have a gift which she did not have. And which you may soon have. But there is soul connectedness that humans do not experience that we do."

"The body dies and the soul leaves," Pedro said. "Is that what you are telling me?"

Antoine raised his head and returned Pedro's stare, and then turned and placed the turn wooden lid back on the coffin. "I have to lower this back in the ground."

Pedro knelt by the foot of the coffin, reached his hands underneath, surprised at the damp, crumbling wood. He looked at Valentina's corpse, scarcely recognizable with years of decay and decomposition.

The clothes she was buried in were tattered, torn and dirtied, covered with mold and black with mildew.

They lifted the coffin, and Pedro was surprised at how light it was. They eased it over to the grave, and slowly lowered it into the ground.

The water splashed at the bottom of the vault.

Pedro knelt next to the grave, looking at the coffin, deep within the earth, covered in dirt. Antoine tossed dirt into the grave, over and over, as Pedro felt tears well up in his eyes.

As the sun was high in the sky and was shining brilliantly on Madrid, Pedro's eyes slowly fluttered open.

Antoine was sitting at the small desk in the hotel room. Jacob appeared in the doorway from the parlor suite.

"I have her remains casketed," he said. "Checked in with *Funeraria Cerventina*. They are holding a coffin for her, and all the arrangements have been made to transport to America."

Pedro sat up in the bed and draped his arms over his knees under the sheet. "I didn't see anything taken from her grave."

Antoine scoffed. "I got what I needed."

Jacob took a small chair opposite the desk where Antoine was working. He sat and turned around to face Pedro, and then back towards Antoine. "I must accompany the casket for the flight from Madrid. But I will see you both in Miami."

Antoine nodded.

"The flight leaves this evening."

Antoine raised his head and looked over towards Pedro. "And you best better get ready soon. We've done what we came here to do. Our jet will be leaving tonight as well."

"We won't be driving to Frankfurt?" Pedro asked, as he flung the sheet off his body and swung his legs to the floor, rubbing his palms over his eyes.

"No," Antoine said. "Madrid is approved. It's just Paris that we must stay away from for flying."

Pedro padded to the bathroom and thought it strange that Antoine did not want to visit his chateau in Lyon, or that Pedro didn't have the opportunity to visit any family while he was in his hometown, but he did respect Antoine's focus on the task at hand.

He didn't see what Antoine took from Valentina's coffin.

The door opened slightly as he saw Antoine just outside, peering through the open crack. "Your Valentina still rests here," he said. "Her body does. And what will allow her to return is what I have, and what you will see when we return to Miami. You will meet the world's finest taxidermist, and we will bring your muse back so you can be inspired once again."

Pedro sighed.

There was a certain mysteriousness about the taxidermist.

The one who had traveled from Tel Aviv, through Italy, and onwards towards France, after as they all crossed the Atlantic towards New York.

When they traveled back to Miami, Jacob had accompanied the casket on a commercial flight, and Antoine and Pedro took the private jet. "The taxidermist I told you about is flying in from Israel," Antoine said as they nursed cocktails together in the middle of the flight.

Pedro looked down at the ice cubes in his glass.

He remembered how they always looked to him, like tiny icebergs in an amber sea. He listened to Antoine's instructions but didn't fully process what he was saying.

His thoughts kept returning to the grave, and to Valentina, her open mouth and her appearance of screaming as her leathery skin clung to her skull.

He leaned his head back and closed his eyes.

She was moving through their kitchen in the flat they shared in Madrid, her eyes were wide, vibrant, bright and full of life. He felt as if he were in a dream when the plane landed, and the car picked up him and Antoine at Miami International.

Although the jet lag he experienced hadn't seem to hit him yet, when the car turned down the familiar Ascension Avenue, and as it drove under the brass sign on the wrought iron gates of the Waxley Mortuary, Antoine finally spoke again.

"Isaiah is meeting us here," he said. "The world's finest taxidermist, of course. Rome has recommended him for bringing her back, Pedro."

Pedro didn't remember much until he raised his head, opened his eyes, and saw they were in Jacob's office at Waxley. Somehow, in some way, he had gone through the motions. He remembered the funeral home, and of course Jacob, but the travel in the plane, and then the car, was as if he was drunk on tequila. He held no memory.

"All of the animals," Isaiah said, slowly, as Pedro's vision came into focus, and he saw them in Jacob's office. Jacob was sitting at the desk with his chin resting on his hands, as Antoine sat in a small chair on the other side of the door. Pedro looked over at him nervously.

Jacob lowered his hand and leaned forward. "But you haven't reconstructed a person? Back from the grave?"

Isaiah turned to face Pedro and raised his eyebrows, making direct eye contact with him. "I was on the team responsible for the Torah," he said as Pedro shifted in his chair. Pedro waited for a moment, looking at his eyes. He knew Isaiah was being truthful; he had heard about the work, and some of the finest prepared, stuffed and mounted animals from Israel and the Torah.

Antoine leaned in closer towards the others. "But a person? Who then would be expected to be living? One who has passed and decomposed for years? And you haven't even asked me why I am doing this."

Isaiah turned and looked at Antoine directly. "We all know why we are doing this, Antoine. Pedro is still part of the uninitiated, but the immortals need him. And his craft. We have the power, and the ability, to bring him back his inspiration."

Pedro met eyes with Jacob, who nodded toward the painting of Schubert which hung behind the desk. Jacob nodded.

The powder.

When Pedro held doubts that he would see Valentina again, he remembered his trip to the House of Voodoo, when he met with LaDonna Mastuer, when she made her promise that yes, he would see his muse again, he would again discover the inspiration which had been lost to him for so many years.

Pedro looked at Isaiah. "Do you do what you do to somehow…evade death?"

Isaiah turned to look out the window, out towards Resurrection cemetery, into the sea of stone statues.

Isaiah remained looking away from Pedro. "I would never ask that," he said. "Death means something different to each of us. And I would never question your reasons for wanting to hold Valentina in your arms again. It's not really about evading death. Taxidermy is an art. Even after so many years. And here, at Waxley, Jacob is going to be a critical part to our success."

Pedro nodded. "Yes. With the crematorium. And she will live again? She will not simply be an ornament?"

Jacob stood.

"Let me show you the crematoriums," he said, reaching for his suit coat and grabbing his keys.

As they filed out into the foyer, Pedro watched as Antoine and Isaiah were having a hushed discussion on the far side, close to the stained-glass gates which led into the viewing rooms.

The office door remained opened just a crack, and Pedro peered inside, watching Jacob as he hung back.

347

Pedro watched as Jacob swung the Schubert painting outwards, revealing a secret storage cubby.

The small glass jar was there.

Jacob had kept his promise, stored the powder for him.

But now, as they had returned from Europe, he knew that he must decide whether to use the powder or Antoine's ritual. Both came with a price.

Resurrection requires retribution...

They quickly proceeded down the slender corridor which spanned the back of the funeral home, walking past the closed, wooden doors, nestled between candelabra sconces on the walls.

Jacob noticed the flicker of the electric candles as Pedro opened the rear door, leading them through the receiving room. As the large elevator opened and one of the staff wheeled body on a gurney, covered with a white cloth.

Jacob turned to them as they piled into the elevator. He leaned close towards Pat, who appeared to be engrossed in his work. "Is number seven ready?"

Pedro, Antoine and Isaiah watched as Pat slowly nodded. Jacob gave him a light pat on the shoulder as they moved further into the coffin elevator.

"Door will open on the other side," Jacob said. "That's where we do hearse loading."

They turned around as the door closed, and they were silent as they listened to the hum of the elevator as it descended.

As Jacob led them down a cement hallway, Pedro stopped.

"What is that?"

Jacob and the others turned around to face him.

There was a deep rumble emanating from deep within the darkened corridor.

"Crematorium is running," Jacob said. "You're going to feel the vibration."

They stopped outside a dirty steel door.

CREMATORIUM 7

"It holds a special power," Jacob said, as he slowly opened the door. It revealed a large dark oven, cold and unused. Several caskets were stacked on the opposite side of the room, yet there was no belt which slid the coffin inside the oven in this crematorium. "The power to resurrect and transform to immortality."

Pedro approached the chamber.

He peered inside, and it looked like any other cremation chamber. It was sloped, like an oven, made of brick and iron, with a large grate in the center.

As he moved his head further inwards, he tilted it to the side.

They were right.

It was seemingly endless.

The darkness enveloped the rear of the chamber, infinite in its grasping. He dared not climb inside, yet part of him wanted to. Jacob said it held the power to resurrect. And transform to immortality. Would he receive the gift he craved for so long if he climbed inside and crawled back towards the endless darkness?

After Jacob met with Claire's family to arrange her funeral, Antoine and Jacob went into the office and closed the doors. As the sun was setting, Isaiah and Pedro followed Jacob's instructions to locate the crypt for the immortals, where Claire would be entombed and wait for the bones.

Pedro slowly followed as Isaiah moved closer to the rusted iron spires along the perimeter of Resurrection cemetery. As he stood and looked inwards at the darkness of the cemetery, Pedro joined him and noticed the reflecting light against the rising stone monuments.

"Jacob told me about the local legend," Pedro offered as they stood next to one another in the glow of the moonlight.

He turned towards Isaiah, and noticed he was studying the graves intently through the opening in the stone wall.

"It must have to do with the mounds of dirt I see next to each grave," Isaiah said, without turning to face Pedro. "And that gives a perfect explanation why Jacob was so secretive about the mysteries surrounding crematorium number seven."

They both paused as they heard the slow approach of footsteps. Pedro felt his heard start to pound in his chest; no one should know they were there.

They both turned as Pedro's mouth dropped open.

Antoine and Jacob were standing just behind them. Jacob held a candelabra, and the flicker of the candles highlighted the weathered stone door. Jacob had a slight smirk on his face and slowly nodded. "Of course, you don't understand why you are really here, do you?"

"If you are going to receive the gift," Antoine said. "And become part of the immortal community, and learn of our secrets, then you must complete your initiation."

Pedro glanced at Isaiah. He looked at him and said nothing, but there was a knowing look in his eyes. Pedro knew. He watched as Isaiah stood next to Jacob. Isaiah had known Jacob for the years when they had met in Rome, when The Inspiriti had insisted that Jacob travel there to meet the world-renowned taxidermist.

It was all there, he could see it in his mind's eye; even as he watched Isaiah approach Jacob in a friendly embrace, he could still smell the coffee roasting in the tiny café outside Paris, back when Pedro was still longing for the gift, and wishing Darius had kept his promise and never abandoned him.

But now, they stood, an ocean away, in the Resurrection cemetery near the one mortuary that worked closely with the immortal community, and he felt like an outcast. They seemed to be their own brotherhood, and he watched them as they stood before him, in a trio of masculine immortality. There was an initiation.

He had to learn their secrets.

But would he be transformed?

Or did they hold a different motivation?

Claire's funeral took place the following Saturday.

Jacob had met with the family in his office on the same day that Jacob, Antoine and Isaiah had visited the mortuary to view the mysterious and alluring crematory chamber number seven. Although Pedro had asked the others about the mystery surrounding the crematorium, he was only met with silence and a stern warning. "You will know when you have received the gift."

Pedro stood on the sidewalk and saw a hearse was parked in front of the steps leading up to the Cathedral of the Gardens. The brown casket was visible through the rectangular rear windows, covered in a nest of white flowers. As a caravan of black limousines pulled up behind the parked hearse, he felt a hand gently touch his shoulder. He moved his neck to the side.

The hand was masculine.

Muscular with engorged veins.

Pedro raised his head and looked up, his eyes widening. He recognized the flowing blonde hair, framing powerful shoulders.

"Tramos!"

It was who he had remembered.

From the days in Rome when Antoine had befriended him and taken him to the trials for the assault of the hooded man in Vatican City with Delia Arnette, who was an immortal of one of the highest statures that Pedro had first learned about from his studies as a student, but also from Antoine.

When looking at Tramos, the one who stood in front of him, his long hair flowing downwards, Pedro remained awestruck; his mouth open, ready to speak but saying nothing.

Tramos smiled a brilliant white smile as his long, golden hair caught a passing breeze. Pedro noted he appeared to be a man, but he knew Tramos was far from that. There had been the days when Pedro had discussed what had happened to Tramos in the past; when the hellhounds had torn him apart in the burned-out shell of Antoine's mansion, a mere few miles west in Coral Gables.

"How…can you be standing here?!"

Pedro caught his breath as he finally managed to gasp some words. "I didn't think she would be gone, but I left her. It was my choice, and only mine."

A flash of Darius pierced his mind, and he was carried back to the humid night in Madrid, when Darius was standing in the small, yellow circle of warm light from the streetlamp which he'd leaned on while studying Pedro.

He looked up at Tramos, who had a pained look on his face.

"You do have to go inside at some point," Tramos said. "I can come with you. I would imagine it's difficult to lose someone like this."

Pedro nodded towards the Cathedral.

A hearse was waiting at the bottom of the steps as the doors opened.

Pallbearers carried a casket on their shoulders, descending the steps slowly, as the mourning crowd followed and spilled out onto the sidewalk somberly.

Pedro let out a nervous laugh. "Ah, she was my psychiatrist."

Tramos nodded. "Indeed. But I do know about your loss, Pedro. Back in Madrid. Are you going to follow them to the cemetery? To get the body which you must claim?"

"Which I must claim?"

Tramos nodded and smiled wanly. "Of course, Pedro. To bring her back, you need a body. Skin, bones and body. Certainly, you've studied it in the code?"

Pedro made every effort to keep his face still. Tramos knew about everything, it seemed.

Pedro thought again of Madrid, and the night when he left Valentina for Darius, as the guilt consumed him. But he needed to take the journey towards immortality; but why had he been unable to take her with him?

Mona Lisa, Becoming a Ghost
A.L. MENGEL

SKIN

BONES

BODY

Mona Lisa, Becoming a Ghost
A.L. MENGEL

TRAVELING FROM FLORENCE

AFTER THEY FLED from the crumbling convent in Florence, Pedro sat in the front seat of the large Mercedes sedan that the Inspiriti had provided them, resting his elbow on the armrest near the door, and watching the mountainsides pass, as Antoine charged towards the chateau in Lyon.

He looked in the back seat; Isaiah was lying still, but his chest was moving.

He was still alive.

Antoine had yet to tell him what happened back in the catacombs beneath the convent in Florence.

He watched at the sun started to sink in the sky, as the rays filtered into the cabin of the car. Antoine was driving in silence; it was as if they were on a mission that was beyond his comprehension.

361

Pedro was traveling with two immortals; they had the experience in these matters far beyond what Pedro could have ever dreamed about.

But he was acting on passion.

He was trying to correct his acting on desire in the past, when he held an infatuation with the immortals.

Yet, despite the time he spent with them, he had never been transformed, despite the gift being promised to him by one of their higher-ranking members. And Pedro still felt desire within his heart, the infatuation, which had governed his life, remained.

Pedro was lost in his thoughts and looked up as Antoine pulled the car through the winding driveway of the chateau.

It was a long drive to Lyon, but they were finally there. Giovanni appeared as he opened the tall heavy wooden front doors, and he headed down the stairs towards the sedan.

Pedro snapped out of his musings and pushed the heavy car door open, as Giovanni and Antoine opened the rear door, and lifted Isaiah out of the back seat.

"The succubus tore out of the catacombs," Antoine explained. "Nearly took all the blood."

Giovanni leaned down close to Isaiah's chest. "But his heart still beats."

Antoine nodded as Pedro watched them carry him up the stairs and into the chateau. He slowly followed, turned around, and closed the doors inwards.

Pedro overheard Antoine in the echo of the soaring, arched ceilings, as they carried Isaiah towards the back guest quarters.

"He must rest for three days and three nights," Antoine explained.

Pedro approached the door to the back bedroom and watched as Antoine and Giovanni lay Isaiah on the bed, placing him under the covers. As Antoine gently eased the sheet over Isaiah, Giovanni rushed over to the windows and drew the drapes closed.

Pedro took a few steps closer to the bed. "Antoine?"

Antoine continued tucking the sheet in around the bed and raised his eyes, looking up at Pedro.

"Is he going to survive?"

Antoine nodded.

"Yes. He has the gift. But the succubae have been an adversary for as long as I have been an immortal. Just like they drain the lifeforce of humans, they do the same for us immortals. They drain us of our blood. Isaiah will live. But he needs to be replenished with the life blood."

After they had spent three days at the chateau, Isaiah emerged from the guest suite. His face still appeared shallow and sullen, but he was alive and moving on his own. Pedro watched as Isaiah sat in the parlor. Giovanni brought them both tea, and breakfast, as Antoine studied his books in the library at the opposite end of the chateau.

After Isaiah had shaken off the ether, Antoine and Pedro sat at the kitchen table with him to review *The Code of the Immortals,* opening it to the pages and drawings about Resurrection.

Their bulbous glasses were nearly empty; Pedro watched as Antoine picked up his glass and downed the bit of dark red wine. He reached over to the bottle which Giovanni had left before retiring to his quarters and winced. "I think we are being told something."

Isaiah hovered over the book, studying the code. His eyes widened. "I see it!" he said, as Antoine and Pedro hovered closer.

"Skin. Bones. Body," Isaiah said, leaning back and crossing his arms.

He moved forward and hunched over the book, extending his finger. "If an immortal desires resurrection, only a member of their bloodline can perform the ritual."

Antoine nodded and stood. "Yes, yes, yes. And the body must be intact, or you can use a proxy, and of course, the bones in the convent in Florence will ensure its success."

"It will?" Pedro asked.

"Of course," Antoine said. "They hold the power of creation, Pedro. That is what is believed among the immortal community."

"Is it true?" Pedro asked.

"The legend says that the parts must be from three separate subjects," Antoine explained.

Pedro listened as Antoine spoke on the phone with the Miami-Dade County Coroner. He didn't know how Antoine would be able to procure Claire's body, but he was insistent that, if the white worm was present, that Claire wasn't dead at all.

There was movement inside the body bag.

That's what was observed.

And was it possible, that perhaps the mysterious visitor that was seen walking into Claire's condo building with her may not have been her killer, but rather her captor?

Would her body work?

Would only the powder work for Valentina? Would the resurrection ritual be a failure?

Claire was buried, if she was even dead.

And would what returned be a physical image of Claire, with the power of the bones of Lisa, and Valentina being lost?

The powder, LaDonna had said, held the power to transform.

To resurrect.

And bring immortality.

He knew that she had died many years ago.

There wasn't much left to resurrect her in full form, but with Isaiah's talent, and Jacob's ingenuity, he felt that this might just actually become a reality.

With the powder, LaDonna's powder, of course.

If, of course, he chose to use it. The powder came with a significant number of consequences, it seemed.

Antoine appeared directly in front of Pedro.

He hadn't even known when the phone call had ended.

"You look as if you are deep in thought," Antoine said. "Of course, I am," Pedro said. "There's so much

367

to do for this, Antoine. And we don't even know if it will work."

Antoine leaned closer to him and placed his hand on Pedro's forearm. "It will work," he said. "She will return."

Pedro leaned back in his chair and folded his arms across his chest. Antoine and Isaiah were discussing taxidermy procedures, and now they had Mona Lisa's bones. And they supposedly held the power which Antoine promised they did. Yet with Darius, Antoine's maker, in the same blood lineage, could Antoine be trusted?

After they had returned to Miami from Madrid, Pedro sat across from Jacob in the front offices of the Waxley Mortuary as a tall Grandfather clock chimed behind them. Jacob sat in a high, leather back smoking chair, leaning on the desk, his hands clasped before his chin. Pedro watched as the door chimed in the foyer. The clap of heels on the marble followed, and the creak of the heavy, iron front doors opening.

She had arrived.

The jingle of her charms and trinkets cut into the otherwise silence of the office, muffled through the heavy wooden office doors, until there was a soft knock. Pedro watched as Jacob raised his eyes.

"Come in," Jacob said. His voice was soft.

Pedro turned as the heard the click of the handle. He focused on Clarissa's jingling trinkets; they sharpened in front of his eyes as he stood in front of Jacob's desk. She placed her hands on her hips. "You've called me here, Mr. Jacob. How can the lovely Clarissa assist you today?"

Jacob cast a glance over at Pedro and leaned back in his chair, looking up at Clarissa who stood in front of the massive, wooden desk, her hands on her hips. Pedro watch Clarissa, noticing her crimson hair; disheveled yet in an intentional style, he thought.

He could tell, as he watched her hastily take the chair opposite of where he sat, and as he listened to the clank and jingle of the many charms and trinkets that she wore, that she appeared nervous and fidgety.

He leaned forward and gestured for her attention. "Are you alright?"

Clarissa turned and looked directly at Pedro. Her eyes appeared wide, and then she smiled, lazily. "I didn't get my ganja today!" she exclaimed. "I always get so anxious! I need that shit." She chuckled and leaned back in the chair, continuing her fidgeting.

Pedro looked over at Jacob who raised his eyebrows and nodded. Clarissa was who she was, and he was confident that there was a specific reason why Jacob invited Clarissa for their meeting. He watched as Jacob stood.

He stood the in foyer and turned as he clasped his hands at his waist. Isaiah stood next to him in the same posture.

Clarissa joined them.

They stood as the mortuary staff appeared behind them, approaching from the rear corridor.

A tall man who wore a white, blood-stained medical coat stood next to the Hispanic woman who had let him in before.

"Are you ready to resurrect her?" Clarissa asked.

Pedro stood in the office, watching them as they all stood in the foyer, their hands clasped at their waists, watching him watching them.

"Come with us, Pedro," Jacob said, softly. "You will become a part of an immortal society that you have always wanted. We need more creatives. More talent."

Antoine nodded.

"Join us," Isaiah said.

He watched as they turned without a word, filing down towards the darkened corridor; and Pedro felt a twinge of uncertainty wash through him.

There was no specific clause which permitted him to rescind his desires, for the immortals were cast in their decision making.

It was apparent to him that destiny had presented a uniqueness to which he had never been accustomed; he had frequently longed for something, or someone, and realized that, sometimes, greatness, and being extraordinary, is an attribute afforded to other people.

Never for him.

And would the participation in a resurrection ritual which would seal a darker destiny for him? Would the powder which he held be a catalyst for his damnation?

Only time would tell.

And as Pedro followed them down the long, expansive hallway which traversed the back wall of Waxley, he saw their determination.

There would be no chances provided for a change of mind.

Jacob led the others, as Isaiah and Antoine carried Claire's body towards the preparation room, where the other staff members were prepping the tools, as her body was wrapped in a white sheet.

Pedro walked behind them as if he were a widower, thinking of Valentina; and in essence, he was, if they had been married. But Valentina had been dead and buried for many years; her body long decomposed, and during the time when she had been dead, he had been following his infatuation; the promise which had never been kept.

As Jacob advanced down the hallway, the candle wall sconce light fixtures illuminated, bathing the corridor in a warm, incandescent glow.

He stopped in front of the last door, at the terminus; he turned and waited for the others, clasped his hands behind his back, as the others gathered around him. "This is where she will be resurrected," Jacob said.

Pedro looked down at the shrouded sheet.

It was of a different woman; someone he had not known other than the brief moments of his being her patient, but he may have wished to have known her. Would what Antoine promised to happen come to fruition?

Would the power that was assumed be there take effect?

Too many broken promises, it seemed.

As he reached into his pocket, and cupped his hand around the small, cool glass jar, he doubted if LaDonna had been honest with him as well.

The Widow was pressing him to visit her in New Orleans, and she clearly held an animosity towards the immortal community.

Jacob pulled a gleaming set of skeleton keys from his pocket, and as he grasped the correct key they jingled against the silence in the corridor.

Everyone stood, motionless, watching and waiting.

As the door swung open, Jacob reached inside and flipped a wall switch, and the room was bathed in harsh florescent light. He turned, gestured for the others to follow, and took a step over the threshold.

Pedro scanned the room.

Several caskets were stacked in the far corner, and a steel gurney reflected the light.

Jacob grabbed a leather pulley and yanked it downwards, as two massive steel doors slip open like a giant reflective mouth.

There was a gurney inside, covered in a sheet; it looked like a snow-covered mountain range.

Antoine gasped.

Jacob looked over at Antoine, shook his head and smiled softly. He approached the gurney and lifted the sheet. There were boxes, books and shiny stainless-steel tools of the funeral trade. Jacob lifted a giant reflective needle.

"This is the trocar," he said, looking over at Pedro. "We won't need this for what we are doing. But I saw that you were looking at it."

Antoine took a step back and shook his head. "I just saw that…"

"This is made out of chrome," Jacob said, holding it up. Pedro watched as it caught and reflected the light. "It's used to pierce the organs. Drains the gas and fluid from a corpse."

Pedro shivered for a moment, watching as Jacob turned his wrist as he rotated the trocar.

An image of Valentina, laying and covered in a white sheet, in a funeral home back in Madrid, as the embalmer held the trocar above her, leaned over her, plunging it in her torso.

He shuddered again.

"This one is a longer one," Jacob said. "Twenty-two inches long. But, like I said, we won't be using this tool."

They headed down to the embalming room, where Isaiah had walked ahead to prepare the taxidermy tools. The thoughts which pierced Pedro's mind were fraught with images of the sea, and the beach.

He had seen her there.

She couldn't be there. It had to be an image his mind conjured up; a result of his anxiety and trepidation.

The souls all seek solace from the sea!

There was no comfort in the crematorium. There was no solace.

He saw her.

Dressed in a flowing black robe as she emerged from the water, slowly, rising towards a dark and angry sky, as the winds howled and the pasty, white limbs thrashed behind her.

She had those dead eyes.

The ones that were clouded and pasty. She slowly approached from the waters as the sea grew angry; waves crashed on rocks and sprayed white foam.

She approached, slowly, methodically, as her long black robe fluttered in the wind. The screams and wails emanated from behind her, as she got closer...until she was standing right in front of him.

I am coming for you, Pedro.

"Pedro!"

His thoughts were thrust back into the present as he gasped for air.

"Pedro?" Antoine asked, as he approached. "Where were you just now? Where did your mind go?"

Pedro regained his breath and looked up at the others.

They were in the bright florescent lights of the preparation room, and Isaiah was now wearing one of the bright lab coats. It was spotless, and he held a small flat metal tool with a long wooden handle. "The is the fleshing tool," he said. He stood in the center of the room, and Jacob stood on the opposite side of the gurney.

Pedro brought his hands up to his forehead and ran them back through his hair. His face appeared red, and his hair near his sideburns was damp. "I...saw her." He looked over at Antoine, who stood on the side wall, his arms folded.

"You saw Valentina."

Clarissa got up from the small, plastic side chair she was sitting on in the corner. Her trinkets jingled as she moved. "That is normal," she said. She moved close to Pedro, placing her hand softly on his cheek. "What did you see? What was your vision, Pedro? You were standing here with us, but I know your thoughts were somewhere else. Where were they?"

He took a breath and exhaled.

"It's the beach. On the desolate sea that smells putrid. I can see them thrashing. They are bodies?"

Clarissa lowered her eyes and pursed her lips. After a moment, she looked up at him. "Antoine can better tell you about the sea."

Antoine hung his head as he spoke of the sea, and the mysterious seven gates which were hidden around the world, which the immortal community was sworn to protect. His eyes welled with tears as he mentioned those souls who had been cast to the sea, who once had the gift, yet thrashed in the putrid water, bound with countless writhing pasty limbs.

Pedro closed his eyes and lowered his head.

The screams pierced his mind.

Pedro put his arm around Antoine. He had never shown any type of weakness to Pedro before.

Resurrection requires retribution…

The voice hissed through his head as Pedro felt a chill run through his spine.

Isaiah lifted the sheet and Pedro gasped as Claire's corpse came into view. It was just like the reports said. Her left eye was gouged out, as if she were shot in the face. Clarissa placed three large, white chapel candles along the side of the preparation table and struck a match. Isaiah snapped on a pair of rubber gloves and looked over at Antoine, who nodded.

Isaiah leaned closer to her eyes and reached his finger inside the gaping hole.

Pedro winced at the squishing sounds as Isaiah moved his finger deeper, and in a circular motion.

His eyes brightened. "Ah, ha! I think I have it, Antoine."

Isaiah lifted his hand, cupping it.

Pedro watched as Isaiah looked at the others, holding his hand out in front of them, and slowly opening it.

"The white worms," Isaiah said.

Pedro took a breath and held it as he watched the tiny, writhing, pasty white worm. They leaned in, and it appeared to be writhing. Isaiah looked over to Pedro. "This is what preserved her," he said. He handed the worm to Jacob who placed it in a jar which he then placed into a small cooler.

Isaiah held a scalpel up and looked at the others.

"Now she may be alive, but I assure you she will feel no pain."

Antoine folded his arms as Pedro could feel his heart race in his chest. He watched, mesmerized, as Isaiah leaned down over Claire's body, making a cut from the side of her head, downwards on the side of her torso, down her legs and towards her feet.

"Skin," Isaiah said. He looked up at Pedro. "She will have Claire's skin. Lisa del Giocondo's bones, which you have, correct, Antoine?"

Antoine nodded. "And of course, Valentina's heart."

Pedro took a breath and slowly exhaled as Clarissa started chanting, calling for a resurrection. He watched as Isaiah removed Claire's skin and carefully, reverently, took it to the sink to begin washing it. Claire's body remained on the table, awash in blood as it drained down the preparation table.

And then he closed his eyes.

He saw Valentina, lying in bed next to him, her smile bright and brilliant, just as it always was in the mornings when they awakened in their bed next to one another, as the bright Madrid sunshine flooded their room. She would always have such a radiance to her that people would ask if she were expecting, yet she never was.

But her smile then slowly faded.

She scowled, shifting her face, easing herself back away from him, pulling the covers up over her breasts. Her eyes widened as she cowered away from him.

Her mouth dropped open as she raised her head and wailed. "Why are they doing this to me?! Leave me at rest, Pedro!"

Pedro gasped as her face shot close towards him, her eyes pasty white, clouded, her skin blackened, her hair mussed and caked with dirt.

They're taking me back to the sea! I cannot be released from the chains!

RESURRECTION

RESURRECTION CEMETERY

THEY LAY HER CASKET in the crypt as the sky was lightening on the eastern horizon.

Pedro shuddered as the grating of the casket tore against the silence of the mausoleum. He and Antoine stood next to each other, watching in the center of the dusty stone mausoleum as Jacob and Isaiah lifted the stone. They grunted as they shoved it in place with a deafening thud, sealing her casket away from the light and earth, wrapping it in stone.

Jacob turned to face them as Isaiah worked on tightening the stone in place.

"She must lay in the casket for three days and three nights," Jacob said.

Pedro turned and looked at Antoine, who was looking downwards, appearing defeated. It had been unlike Antoine to be so quiet in the years that Pedro had known him, but recently, Antoine appeared to be misguided. Possibly longing for his own maker, Darius.

"So, you say the bones have a power? Our trip to Florence, and nearly losing Isaiah is not for naught?"

Antoine raised his head and looked over at Pedro.

Pedro thought Antoine's face appeared tired.

He was the most human looking immortal Pedro had ever remembered seeing throughout his life. His skin did not appear angelic or statuesque; his forehead glistened with sweat, and there was a splotch of dirt on his cheeks. Antoine nodded. "Come back to the mortuary, Pedro. We will wait there. Some time will pass."

They all filed out of the crypt, as Jacob closed the rusted wrought iron gate, turning the key in the lock. He turned to the others as they made their way through the cemetery, amidst the sea of rising stone markers and artistic, weathered monuments. "Now we wait," Jacob called, from the ahead, without turning around.

As they walked through the dense forest which separated the mortuary from the cemetery, their footsteps crunched through the leaves and snapped broken twigs. Pedro turned and watched Antoine, as his face appeared to be shifted with worry. He was still looking down, appearing to study each step he took in great detail. As they approached the gardens which surrounded the funeral home, Antoine looked up and cast a glance towards Pedro. His eyes were intense. "Did you use the powder?"

Pedro stammered for a moment.

Antoine was more insistent. "Did you use it?"

Pedro took a short breath, holding it, as he looked ahead at Jacob. Antoine glared at him, waiting for an answer. Pedro shifted from foot to foot, as Antoine folded his arms. "*Did you use the powder, Pedro?!*"

Antoine lowered his arms and let out an exasperated sigh.

"It doesn't come without a cost, Pedro! It comes at a great cost to the immortals – a community you have been desperate to be a part of, I might add – but also what returns from the grave! You know the coven at Haddon House is a formidable threat. They hold their own intentions and have a deep connection with

LaDonna and her subjects. But I will not, as your mentor, cast anger at you. Because you are learning. You remain the student. And I know I gave you permission to go to New Orleans and conduct your research."

As they rested in Jacob's residency above the mortuary, and as the day transformed back to night, Pedro stood at the window in Jacob's living room, which overlooked the cemetery. He saw the small crypt in the thick of the overgrown trees at the edge of the graveyard, and stood, watching, and waiting.

Antoine appeared anxious when they were preparing to return to the crypt at the end of the third day. Pedro watched as he stood at the kitchen sink, running the water and splashing it on his face.

"Antoine?" Pedro asked. "Are you alright?"

Pedro watched as Antoine turned around; his eyes were bloodshot and his face pale. He had not seen Antoine in this state, nor had he experienced anyone in the immortal community to hold such uncertainty.

There had to be something more.

He watched as Antoine joined Jacob and Pedro followed them as they headed down the long, winding stairs into the marble laden foyer below, past the long corridor which led to the embalming and crematoriums, and over towards the expansive front doors past the offices.

Antoine knew something.

There was a change in his behavior.

Pedro watched as Antoine remained silent. Antoine looked down as Jacob placed his hand on the brass handle. Antoine raised his head to look at the others.

And then Antoine finally spoke.

"The winds have started," he said. "They will have begun their assault by now."

Isaiah shifted towards Pedro and leaned close to him. He spoke softly, almost in a whisper. "Then we best be careful!"

The clouds raced across the sky as the sun sank into the horizon, igniting the fiery crimson palette; the winds were whispering her name *Valentina…*

Lightning crashed from a dark storm cloud which billowed outwards against the sunset; as the sun sank and the sky darkened to a deep shade of blue, the flash of the lightning and the winds returned. The winds tore through the treetops, and the leaves and twigs blew through the cemetery and swirled as the wind caught them.

Pedro wandered through the residence above the mortuary, wishing he could rest. But sleep would not come to him this evening. The deed had been done, as had the ritual, and the resurrection would soon follow. He grabbed a throw pillow and wrapped it around his head, covering his ears.

Pedro sank into the sofa as the twilight faded to darkness, and as he gazed out the window, the haze of the whiskey numbing him, he saw the flashes of lightning in a silent, thunderless storm, far in the distance.

He froze as he heard the whisper again.

Valentina…

390

He scanned the foyer, peering into the darkness as he gingerly set his glass on the table. The chandelier hung like the silhouette of a skeleton wrapped in a fetal crouch; he gasped as the lighting flashed again, bathing the foyer in a blast of bright, white light.

Jacob nodded and looked towards the others, as they huddled by the doors. "Are you all ready?"

Pedro watched as Antoine looked up making eye contact with him. "You will see," he said. "That resurrection requires retribution."

As thunder rumbled above, a crash came from downstairs followed by the pierce of broken glass.

Antoine rushed towards the door. "She's here! It's happening!"

Jacob and Isaiah charged into the living room behind Antoine as Pedro felt his heart race in his chest. Pedro joined them at the head of the stairs and saw the elongated shadow on the marble below. Jacob reached his arm across their chests. "This cannot be…"

"What came back?! What is this, Antoine?!"

Pedro stood as the others charged down the stairs. "Pedro, get down here!" Antoine's voice boomed from the foyer. The authority was there. Antoine was back.

"Get her to crematory number seven!" Jacob screamed.

Pedro shook his head for a moment, and then ran down to the foyer. He stopped and his mouth dropped open. There was a gaping hole in the front; the doors splintered and crashed to the floor.

Valentina.

But it wasn't Valentina.

She was a woman, reconstructed. Sewn together, yet still dead.

Her skin was dead and pasty, her eyes clouded and white. Jacob and Isaiah rushed forward, pushing her out the front door, as they spilled through the broken frame.

Antoine's eyes glared crimson red. His head snapped towards Pedro. "*This was not supposed to happen! You did use the powder!*" Pedro followed as Antoine rushed towards the others.

They were holding her down as she writhed on the front porch, her legs splayed, ripping her black skirt.

Antoine snapped his head around. "Get her leg!"

Jacob and Isaiah held her arms as Pedro grabbed her leg. It flailed as he struggled to control her power. He looked over at Antoine. He held the other leg, and his face had softened. "You must gain confidence, Pedro."

And then she stopped writhing.

The storm silenced and the winds abated as they heard the approach of footsteps.

They turned.

Her long, flowing gown dragged on the pavers as she approached, clasping her meaty arms together in front.

She wore a crown of thorns.

"You must realize," she said, "that when you use the powder I give, that the portal opens. And what can come…may not be what you expect."

Pedro gasped. "You did not tell me about this!"

LaDonna approached the steps and placed her hands on her hips. "Our Queen Reynalda has been governing the lost sea for far too long. Her sentence is now finished."

An image of the beach and the writhing pasty limbs flashed through Pedro's mind. He saw Valentina rise from the waters, staring at him with those dead eyes. Clouded. She wore the habit of a nun, and as she approached the scars.

Screams wailed and the pasty dead souls charged through the waters and spray of white foam, grabbing her, tearing the skin from her bones.

"Her destiny is to be in the sea!" LaDonna boomed.

Pedro was thrust back to the present.

They each remained holding a limb as LaDonna reached her hand out towards Valentina. Pedro felt his arms weaken as she levitated, upwards, and he saw the others watching, as if mesmerized. He could not speak. He could not move. But they watched as the body lifted higher and levitated over towards LaDonna.

"You gave me the bones of a nun!" LaDonna said, laughing. "And she will be under my control!" She looked up at Pedro. "You see, the powder did work, as I promised you. And now we will have our Queen once again." She looked at Isaiah and Jacob. "Thank you for all of your hard work. It was most appreciated."

LaDonna Mastuer retreated with Valentina, and they were able to move again. Jacob clenched his fist and opened his hand and made a fist again.

They stood on the porch as the winds strengthened. It was if a hurricane was approaching, as they tore through the gardens.

"Get inside!" Antoine screamed as they turned and retreated towards the winding staircase. The chandelier rocked as the winds fought their way inside. They spilled up the stairs and tore into the living room. Pedro flopped on the couch as Isaiah and Jacob ran to the windows yanking the curtains shut.

Antoine leaned down.

His eyes were intense.

"Don't you see?! This is the result. *You ignored my warning!*"

Pedro watched as Antoine shook his head and went to assist the others. He sat, fumbling with his hands in his lap, as he listened to the winds howl outside.

They waited inside the mortuary for what seemed like days, but as Pedro wandered slowly to Jacob's office and looked up at the grandfather clock as it ticked patiently, it had only been mere hours. The darkness outside seemed eternal; unforgiving. An undeniable force, as if it were bathing the mortuary in a skeleton which hugged them in a demonic embrace; they remained sequestered.

Jacob returned to the foyer.

Antoine sat underneath the massive, ornate mirror which hung above suede and brass benches which lined the wall. He leaned his head back, his eyes closed, his arms draped over his knees. Antoine's forearms still glistened with sweat, marred by dirt.

Isaiah assisted with holding large sheets of plywood against the gaping hole in the front doors as several of the staff members hammered nails into the frame as Jacob paced in front of the large, round mahogany table the center of the floor.

Pedro took a few cautious steps into the foyer and looked down at Antoine. He opened his eyes and looked up at him. Antoine no longer appeared angry, his face was tired and defeated. "You see?" he asked. "What I told you?"

Pedro approached and knelt next to Antoine.

"The only thing the power guarantees is that the body will resurrect. No Valentina. Nothing. LaDonna had you all along, Pedro."

"Then why did you allow me to go to New Orleans?"

Antoine leaned his head back on the wall again and sighed. "Because Pedro. You must learn. You must realize that your decisions, however noble they may seem to you, have consequences. Will you get your muse back? Only time will tell."

Pedro hung his head and closed his eyes.

"I may be a mentor, Pedro. But only you can demonstrate that you are understanding the lessons. By your practice."

Pedro opened his eyes and watched as Antoine rose to his feet. He looked over at Isaiah who approached the others as the staff left from hanging the plywood.

Jacob stood on the opposite side of the table, his arms folded, his eyes raised towards Antoine.

"We must travel to where the lights of the night soar across the skies," Antoine said as he looked down at Pedro. "And we don't have much time to reach her. Get up. We have to get going immediately."

Their flight was delayed by three hours, and they sat in the crowded and busy airport terminal, wishing they hadn't made the choice to use a commercial flight to fly the many hours long route to Anchorage from Miami. Pedro snapped his head over towards Antoine, who returned with two steaming cups of coffee. He handed a cup to Pedro, who reluctantly took it.

"We have to keep alert," he said. "No potions, no drinking."

Pedro started to take a sip of the steaming, hot beverage, as he heard Antoine mutter under his breath. Antoine turned towards Pedro. He looked down as Antoine handed him his ticket. It was stamped with "VIP First Class".

"Didn't have time to arrange the jet, so I'm sorry. But we'll have some room."

Pedro took the ticket and slowly nodded.

"And there's something that I want you to do on the flight."

Pedro raised his head and made eye contact with Antoine.

"I want you to write," Antoine said. "You have all the tools that you need. And plenty of time on this flight. You have all of the pain and loss that you can imagine from this journey we have taken together. You don't need Valentina to write, Pedro. She can inspire you from wherever she is now. Because your inspiration, and your talent, comes from within."

Antoine pointed at Pedro's chest as boarding was called.

As they settled into their seats, Antoine turned towards Pedro.

"Do you remember what Flavio said?"

Pedro remembered the small, boisterous man, and the Hotel Cellai, back in Florence.

It seemed liked a lifetime ago. The walk underground seemed dreamlike, but he did believe that it happened.

"It happened," Antoine said. "But you remember what he said. Why the Inspiriti exists, right?"

Pedro nodded. "They are the guardians of the gateways."

"There is one in the arctic circle which has a significant draw. It's where the light dances in the sky, guardians of the ice grave."

"And you think that LaDonna went there?"

Antoine took a sip of his coffee and nodded.

"I know that she's there. The ritual requires it. And if the witches want Queen Reynalda to return from guarding the sea of souls, the ice grave is the only portal from which someone of her stature can enter the world."

Pedro shivered as the plane started backing up.

He leaned back, and settled into his seat, closing his eyes. He felt sleepy as the rumble of the jet engine, as the plane barreled down the runway, slowly lulled him to dozing. He could still hear the announcements in the cabin, the light chatter from nearby passengers, and the *bong!* as the seatbelt sign flashed off once they were cruising.

He looked over at Antoine.

His eyes were closed, and his seat was reclined, but he doubted that he was sleeping. Antoine rarely did. And rarely needed to. But Pedro knew that he felt exhausted, yet the adrenaline which pumped through his veins denied him sleep.

Not that he needed any.

Antoine's words replayed in his mind. *Use this time to write.*

He reached down in his bag, and drew out a large, yellow legal pad.

That would have to do.

Antoine insisted that he already had the talent, so now it was time to put it to the test.

There wasn't much left.

The winds lightened but still whispered across his ears as if the orchestra was warming up, at the point of readying to play. But Pedro knew.

They would be just through the trees. The dark forest which surrounded them, catapulting them into captivity.

She hadn't had much time to walk with the immortals, but he knew the purpose had been driven by a darker force, as Antoine had warned.

"Pedro!" he hissed.

Antoine was not much farther up. A few stones, hiding behind the largest markers, just as he was. But it didn't matter. She guarded the exit.

He could see Asmodai's towering silhouette as the light brightened in the distance. They both looked and gasped as it intensified. Antoine turned to face Pedro. "You have to *move!*" he said as the winds intensified.

Pedro knew.

Antoine had been through this before, in a different time, with a different immortal.

Back in the days of Darius, in this same, lonely, forested cemetery in the forests and farmlands that wound their way through France.

Darius, are you there?

Pedro flipped the pages and repositioned his pen.

He lost his awareness of how long the flight had been; as the flight attendants offered dinner, and evening cocktails, he ignored it.

His one focus was the page.

Are you there, Darius? Are you still alive? Do you hear me calling you?

He waited, staring out into the darkness. Waiting for the mist, the clouds, the destiny.

Someone was out there.

He could sense it.

His limbs tingled as his hands became furious, reaching outwards, feeling towards the nothingness, grasping it, drawing it towards him, pulling it closer.

There was something out there.

It was time to create.

As the plane touched down in Anchorage, Pedro stared at the legal pad. It was filled with his writing, along with a second pad, which sat underneath the table. Antoine looked over at him and nodded in approval.

"You see? The talent is within you, Pedro."

Pedro stared at what he had written.

There were too many years of following a broken promise and an indulgence; this was his true calling. He closed his eyes as they caught a train which traversed across the Land of the Midnight Sun, as the terrain was called. They headed farther into the snow-covered mountains as darkness fell across the land.

Pedro leaned his head against the window, watching his reflection in the darkened glass stare back at him, wondering how far the journey would be, to the seventh gateway, the ice grave. How far from the solace would he be, when the winds would cry their song of anger?

The eyes appeared in the darkness.

Deep within the forested mountains, through the falling snow, they watched him. The methodic sway of the train car lulled him into a somber state; he leaned his head against the seat, his eyes feeling heavy, but the eyes continued to watch him.

They were crimson orbs deep within the black forest.

Watching.

Waiting…following. He snapped awake as a chill ran down his spine.

"The aurora borealis is active now," Antoine said. His words seemed distant against the quiet car. Pedro concentrated on his breathing as the eyes disappeared.

He shifted in his seat, turning to face Antoine, who was sipping on a cup of tea. "Is this part of the ritual?"

Antoine nodded.

"Is what we're doing…evil?"

Antoine placed his tea down on the saucer with a slight clink. He pursed his lips together and looked over at Pedro. His eyes felt piercing yet knowing. There was experience in those eyes. "I know that Darius came to you," he said. "Didn't he?"

Pedro nodded slowly.

"After he passed. There's more that I know, Pedro. It's part of our gifts, of course. And the Darius I know would want to come back to this world."

Let me walk in this world again…

"He promised you the gift, Pedro. But it won't be him that will be returning. LaDonna believes that Queen Reynalda will be able to return in Valentina's new body. But the powder leaves out one key factor of returning to the world from the seventh gateway, Pedro."

"What is that?"

UTQIAGVIK, ALASKA

The train hissed to a stop at the tiny terminal.

Pedro slowly opened his eyes into the darkness, but the small iron lamp posts shone a dim yellow halo around the small, wooden buildings, slender walkways, and old, rusted pickups parked nearby. It was as if they had stepped back in time, into an old, rusted, forgotten city at end of the earth, which the world and time had neglected.

He watched as they exited the train, wandering through the mud and snow-covered streets. The snowflakes fell angrily, and the winds howled, ushering in the relentless winter.

It was the city next to the frozen ocean; a land where the darkness grasped with a stronghold in stark contrast to the midnight sun, where the winter refused to be worn, and the residents brought a warmth which they exuded, bathing the chill with friendliness.

As they walked away from the tracks, a man stood, his hood covered his head. The fur which lined it appeared as if he were hiding within the fur in the curved shaped of an igloo; but as they approached him, he raised his head, his face emerged from the darkness, and he smiled as his brilliant white teeth caught the light.

"Antoine!" he said. "Welcome to Barrow! This is truly the end of the earth, my friend."

He and Antoine embraced, and then the man turned and looked at Pedro. "And this is the new recruit, Antoine?"

Antoine nodded, leaning close to the man, as Pedro watched, listening, but not hearing what they spoke of. The man looked at Pedro, as his face livened.

He reached outwards. The man wore a heavy mitten, and Pedro shivered as he accepted it.

"Nanurjuk," he said, looking at Antoine and then back over to Pedro. "I am the owner of the King Eider Inn. Just a short walk from here. We will warm up in there by the fire with plenty of American whiskey. And then we will head out there!"

He turned and pointed towards the darkness.

A field of stars above twinkled and glistened against the blue reflection of the ice; it was the sea which remained forever frozen. Yet, under the reflective green light which danced across the darkened skies, it was if the aurora borealis was a beacon.

Guiding them there.

To the ice grave.

It was what Antoine spoke of and it was what LaDonna mentioned back in New Orleans. There was a grave, a gateway, made entirely of ice. Where the coldest of hells would reside, where the demons danced, and the Queen would reign over the souls trapped in the dark, murky waters.

Pedro thought he was in a dream as he and Antoine prepared for the journey outwards on the frozen sea.

As the lights soared across the darkened sky, they walked on the ice, their boots crunching in the hardened snowpack.

He followed Antoine as the chill of the wind bit at his face. It was a cold which he had never experienced before, and probably would not encounter again. But Antoine had said the chill of hades was significant, if not more so than what they were trekking through at the top of the world.

He focused on his feet, wearing the heavy boots which Nanurjuk provided, while he so graciously bowed out from accompanying them. "I know what resides there," he said, slowly, and quietly, earlier as they sat in the lounge at the King Eider, nursing their whiskeys.

Pedro took a breath and examined his ice cubes, floating in the amber liquid. Antoine started speaking to Nanurjuk, but Pedro wasn't listening. His mind was out in the dark, frozen sea. Under the guidance of the dancing lights of the aurora borealis.

That's what they had said.

The dream became.

Destiny fought through the wisping clouds which fought across the sky, the words abounded in his mind, flowing through his thoughts.

He was no stranger to deception. There was no murder in his heart. He needed only to look ahead, and forge the path, towards the light, which came soaring upwards towards a darkened sky.

"A destiny of angels," Antoine said.

Pedro didn't ask for an explanation. And he didn't want a war.

"Sometimes it chooses us," Antoine said.

They stopped walking and looked ahead.

Pedro squinted, as it remained in the distance; but he saw a flicker. It could be a flame, a delicate glow far ahead. Antoine turned and faced him. "The light will guide us," he said.

As they started to crunch through the frozen snow and icepack again, Pedro watched his feet, in the heavy, black boots, imaging the raging, frigid waters just beneath the icy surface. He looked up as the colors leaped forward, reaching downwards towards the flame, and then his heart thumped in his chest.

She was there.

He could see her long, flowing black robe which she was wearing when LaDonna had taken her from the mortuary.

Then he watched as she was watching him; the distance remained great, yet the closeness of her eyes was piercing.

He started running. "Let's go, Antoine! I see her there!"

Antoine ran and followed behind him. "No, Pedro! That isn't her!"

Pedro remained focused on Valentina, as she rose from the icy surface, the light emanating from behind her, as the colorful wisps in the dark skies reached downwards towards her, wrapping around her, bathing her in color and light.

"That is false light, Pedro!"

Pedro focused on Valentina, who rose from the ice like a phoenix, rising to the sky, as the lights danced around her. He locked eyes with her, looking down to him. He ignored Antoine's footsteps behind him; his calling seemed distant, insignificant.

You will have all the talent you can imagine, Pedro…

"Yes!" he cried out, as he fell to his knees.

Antoine stopped next to him, knelt and grabbed his shoulders. "Snap out of it, Pedro!"

But he did not listen.

A ring of fire ignited in the center of the icefield, as the cavernous ice sloped downwards.

Pedro watched as Valentina sank into the dark cavern, deeper, until she had disappeared. Pedro snapped his head towards Antoine. "We have to go after her!" he cried.

"No!" Antoine said. He grabbed Pedro's shoulder, holding him back. "If you go down there you will lose your mind, Pedro! It's trickery. She isn't really there. Don't let yourself be lured down there. Don't!"

Pedro turned and grabbed Antoine's neck. "Then transform me! *Keep the promise!*"

413

Pedro gasped and cowered down. Antoine's muscular arm pinned him to the ground. Pedro's heart raced in his chest as he looked up into the red glare of Antoine's eyes. He was monstrous, beastly muscular, with enormously engorged veins.

His voice had deepened. "If you want this, I will give it to you. *Take the gift!*"

Antoine pinned Pedro down, his muscular body holding him to the ground. Pedro's clothes tore and shredded. Pedro cried out, writhing beneath his massive frame.

He pierced his neck, and Pedro closed his eyes as the hot blood poured down his neck. His eyelids quickly became heavy, as he watched Antoine move closer to his mouth.

"*Take my blood!*" he said. "Experience the blood lineage. This is your destiny, Pedro. You will have all the talent in the world you could ever desire..."

As Pedro slowly drifted off, he turned his head towards the icy cavern.

She was there.

The Valentina he always remembered, back in Madrid, twirling in her flowery sundress, smiling with brilliance, her hair clean, flowing; he thought she smelled of lavender.

You will have all the talent you could ever Desire, Pedro...

And then there was darkness.

SCENT OF THE GRAVE

PARIS

THERE WAS A TIME when people believed their destinies had been pre-determined. Perhaps from before their birth in the human form; and others, they thought, when they had been transformed into immortality. The path that they each followed led to a unique location, apparently selected for each of them.

But there were anomalies, which served as distractors, leading the one who takes the journey off the intended path, and towards a different direction. At times, the direction could be an improvement on the journey, a necessary deviation. But there were also other times when one could be led astray, in a vast and incomprehensible fashion, without a learned and specific approach to a corrected path.

Some people say that, when a person dies, whether or not they once possessed the gift of immortality on Earth, that the soul becomes attached to the physical world, and hesitates in taking its journey towards the spiritual.

Pedro thought about the lectures, and what they had told him.

"There is so much art to experience in this world, Pedro. In all forms. Books, music, paintings, sculptures...because humans have the gifts of reason and appreciation, and purpose, they will continue to create."

Antoine was leaning over the bed, looking down at him. "Are you rested now? Do you feel refreshed and renewed?"

Pedro sat up in the bed, as the thought pierced his mind. *I cannot write without my muse. And my muse is lying in a coffin.*

Antoine leaned back and shook his head. "That's enough of those dark thoughts," he said. "Yes, she is lying in a coffin. But now, you are extraordinary. You always were. You didn't need the gift. But now that you have it, it's up to you to make the best of it."

Pedro had no memory of what happened after Antoine transformed him on the ice grave.

He remembered the sacrifices Antoine made to help him realize the potential he had. But the gift had been given, by Antoine, and now, he was grateful.

There is something mysterious about a grave; in particular, when the grave is fresh, and the mound of dirt is elevated above the grass, as flowers lay on the top of the mound, still fresh, not yet wilted or browned. Perhaps the person lying in the casket below hadn't realized that they were going on a journey as recently as the previous week. And in other situations, the grave could be fresh, yet the person could have long left the world.

Thoughts raced through Pedro's mind as he drove the closer to Les Enfantes. He had heard that Valentina had come to America. LaDonna was still rumored to be controlling her, and he kept shaking his head in disbelief that they had been close to one another the entire time.

Had it really been her?

It didn't matter now, he knew.

He could still hear Antoine's words in his head.

"I will give you the same satchel and pickaxe that I used."

Pedro looked down at the satchel.

I cannot write without my muse. And my muse is lying in a coffin.

Was it time to resurrect again?

He raised his eyes to the rearview mirror and saw the brown bag on the rear bench seat. He was going through with this; now was the time, and he could only do it alone. There wasn't much time before the sun would rise and the sky would lighten. He glanced at the clock. Just past midnight. It would have to be enough time to dig and drag the body out. The sun would certainly be rising by then.

He sighed and shook his head.

No, no. He wasn't going to do it. He was already being called "The Resurrector" in immortal social circles, and others had been approaching him, particularly back in Miami, where he had formed a bond with Jacob Benjamin over at Waxley Mortuary.

The powder would no longer be used.

Antoine had said that he could use the chateau, assist the others, bring back the long-lost. But not if he used the powder.

Of course, it was hours from Paris, because that was where Pedro wanted to be. Despite the loss of the Jefferson Majestic theater, the immortals remained a significant force in Paris.

And then there was the time, when he stood in the *Louvre*, once again, as the sun started to set in the western sky. He again stared at the painting, at the work of art.

Mona Lisa.

They had said that she was da Vinci's masterpiece; it was argued, and many agreed.

It always was, and always will be.

She was always thought to be a painting, but now, she was so much more.

Yes, there indeed was power in those bones.

Had he followed the path he had been on, had Antoine not executed the promise, where would the destination be?

Pedro knew it had been a correct assumption. But now, he knew, there would be another reign of the immortals. There would be a time when Ramiel would invite him back to Rome; when the Monsignor would invite him to the catacombs beneath the chapel, and *The Inspiriti* would rule over the immortals with a strong and regulated arm, as it had in the past, when the immortal population was much larger and stronger. During the years when the immortals were greater in number.

But not today.

"I will never run from the ghosts again."

Pedro knew. It was time. His selection had been made, and the others agreed. There were far too many ghosts. The spirits had been active, now it was time to keep them quiet.

Was there destiny hidden in the painting?

Could there have been something – a single line in the code, perhaps – which he had incorrectly interpreted?

Perhaps, he knew that. As the p.a. system announced, in French, that the museum would be closing in fifteen minutes, he continued to gaze at the painting.

There would be more time; the meaning remained; a metaphor grasped him; the destiny was certain.

He turned and navigated the crowds as they quickly started to disperse.

There was no reason to remain in the museum any longer. The Louvre had served its purpose. He turned one last time to look at her.

She had done her full duty; proved her diligence.

Offered her continued inspiration.

Until the doors swung open, and he stood, watching the others who stood outside the pyramid in the chill of Paris in winter, he watched as the tiny clouds emitted from their mouths as they spoke and rushed and laughed and smoked.

But was there destiny in the painting?

He stood, pulling his coat closer, warding off the chill; the workers were up on ladders removing the Christmas decorations from the lamp posts. He tied the waistbelt together and froze when he felt a hand gently touch his shoulder, and speak in a masculine, articulate tone.

It was a voice he had heard before.

"I am meant to be heard by you, and only you."

THE END

Did you enjoy Mona Lisa, Becoming a Ghost?

If so, please leave a review on Amazon, Barnes and Noble, Goodreads or the outlet at which you purchased this novel. Independent authors, such as myself, most sincerely appreciate reader feedback. It helps us with our storytelling, so we can craft stories for readers years into the future.

With Love, A.L.

BALLET OF THE CRYPT DANCER

NOW AVAILABLE WORLDWIDE FROM PARCHMAN'S PRESS

RAMIEL ALWAYS WANTED to tell the story of The Crypt Dancer, and of the massacre, and of the witches.

But there was no one, for years, who wanted to listen. In the days before he became an immortal, as he wandered the outskirts of Rome, he had heard about the mystery of the everlasting kind. A young man preparing for the seminary, he wondered about the fascination with the immortals, those despised creatures. Why were they loathed so much? Was there an unseen threat towards humans which was insurmountable, inconsolable?

He found it unusual that there could be a population apparently impervious to death, and disease; that those eternally youthful could coexist with humans and seem to appear ageless, despite the passage of time. He witnessed some of the countless discussions about the immortals, throughout the city and across the world, that those with what was called "the dark gift" may be supernatural; ghosts, demons, wizards or witches…but certainly not human.

And must not be accepted into society.

As a boy, he would listen to the dinner table chatter, as rumors of another kind increased, about the threat of the immortal population, who lived in the same cities and countries as mortal humans did. But Ramiel had never encountered one of the legendary immortals directly until leaving his parent's home, when he left to join the church.

It was there that he discovered an apparent truth; that there was some certainty in the rumors. That there were those in the population who appeared ageless, as if frozen in time, yet otherwise indiscernible. He had matured into a young man of robust, yet slender build, and while he was in the priesthood, he watched the others. There were those who had angelic faces which far unmatched their chronological years; as a mortal man, his appearance was also youthful, strong, with brown shoulder length hair.

He could have been one of them.

But in those days, he wasn't.

There were those who harbored some of the characteristics which he'd heard mama and papa discuss with their friends at dinner parties when he was still a boy, while they were planning ways to extricate the immortals from society. Perhaps there was a jealousy, Ramiel had thought.

But certainly a fear of the unknown.

Immortals were eternally youthful, despite the passage of years, sometimes decades; charismatic, with the ability to convince one who is unsuspecting to become infatuated with their gifts and powers; and malevolent, with doctrines that must be followed unequivocally, bringing swift and cruel justice for those who disobeyed.

431

Ramiel's time with the church may have been a foreshadowing of the events which would follow; the monsignor was a loyal tutor yet misguided.

And then there was Cristofano.

A fellow Italian, from Salerno, on the Mediterranean coast, Ramiel grew from a boy to a man completely unaware of their destined connection through the enlightened tapestry of immortality, and the secret society, the Inspiriti.

He knew nothing of Cristofano's existence, until he had been introduced to him while under service at the Sistine Chapel, under the guidance and tutelage of Monsignor Harrison. It was Cristofano who was the one who introduced him to the mysteriousness and pleasures of the Inspiriti, and immortality, and the dark gift.

And who transformed him.

Yet after Ramiel's days in Paris, which followed his time in Rome, and the massacre at the theater he had been destined to perform, there had been a period when his loneliness had consumed him. As if the immortals were secretly despised, his thoughts would frequently drift towards those who hunted them. It wasn't only those who burned the theater with angry, flaming torches; those who ignited the curtains and destroyed any immortal with fire who was unable to flee; it was, he thought, possibly a threat of annihilation which originated from their own kind.

But why?

It was those thoughts which brought him to America, not only to find an inner sense of purpose, but also to reach forward on his journey as an immortal and as a man.

He formed his story.

He knew some of the others who had comprised the cast at the theater, and some who contributed to the events of the massacre; the events were soul defining. What purpose could come from an immortal, dragged through the rear gardens in flames, who was unable to die? Whose consciousness would endure in the coffin, for eternity, with seldom relief from the lonely torment?

If any.

Where the dreams that he held, each night when he lay in a coffin, just as he was taught by his maker, were just simply dreams. That there was nothing on the other side that he could sample when he closed his eyes; that the dreams, tiny snippets of death, were simply that. And that his soul was just as darkened and stained as the others, and despite the many beliefs that he'd carried since he was a boy, the conclusion was that once he closed his eyes, in that sleep of death of which immortals were comprised, there would be a simple drift towards solitude, silence and darkness.

But there was death in the solitude.

The immortals burned in the massacre; the awareness was the punishment. When the flames charred their skin as it melted from bones, and the stench of burning flesh permeated the air, the immortals may have pleaded for the solitude of death, which in the torment, would be a respite, which the immortals would never receive.

Ramiel knew the story must be told.

The massacre happened.

The Crypt Dancer was real.

And the witches had evaded detection for years. But as he mentioned it to others, be they human or immortal, he got brushed off.

Until one immortal, Delia Arnette, knocked on the estate door in Coral Gables, in Florida, during his time in America. It was a southern city with brilliant green lawns and soaring, shaded oak canopies; hanging Spanish moss which swayed in slow afternoon breezes. A suburb of Miami that reveled in its plantation dreams.

The estate, in possession of the immortals for generations, was once occupied by Antoine Nagevesh, a coffee harvester from Sri Lanka who had been discovered and brought to America. Nestled on the corner of Andelusia and Anastasia, the soaring Corinthian columns were unmistakable from the streets, as the home was known as the mansion of luxurious overstatement by the locals.

Ramiel padded through the kitchen as he heard the door chime.

The foyer remained unscathed from the fire, yet the distinct smell of charred wood hung in the air, as sheets of plywood covered the winding staircase. Ramiel was occupying the estate to oversee the renovations. Antoine had left Miami, with his maker, Darius Sauvage, to return to their chateau in France, after the fire had devastated parts of the mansion.

As Ramiel parted the lacey curtains on the skinny, rectangular window next to the double wooden doors, he saw the small woman, the one who had been introduced to him as Delia Arnette.

She was one of the immortals who had originated from a coveted bloodline; one of those with the time gift, who possessed the ability to appear in different time periods across oceans and continents, in altered appearances – exhibiting variations in age, physical stature, and demeanor – which, Ramiel had learned, was a gift exclusive to those selected to the blood lineage of Claret Atarah, rumored to be the eldest of the immortals.

But the woman who stood on the long, wraparound porch, in between the columns, in front of the rocking chairs, did not appear as the same Delia that he had expected. Her hair, snow-white; her face, lined with wrinkles, and her short stature all brought on the thoughts which pierced Ramiel's mind. Had The Hooded Man gotten to her too? Was his global virus of wrath impossible for her to resist with its temptations?

She clutched her slender, black umbrella close to her chest.

She had been one of the most peculiar of immortals, Ramiel knew that for certain. He'd heard of her, back in his early days in Italy, not far from Rome. She was known, in the mortal communities in which Ramiel had grown and studied, that she was a woman who frequented Rome, and also Paris, and it was rumored that she was "one of them". When he was still a boy, and when he was infatuated with the immortals, he had heard Delia's name mentioned...even in the supernatural classes he had taken in secondary school which had studies of the immortal population as course electives.

It was Delia's name which had been mentioned, in the texts and the main doctrine, *The Code of the Immortals*, which had been published in an undisclosed location, by a mysterious publisher called Parchman's Press. And, it was told in the classes, that only one copy had been created, and that the book had supernatural powers. The students were instructed to avoid the book at all costs; that it was spawn from Satan, that only evil resided in the book. The book, which was housed in Rome, Ramiel suspected, had not been the original, for it would have then diluted its power. But the book mentioned her, in several instances.

In the days when Ramiel had been studying the immortals, Ms. Delia Arnette had been youthful and vibrant, at least from the photos that Ramiel had seen. Most photos were crude, in black and white, and taken when the camera had just been invented. They were often in books, but sometimes in periodicals. Newspapers mainly. But she was young; elegantly styled hair, voluptuous lips.

That was how Ramiel viewed an immortal.

They were strong, forceful. Undeniably attractive, physically. The males endowed with a lush presence, muscularity and charisma; the females with the power of seduction, persuasion and supple physical features; voluptuousness.

The power of seduction, but more often persuasion, was a gift afforded to all immortals. It allowed them to take command of a room with ease. There was something about them with which most humans had become enamored. Those had offered myriad theories. Some had been that mortal humans harbored jealously towards the gifted ones who had been bestowed supernatural powers.

The immortals, though, had always been human at one point, and when Ramiel had first taken notice of

Delia, he was a mortal human himself. And when he stood in the foyer of the Miami estate, as he watched the small, frail woman reach out for the lion crest knocker once again, he grabbed the bolt and turned it, slowly opening the door.

She nodded and smiled. "Ramiel, I presume. May I come in?"

PARCHMAN'S PRESS

Excellence in Fiction